LADY FEARFUL

A Series of Senseless Complications
Book Seven

Kate Archer

ARE YOU SIGNED UP FOR DRAGONBLADE'S BLOG?

You'll get the latest news and information on exclusive giveaways, exclusive excerpts, coming releases, sales, free books, cover reveals and more.

Check out our complete list of authors, too!

No spam, no junk. That's a promise!

Sign Up Here

www.dragonbladepublishing.com

Dearest Reader;

Thank you for your support of a small press. At Dragonblade Publishing, we strive to bring you the highest quality Historical Romance from some of the best authors in the business. Without your support, there is no 'us', so we sincerely hope you adore these stories and find some new favorite authors along the way.

Happy Reading!

CEO, Dragonblade Publishing

Additional Dragonblade books by Author Kate Archer

A Series of Senseless Complications
Lady Ferocity (Book 1)
Lady Graceless (Book 2)
Lady Impatience (Book 3)
Lady Dramatic (Book 4)
Lady Liar (Book 5)
Lady Suspicious (Book 6)
Lady Fearful (Book 7)

A Very Fine Muddle
Romance Me, Viscount (Book 1)
Be Daring, Duke (Book 2)
Stand With Me, Earl (Book 3)
Sweep Me Up, Baron (Book 4)
Write for Me, Marquess (Book 5)
Convince Me, Viscount (Book 6)

A Series of Worthy Young Ladies
The Meddler (Book 1)
The Sprinter (Book 2)
The Undaunted (Book 3)
The Champion (Book 4)
The Jilter (Book 5)
The Regal (Book 6)

The Dukes' Pact Series
The Viscount's Sinful Bargain (Book 1)
The Marquess' Daring Wager (Book 2)
The Lord's Desperate Pledge (Book 3)
The Baron's Dangerous Contract (Book 4)
The Peer's Roguish Word (Book 5)
The Earl's Iron Warrant (Book 6)

PROLOGUE

ROLAND NICOLET, THE Duke of Pelham, had spent a great many of his middle years launching daughters out of his house. As he was in receipt of seven of those individuals, he'd been a regular Sisyphus toiling to get his rock up the mountain. That rock was just now teetering at the summit and ready to tip over the other side and never trouble him again. He had one last daughter to launch and then an empty house would soon be his. His dream was finally within reach!

Of course, were any of his array of daughters to hear these thoughts spoken aloud, and they often had, they would decry them as the worst bit of nonsense. The truth was, he rather missed the chaos of seven bright-eyed girls running roughshod over his peace. However, he knew his duty and that was to see them all settled creditably.

That duty had turned out to be no easy task either. When he'd contemplated the project, he'd viewed it as a leisurely stroll down the paths of a well-manicured park. Once he was actually in it, he realized it was more like having to hack one's way through an Amazonian jungle. It *should* have been a leisurely stroll; his girls were all comely and well-funded and what else could possibly be required?

Apparently, what was required had been tears, laughter, ups, downs, circle rounds, hopelessness, hopefulness, declarations of spinsterhood, vows to give him up, vows to never give him up, packing trunks, unpacking trunks, he'd never, he might, he would, he wouldn't, he couldn't, he did. Several of the gentlemen had almost died in the attempt to court one of his daughters and the rest, if not in mortal danger, had been severely shaken by the experience.

Nevertheless, six of them had been settled and that just left Valor, his youngest. He could not even guess what that girl would have up her sleeve. Considering it had been a monumental effort to even convince her to agree to go to Town, he was confident it would be a spectacular sort of nonsense.

He'd enjoyed a few years of relaxation as his youngest reached maturity, but now it was time to gird his loins once more and hold on to his hat—the Dales were to be left behind in favor of Grosvenor Square and a new season was set to begin.

If he were a religious man, he might have sent up a few prayers about it. As he was not, he ordered his vicar to do it for him.

CHAPTER ONE

A Remote Estate in the Yorkshire Dales, 1811

VALOR NICOLET, THE last of the duke's daughters, had been dreading this moment all her life. She was to go to Town as a lady out in society. She'd never wished to be out, she wished to be in!

She'd been scheming to avoid being out most of her life. Valor had done everything she could think of to keep her sisters at home and her family as jolly as they always had been before they'd begun going to Town. However, one by one, they'd all married, leaving her behind.

When it became apparent that she could not stop them from leaving, despite her ever more outrageous efforts, she turned her thoughts on how to at least save herself from being forced out of the Dales and into some strange household with some strange man.

That had been the start of her campaign to remain by her father's side as his hostess, forever. He, she, and their dear Mrs. Right could carry on as they had always done. She'd even had hostessing clothes made. At least, her idea of what the hostessing clothes of a mature matron might look like. In retrospect, she was glad she'd grown out of them, as she could see now that they had been rather dreadful.

After Winsome had wed, she had visited that household for some months and then she and her father had retreated to the quiet and safety of their house in the Dales.

She'd tried out several gambits over the years to convince the duke that she ought never leave. One, taking over the buttering of his toast and explaining that nobody but herself did it just right. The duke explained that he wished for a more suitable future for a duke's daughter than "butterer of toast." Two, making comments about the duke's supposed frailty and wondering how long it would be before he was entirely incapacitated and needed a nurse. As he was a hale and hearty individual, that was not as convincing as she'd hoped.

In a fit of desperation, she began pretending she was consumptive. She'd gone so far with it that eventually she was being wheeled out to the garden in a chair to take in the air. However, the boredom of it finally did in that plan and she had been forced to stage a miraculous recovery.

As she was trying out various machinations, her father was broaching the subject of a season more times than she could count. He'd even ignored it when she was, for some weeks, in a wheeled chair and pretending to be slowly fading from life.

His reasoning was rather frightening. Her idea that she, the duke, and Mrs. Right might live together forever was physically impossible. He would die, Mrs. Right would die, and then her worst fear would come true—she would be left alone to face a strange man. She'd never set eyes on the duke's heir and none of them knew what he would be like.

He might be cruel, and he might even bring a cruel wife. Valor would be seen as the worst possible inconvenience. The estate would no longer be hers. She would be an interloper with no claim. What was likely to happen to her?

The duke speculated they would not throw her to the road as that would reflect badly on them, but they would leave her in the Dales alone for long stretches as they certainly would not take her to Town for the seasons. She would be an expense they would not be eager to pay.

One of her sisters could take her in, but then they all had their growing families to contend with. It would be decided that she ought to stay in the Dales, as that house had always been her home. She was not really convinced of that; she thought any of her sisters would take her in. But it did raise the idea of being a burden on them, which she did not like. She'd have to stay in the Dales if she wanted to avoid it.

There she would be, alone in the Dales, left to listen to the sounds out of doors that frightened the wits out of her. The foxes' screams in the middle of the night had always terrified her. These days, she was now intellectually convinced it was a fox she heard, but her heart could not dismiss that it sounded like a woman being murdered. After all, if a woman *were* being murdered how would she ever be saved if everybody just presumed it was a fox? At least she'd given up accusing the vicar of somehow being involved in the murders. She sensed he was grateful for it.

Her father pointed out that when this new duke's children came, she might be pushed into acting as their governess, as so many spinsters before her had been. Suddenly, it would not be seen as convenient to have her at table, as the children needed her more. By slow degrees, she would be made a servant and slowly disappear from view.

It was a very grim picture the duke painted. And then, time did some of the work for him. She did grow and mature by degrees and she did find she rather desperately wished for children. Her thoughts continually drifted toward what sort of mother she might be and how interesting her children might be and how in her last years she might be surrounded by grandchildren. She'd grown up in a house near bursting with people and she began to think becoming a lonely spinster held less charm than it had done. She did not want to care for somebody else's children, she wanted her own.

In the meantime, she longed to see her nieces and nephews. Grace's boy, Miles, had even begun to write her letters. His last outlined how he intended to marshal his cousins into an army of sorts, and should she have her own children then of course they must be a part of it.

Isabelle was seven and would have a lot to say for herself.

Lily would be turning five and was there a more charming age?

Serenity's Daisy and Verity's Henry were both two, which was of course an awkward age. The positive of it was that it would not last forever.

And then the most recent arrival, Winsome's boy Leland, who was using all his time these days in figuring out how to get on his feet. She wished to see them all!

She even began to think that having a husband might be favorable too. She really could not even say how that idea had begun to seem a good one. At one moment she was positively revolted by the idea of Mr. Stratton staring at Felicity while she slept, and horrified that her sisters' husbands were in the same room with them while they were trying to sleep. How had the revulsion and horror slipped away and been replaced with a curiosity? It was a very strange thing, but it had.

She'd first noticed this development when she'd seen a peddler going by in his cart. Next to him had been a simply dressed but very handsome young man. She'd wondered what it would be like to kiss him, which had taken her entirely by surprise.

However, this new idea of a husband could not be just any man. He had to be the right sort of husband. Other ladies might be impressed with derring-do, manly action, loud voices, and the amount of space a man seemed to take up. For herself, she would look for a rather quiet and gentle individual. She wished to live peacefully somewhere with as little excitement or danger as possible. She wished to walk her horse, not gallop it. She wished to be assured that the screams out of doors were only a fox. A quiet yet protective baron with staid habits and no ambitions might be just the thing.

Valor had even begun to be hopeful that such a man existed. The duke had assured her that it was so. He further added that she would likely have very good luck with those sorts as they were often overlooked in favor of more forceful and strong-willed gentlemen. She'd begun to imagine a very handsome gentleman who liked to read and collect books. Perhaps he might have an insect collection and would stare at his butterflies all day. Or he might collect coins or even snuff boxes as Lord Petersham did. He was softspoken and not prone to a temper. Though also, he must be strong, he must be her protector.

That really was it—a strong and protective, yet quiet and calm, rare books collector.

Just now, the duke came jogging into the dining room waving a sheet of paper. "Well, Val, Lady Misery has not let us down."

Valor knew very well that her father had been eagerly awaiting a letter from her aunt, known to the wider world as Lady Marchfield. That lady, insistent that a duke must have a butler when they were in Town, had been in the habit of installing them.

The duke did not wish for a butler. His household was run perfectly well under the management of his housekeeper, Mrs. Right, who also did not wish for a butler. So it would begin—a butler would be installed and Mrs. Right would uninstall him in the most amusing way possible.

The duke took his chair. "Listen to this," he said, "she sends one Mr. Hubert Huberville. She says he's been dismissed without a reference from two households and is so desperate we will never get rid of him. He'll hang on like a barnacle to a boat. She writes that our diabolical housekeeper is finally to meet her match."

The two footmen, Charlie and Thomas, snorted at the sideboard. They knew as well as everybody else that it was always a mistake to underestimate Mrs. Right's creativity and determination in getting rid of a butler.

"I cannot imagine our Mrs. Right ever failing to eject a butler. My poor aunt," Valor said, "she would be happier if she gave it up. She is always to be disappointed that her man does not succeed."

"She would not be disappointed if she would stop sticking her nose into my affairs. In any case, this butler gambit has turned into a battle for the ages between us so I suspect she cannot face giving it up. And look here, another bit of good news—you will not have to don that ridiculous court dress and make your curtsy to the queen. Queen Charlotte will not hold a drawing room this year. She's probably too shook up over the king's condition and that profligate son of hers being named regent. I'd be shook up too if I were her."

No curtsy. That was an enormous relief. She'd seen what Winsome had gone through, encased in a cake of a dress and having to be made a spectacle of.

"I, for one, am happy to skip over that palaver," the duke said.

"As am I," Valor said. "I was going to be sick on the day, anyway. The consumption was going to come roaring back. I had a whole scheme set up where I would wet a small towel, hold it over the fire, and hold it against my forehead. Then I would ring my bell and it would seem as if I had a terrible fever. Now I do not need to go to the trouble."

The duke laughed. "Chin up, my girl. We leave tomorrow morning and you will have Mrs. Right and Sir Galahad by your side."

The "sir" in question, a chubby pug, was just now lying under the table in case anything was dropped there.

Valor thought she might take comfort in that. The two beings in the world who knew all her secrets, their housekeeper and her dog, would be by her side to prop her up. Then her sisters would be there to surround her when they got to Town. They'd all written letters of encouragement, sent news of her nieces and nephews, and claimed they would have a jolly time together.

It must be enough. She took a deep breath to calm her anxiousness. It might be all right. Possibly. If her rare book collecting baron was out there somewhere.

WESTON NICOLET, VISCOUNT Tramondeley and heir to the Duke of Pelham, let the mainsail luff as they drifted toward the dock. The sun was on the rise and the French vessel they'd harried and teased all night sat far on the horizon. It was a fine morning on the Cornwall coast.

His valet and crewman, Stockton, got the jib down and leapt onto the pier with the bowline while Weston took the stern line. They were bringing in the *Athena*, a Bermuda sloop, after a long night of sailing. Weston had built her for her speed and agility and she was painted a very dark blue and her sails were dirty gray. She was aptly named—just as the goddess Athena was known to do, the sloop donned her cap of invisibility while they were out on their nighttime prowls. If Weston chose to show himself, he'd light a lamp for a brief moment and then snuff it, blending into darkness once more. Even in the dawn light she was hard to spot—the waves and heaving sea and her matching colors making her as one with it.

It drove the French positively mad.

He'd been sailing since he was ten years old. Several years ago, he'd been out at night just for the fun of it, he and Stockton practicing navigating by the stars. A looming shadow had come out of nowhere and they found themselves outrunning a French frigate by tacking every which way and counting on their nimbleness to get away. Since then, he'd turned the tables and been tracking French activity along the coast and sending messages to Sir Peter Parker, Admiral of the Fleet.

Weston had become aware that the French called him "Le Moustique," or the Mosquito, for how he buzzed around them and let them know they were seen. The admiral had also written to him that perhaps the greatest benefit in the whole scheme was that the superstitious French sailors began to see the Mosquito as a messenger of some sort of doom on the horizon.

Weston tied off the boat and hopped into his waiting carriage. As they made their way back to the house, he and Stockton passed a jug of hot coffee between them.

The house, his childhood home he supposed he'd call it, was a lonely structure high on a cliff and overlooking the sea. It was relatively empty of people inside, but for Lord Ledderbey and a skeleton staff. The lord was an old family friend and when Weston's mother and father passed there had been nowhere else to go as Weston was thought to be too young to leave to his own devices and had flat-out refused to be sent to Eton.

Weston might be the Duke of Pelham's presumptive heir, but that gentleman had not had an interest in taking him in. He assumed the duke was annoyed that the entail would force his estate into Weston's hands rather than his slew of daughters and the title would go to him too, in the natural order of things. He'd heard that his father and the duke had never seen eye to eye on anything, so it must be particularly irksome.

For all that, he was not sorry about his circumstances. Lord Ledderbey was a kind, elderly gentleman who'd never kept him on a tight leash and so he'd stayed long after he might have left. Really, the gentleman did not generally know what he was up to at all. He'd only in the past year found out about Weston's night sails, though they'd been going on since he was sixteen.

When he and Stockton reached the house, which ought to be quiet at this early hour, they found Lord Ledderbey pacing the great hall in his dressing gown.

Weston rushed forward to the old gentleman. "What's happened, my lord? Are you ill?"

"If I am, I would not be surprised. Thank heavens you are home, my boy. Never have I spent such a night in my life."

Weston surreptitiously glanced around and scanned the windows. He'd always had a worry that the French might find his exact location, land a dinghy, and come to the house. He was certain they knew where he docked his boat, however, the house was some distance from the pier. Anybody attempting to see where he went through a spyglass after he disembarked would not find success—the carriage would disappear behind a hill and be lost. For all that, they might put a man on the ground and figure it out someday.

He nodded to Stockton and his valet began working his way through the rooms looking for anything amiss.

"Come, my boy, into the library," Lord Ledderbey said, shuffling in that direction.

Weston took him by the arm and helped him there. The old man collapsed into a chair. "First," he said, "there was a pounding on the door sometime past two. Poor Jeremy answered it, scared out of his wits. Here is what was handed to him by a messenger on a fast horse."

Lord Ledderbey handed over a sheet of paper that looked as if it had gone through the wars.

Viscount Tramondeley

It is with regret that I inform you that Admiral Peter Parker is dead. (Natural causes. As you know, he was ill for some time) I am his personal secretary and have been aware of your communications to the admiral since the beginning. Do not send any further dispatches here, as I do not know who will step into the post. I am making inquiries into where your valuable insights ought to be redirected. Though, as you will soon see, perhaps they ought not be directed anywhere at all just now.

The admiral was in receipt of information only yesterday that he'd intended to communicate to you at the earliest possible moment. He did not get the chance, so I will do so now. He was alerted to the idea that the French know your approximate location and there is some idea of them attempting to locate you. Beyond that, we do not know their plan. Is it to destroy the Athena? Or perhaps make an end to the Mosquito himself? The admiral was intent on you moving locations and did have the opinion that you ought to pause your activities for some months to perhaps give the idea that their problem with the Mosquito has ended.

The admiral was quite fretful over this and took the threat very seriously. I urge you to vacate that location, at least for the time being.

Regards,
Lawrence Cadwalker, Former Secretary to Admiral Peter Parker.

Weston folded the letter. He could not say he was surprised to hear of the demise of the admiral, though he was sorry to hear it. They had been corresponding with one another for years and he had noticed over the past months that the admiral's penmanship had begun to deteriorate and appear shaky in nature. Weston would miss him indeed. He'd been only seventeen when he'd sent the first report and had a time of it convincing the admiral that it was true.

"Now, my boy," Lord Ledderbey said, "far be it for me to open your private correspondence. However, when that correspondence arrives in the middle of the night while you're out drifting round in the darkness on that little boat of yours, that is another matter. I'd thought maybe it was the news that duke of yours was finally dead, which would have been welcome all round."

Weston nodded. Lord Ledderbey had been a friend of his father's, so was forever aligned against the duke. The fact that His Grace never bothered with his heir only cemented his ideas. Weston, himself, did not harbor any particular feelings for the duke one way or the other, but for a bit of annoyance, though he absolutely did not wish him dead. He was not ready to take on the ducal mantle; he had too much else to do.

"I think we will have to move, at least for now," he said, "and I am sorry for that. I've put you in a terrible spot."

Lord Ledderbey waved his hands. "All for England, what right do I have to complain about it? But that's not the end of it. I'd just recovered from the shock of that first missive when another turned up just before dawn, and it's a corker."

Lord Ledderbey handed over another sheet of paper, this one looking far more pristine than the first.

Weston unfolded it.

Tramondeley—

I suppose I ought to have written before now, but boys are never up to much so I thought I'd wait until you reached your majority. In any case, better late than never, eh? Well, here you are and I look forward to seeing you in Town this season. I understand Ledderbey does not keep a house in London so I've rented you one. It's on Grosvenor Square, number four, fine address, we are there too, just across the square. It's furnished and up to the mark so all you need do is turn up with your staff. Bring Ledderbey along if you like.

Turn up as soon as is convenient, the house is ready and a porter will let you in. We will not arrive until the eleventh, come to dine on the thirteenth.

Pelham

Good lord, the duke had finally decided to get in touch. What did he mean, he'd rented a house? It seemed rather high-handed. Weston had no intention of going to Town. He was far too busy here.

Weston paused. He was too busy here, but now he must be elsewhere. Even if he were willing to take his chances, he could not leave Lord Ledderbey in danger. He could not go out at night, leaving the old fellow here alone to defend himself from an attack. The old fellow was deeply shaken over only letters arriving in the night, he'd fall over dead if the French breached his doors.

"You see how it is, I think," Lord Ledderbey said. "I'd been pondering where we ought to go and then that mad duke writes that he's rented us a house."

"Why has he done it, though?" Weston asked.

Lord Ledderbey shrugged. "Who knows. From what I know about that individual, predictability and sense are not his strong suits. Your father always said he was eleven eggs short of a dozen."

"I do not like this," Weston said. "Am I to go to Town and swan around like a weak-minded dandy with no thought for anything but amusement?"

Lord Ledderbey snorted. "I cannot quite picture that. However, presenting yourself for a season is not the worst idea in the world. For one thing, you'll make connections, far more than you ever could living in our lonely outpost. For another, you are getting of an age to consider marriage. Every likely lady in England will be found there. That's been on my mind for a while, actually."

Weston did not say so, but marriage had been on his mind too. He'd just been too busy to do anything about it. As well, he was not certain what sort of lady would like to live on the coast of Cornwall and wave off her husband at night as he set off across a dark ocean in a small sloop. He supposed she'd need to be a stalwart sort and having never set foot in London he was not certain how many of them existed.

"In any case," Lord Ledderbey said, "I believe we can view this as a two-birds-with-one-stone situation. We cannot stay here, and the Duke of Pelham has conveniently rented us a house."

Weston nodded. As improbable as it was, he could see no other solution. Hours ago, he'd been happily harrying a French ship and now he was to go play nice in Town with the duke who had ignored him all his life. What a world.

Stockton returned from his touring of the house. "Everything is in order, my lord," he said.

"Excellent. Now hold on to your hat, Stockton. We depart for London on the morrow. I'm to have a season, apparently."

"*London? A season? In London?*"

Those questions were posed in a tone of utter disbelief. "Go get some sleep and then get the trunks packed, I'll tell you all about it later."

Stockton, ever the disciplined navy man, recovered himself,

nodded, and set off to do his lord's bidding.

"Do you suppose we'll really have to go to Pelham's house for dinner?" Lord Ledderbey asked.

"I imagine so," Weston said.

"Careful there, the duke might be thinking of a match between cousins," Lord Ledderbey said. "I believe the youngest of that parade of women is not yet wed. At least, so says my sister in her ongoing effort to send me gossip I do not want."

Weston laughed, the first time he'd done so all morning. If the duke had any ideas of a match, he was indeed eleven eggs short of a dozen. The very idea that he'd take on a duke's daughter was absurd. He'd already met one of their ilk and had not enjoyed the experience. A lady raised in a ducal household would be far too particular for his taste. That sort imagined the whole world admired them. Let her find a delicate dandy who handed out posies of compliments and they could prance preciously through life together.

The duke might have rented him a house, but that generosity would not buy him any influence over his heir.

CHAPTER TWO

DAMIANO VERDICCIO, CONTE di Conpressio, eldest son of the Marquis di Rossi, currently found himself in the barbaric land of England. He'd been here before, of course. He had some relations that were English. His father even had an estate in Hertfordshire that they left a steward to manage, as apparently one could not demand respect in England without the land to back it up. He had been for several years sent to Eton. This schooling had not been to turn him into an Englishman, but rather to make him fluent in their harsh language. Those were some long years, forever hiding his disdain for plodding English habits and food and pretending he was delighted with all he saw. He was, to his core, continental—a pleasing mix of Sardinian and French.

Now that Napoleon had made himself King of Italy, Damiano leaned more heavily on the French side as a matter of convenience. If and when Napoleon was defeated and gone, he'd lean more to his Sardinian side. For now, he made himself useful to that obnoxious little sword-swinger, as he had every intent of keeping his father's vast estates intact. Napoleon had not conquered all of Sardinia yet, but he controlled an area close to his father's land. They would placate the little man for the moment. Dictators, profiteers, and usurpers might come and go, but his family's holdings were eternal. At least, he would see to it that they remained so under his watch.

So far, he'd been successful, though it had tried his patience endlessly. He'd been forced to deal with one of Napoleon's short and irritating attachés forever giving him orders and advice. Monsieur Bernard spoke to him as if they were equals; Monsieur Bernard had moved himself into the house to be on hand at every possible moment.

Monsieur Bernard even dared to speak directly to the marquis on occasion and Monsieur Bernard had no idea how many times the marquis had directed the maggiordomo to poison the little man's drink. Each time, Damiano had been forced to put a stop to it before Monsieur Bernard fell over dead. These days, if he heard Monsieur Bernard had again had the temerity to speak to the marquis, he just cancelled the order for poison he knew was coming. His father could not fathom why that presumptuous person was not dead already. The entire situation was tiresome.

If he could, he'd run Monsieur Bernard through with his sword and pitch his lifeless body to the road. Perhaps he would someday, or he'd let the marquis poison him, but not right now. For now, Napoleon and his cronies used Damiano for his ability to appear nearly anywhere, including England, thanks to his relations there. Due to his station, all doors were open to him. These French idiots might not like that he had a title, but they put up with it for their own purposes. He put up with *them* to keep his father's estate out of their hands.

This particular directive was a bit different though. For one, he was sent to England. For another, he had left Sardinia with two separate missions from two entirely different quarters.

The attaché required that he discover more about the operations of the Mosquito, an ongoing effort to harass the French fleet. This harassment only occurred at night and seemed only to be one small sloop at a time. It was not that the effort posed much danger to a frigate, or even that the sloop was most certainly tracking locations. No, the larger damage this operation was causing was unease within the ranks of seamen.

A few coincidences of the Mosquito appearing at night and a

ship sinking in the days afterward had created a mystique of terror surrounding that sloop. The crews whispered that when the Mosquito was seen, death was soon to follow. A stupid little boat had somehow become a harbinger of doom. Seamen always had their eyes out for it—that blink of a lamp that signaled it was nearby. Imaginations had begun to think they saw flashes of light everywhere. Whole crews, convinced they were soon to meet their maker, dragged heels and wrote last letters to loved ones that they were certain would never be delivered.

It was all nonsense, he had no doubt, but the men entirely ignored it when the sloop harassed them but their ships did *not* sink. They only had eyes for confirmations of their fears. Nonsense or not, when you expected men to fight you could not allow them to begin believing that unseen dark forces were at work against them. Especially not seamen, as they were in general prone to superstition.

So, how many people were involved in this Mosquito operation? How many of these sloops were sneaking around? Who led the operation? He'd been given the location of the pier that was thought to be the location of at least one of the sloops but that was all he had to go on. After the outstanding questions had been satisfactorily answered, he was to cut the head off the beast, which ought to send the rest of them involved scattering for the hills.

He had agreed to manage the matter if Monsieur Bernard would take himself elsewhere during his absence. He claimed the marquis did poorly and did not like company when he was in such a state. Monsieur Bernard would remain ignorant of the fact that if Damiano was not there to turn round the orders for poison, Monsieur Bernard would soon find himself toes up.

Damiano's plan was to base himself in London at Lady Tallifer's house until it was time to strike. She was a cousin of his father's and had been happy to provide him with a room. She was a rather silly woman, but that was probably for the best. When he needed to disappear to Cornwall to deal with the Mosquito, she would swallow whole whatever flimsy excuse he gave her. In any case, he had need to be in London for a time to execute the other duty given him.

The marquis had directed that he was to find himself a well-connected English bride. A duke's daughter, if possible. A princess would have been ideal, but Princess Caroline was too young, Princess Amelia was dead, and the rest of them too old. It would have been hard if not impossible in any case to get such a thing through the various hoops that must be jumped. A duke's daughter was far easier to achieve and there were three of the right age drifting round London this particular year. He would put on his pleasant manners and his best coat to get it done. His father was depending on him.

The Verdiccio family, unlike most of their equals, believed in hedging their bets. They'd long built alliances across nations rather than across Sardinia alone. Other Sardinian families wished to knit together and form an impenetrable club of sorts. They turned their noses up at anyone not of long Sardinian heritage. The Verdiccios cast their nets and webs over mountains and seas. If one place proved impossible, there was always someplace else to go. With Napoleon having great success on land and less success at sea, an island was an ideal choice just now, and what other island was more suitable than England?

As his father always said, were Sardinia to cease to exist, they would relocate to their estate in Hertfordshire, shorten their name to Verdic, take up fox hunting, stock their cellars with the substandard wines the English preferred, and carry on.

Damiano sighed. The whole venture was likely to be exhausting. He must wed and murder on the same trip. No rest for the weary, he supposed.

Nevertheless, he would get on with it. Just now, he was poised to have a perfectly natural and accidental encounter with one of his quarry. He'd been tracking the Duke of Pelham's movements and was informed of which inn he would stop at on the last night of his trip to Town. He would happen to be there too. A daughter was with him, Valentine or Violet, he thought her name was. Perhaps he could make quick work of that half of his reason for being in cold and damp England.

Rather cleverly, he'd arrived at the inn two days ago and reserved the only private dining room in the place for the entirety of his stay. The innkeeper had been leery, as he did expect the Duke of Pelham and that duke would expect to have the room. However, leeriness was always overcome with the right amount of money. This particular case proved rather easy, as it seemed the innkeeper was acquainted with the duke from past years and was not an admirer. Damiano was informed he ought to refuse to put any credence into half of what the duke said, especially anything to do with dishes nobody had heard of or a made-up holiday called Captain Cook Day.

As always, the English managed to take eccentricity to new heights.

Nevertheless, when the duke arrived, Damiano would make a great show of being a generous individual with the most delicate manners imaginable by insisting they must take the room for their convenience. The English were hilariously susceptible to flattery and he planned to use that to his advantage.

VALOR PEERED OUT the carriage window. Day by day, they'd inched their way toward London. This was their last stop overnight. On the morrow, they'd positively be there.

She had soothed herself rather satisfactorily over the idea, she thought. She'd simply decided that she would only consider a gentleman who was both strong so he might protect her, rather quiet, and had a habit of quietly collecting something, whether that be coins or rare books or some other thing.

Of course, her father had gone a long way in making the trip pleasant. He'd dropped the last trip's gambit of pretending it was

Captain Cook Day and reciting a poem he'd composed himself before revealing he'd made the whole thing up. This year, he'd taken to hinting that he'd noted a secret spy for the French creeping round the neighborhood and then collapsing in laughter when the staff at an inn began to appear worried over it. Valor could not work out if they were worried because they thought it might be true or whether they worried because they wondered if the duke had gone mad. Either way, it had been amusing and it passed the time.

The carriages had stopped and one of the grooms helped her and Mrs. Right to the ground. He reached in and got hold of Sir Galahad and put him in Valor's arms, that dog not liking to walk anywhere if he could just as easily be carried.

They followed the duke inside and found him looking askance at the innkeeper. "What do you say?" the duke asked. "Certainly we must have the dining room."

"It is unfortunate, Your Grace," the innkeeper said nervously, "but Count di Compressio has reserved it since he arrived."

"A foreigner?"

"Yes, he is, though I understand he has connections to England. What could I do? He all but insisted."

Just then, Valor spotted a rather marvelous looking man approach. He was tall and slender with thick dark hair and an aquiline nose. His clothes were usual, but somehow different. His coat's lapels were the smallest bit wider, the buttons somehow more restrained, the material seeming a very fine wool. His waistcoat was more colorful than she was used to seeing, yet not loud or off-putting. His boots were impeccable, one might fix one's hair in their shining reflection. His whole person gave off the idea of sophistication and elegance.

"Your Grace," he said with an elegant bow. "Conte di Compressio. Forgive me for overhearing. I understand you are experiencing trouble."

The duke turned to him and looked him up and down. "I am, rather."

"This cannot be permitted to proceed," the count said. "A duke of England inconvenienced? It is too absurd. No, I will not allow it. You must have the room, I will insist on it."

"Ah, there now, very good of you," the duke said, seeming far more cheered. "All problems solved."

"Most satisfactorily," the count said. "I can easily take myself to…some charming corner…out here. It will be most pleasant, I'm sure."

The duke looked the count over. "Here on your own, are you?"

The count nodded. "But for my valet. I arrive from Sardinia and travel to London to stay with my cousin, Lady Tallifer, and then see to my father's estate in Hertfordshire."

"Tallifer, you said?"

The count nodded. "She is a dear lady."

"Yes, I suppose she is. She's a good egg," the duke said. "Well now, I can't see a cousin of Lady Tallifer's being kicked out of a dining room, even if you are a foreigner. As it's just you, join us for dinner."

"I am most obliged, Your Grace," the count said.

There was a quiet self-assurance to the gentleman. There was a sense of calm about him. Perhaps all continental gentlemen were so? Valor did not know, as she'd not met any. She did note his English was rather perfect, which was surprising. She'd been told her French was middling at best and her accent hard on the ears. She spoke no Italian at all. She'd found it very hard to learn as much French as she had.

"This is Mrs. Right, and my daughter, Lady Valor Nicolet," the duke said.

The count swept into an elegant bow. "Mrs. Right, charmed. Lady Valor, my honor. May I say, that pug is clearly the result of excellent parentage. Rarely do I see a dog of that breed so well composed in form."

"I have always thought so," Valor said, much surprised by the comment. She was gratified that the gentleman perceived the worth of Sir Galahad. So few people ever did, despite her pointing it out.

"Ladies, until this evening," the count said, before taking himself off.

Valor was a bit taken aback. Had anybody told her that a strange gentleman was to dine with them, she would have been very opposed. And yet, she was not so opposed. She began to wonder if perhaps the count collected rare books.

"Papa, the count seems very nice," she said.

"Does he?" the duke said. "A bit delicate for my taste, but I suppose there is no harm in him."

Delicate. Yes, perhaps that was why she felt comfortable in his presence. She supposed she did not mind a bit of Sardinian delicate.

"Come, love," Mrs. Right said. "Let us proceed to our room and settle in before dinner."

Valor nodded. Dinner was looking to be more interesting than she'd expected. She hoped her father was not planning on fooling everybody about the French spy he'd allegedly seen. It might startle a delicate gentleman like Count di Compressio.

Sir Galahad yawned in her arms. She gazed down at him. "You really are well composed," she said to the chubby little dog. "Finally someone has noted it."

As Lord Ledderbey traveled with him, and as that lord was getting up in years, Weston saw to it that they accomplished the trip to London in easy stages. He was not sorry for it, as it turned out. They'd had early and leisurely dinners at the inns where they stopped and Weston had more conversation with his guardian than he'd had in a year.

He discovered that Lord Ledderbey had been rather fretful over Weston's way of life. It was not so much the danger of sailing around in the darkness as it was how much of a young gentleman's training had been somehow missed. His education in the usual subjects had not been formal but it was well enough, the lord having an extensive library. But the niceties of society had not been as successful. He brought up dancing specifically and regretted that he'd not hired a dancing master or encouraged Weston to attend the local assemblies.

Stockton, being more friend and accomplice than a valet, had attended these dinners. He'd nearly fallen off his chair when dancing was brought up.

Dancing. My God, was he expected to dance while in Town? According to Lord Ledderbey, he would be. They had not come to any conclusion about what ought to be done about his utter lack of the skill.

The carriage had made its way through the crowded streets of London. It was *too* crowded, in his opinion. Why did people not spread out more? Why jam themselves into one town like mackerel in a bucket? He'd just got here and found a distaste for it. It smelled, for one. The air did not feel clean, for another. And there were far too many people, for yet another.

Stockton stared out the window with a grim expression. He was a sailor at heart and clearly did not care to be landlocked.

"Gracious, I have not been to Town in an age," Lord Ledderbey said. "I find all this mad activity rather invigorating."

Weston peered out the window in response.

"Ah, we near the square now," Lord Ledderbey said. "If it is as I remember, it is a haven of peace surrounding a very pleasant square of greenery. And then, we are very close to the park, too."

Lord Ledderbey was right. Grosvenor Square was not half so busy as what they'd passed through so far, and the trees of the square did soften the harsh impressions of the town.

"Here we are," Lord Ledderbey said. "Well, it looks to be a fine house. I suppose we must venture inside and see what the Duke of Pelham has decided to rent for our convenience."

A porter noted their arrival and had the doors open. The

carriages carrying Lord Ledderbey's staff poured out and that staff all scurried to where they were needed under the direction of Malberry, Lord Ledderbey's intrepid butler. Trunks were unloaded, Cook very determinedly marched to the kitchens to discover what he would be dealing with, the housekeeper corralled the maids, and the footmen began the process of figuring out which trunks went where.

Weston gave his arm to Lord Ledderbey and helped him inside.

He must admit, it was a fine house. It was not as sprawling as the house in Cornwall. Lord Ledderbey's ancestors had added to that edifice several times and so it had grown by degrees. However, there was something about the compactness and order of this house that Weston liked.

They moved through the rooms, examining the accommodations. The drawing room was a very good size and overlooked the square.

"Ah, there is a well-stocked library," Lord Ledderbey said. "I shall be quite content."

It was indeed a fine library. There was also a music room, which would get no use at all as neither of them played an instrument. There was a smaller salon for what Weston supposed would be used for tête-à-têtes of the womanly variety. They came upon a good-sized dining room. And then a very large ballroom at the back of the house.

"You see," Lord Ledderbey said, "they've even got a ball-room, most London houses do."

Weston nodded. The Cornwall house had a ballroom too, though it was currently used for storage.

"My lord," Malberry said, hurrying in after them, "this was left on the mantel in the drawing room." He handed over a folded sheet of paper.

"From that duke, no doubt." Lord Ledderbey said.

Weston was equally certain it must be from the duke. The only other person to know that he'd relocated here was Lawrence

Cadwalker, the admiral's old secretary. Weston did not know what use he could be to the new admiral, whoever he might turn out to be, as he would be trapped in London for the time being, but he would not be here forever. As it was, he did not really expect to hear from him or anybody else until he'd returned to Cornwall.

He unfolded the paper.

Tramondeley—

If you are reading this, I can safely assume you have installed yourself in the house. Several things to note: I have stocked the wine cellar and a grocery order will be put in as soon as the porter has received you into the house. (Yes, I realize your butler will be offended at not choosing the wines himself and your cook will be apoplectic and disdainful of a grocery order he did not compose himself, but that's your problem, not mine!)

I have also arranged for the rooms over the stables to be kitted out and plentiful ale delivered so your coachman and grooms don't stage a revolt. The house staff will find several bottles of hock in the servants' hall to smooth their transition to Town. If they complain after all that then I do not understand what sort of people you employ!

We will have a family dinner on the thirteenth. High time you met your cousins and I have an astounding supply of them. The once removeds are growing too and will make a brief appearance. Though he is not family, bring Ledderbey if you've dragged that fellow to Town. I am well aware that he does not hold a high opinion of me, but I never do care what other people think. We dine at eight.

Pelham

Lord Ledderbey had read the missive over his shoulder. "He is a case all his own," the lord said.

Weston nodded in agreement. Though, he was rather admiring of the duke's care for his staff. He'd not expected that. He was not certain what he *had* expected, but the duke sparing a thought for those below him had not occurred to him. He expected the staff would be at least somewhat mollified. "You will come to this dinner, will you not?" he asked Lord Ledderbey. "You will not send me there on my own?"

"I will most certainly come. I would like to get a look at this duke."

"And his endless supply of daughters."

Lord Ledderbey nodded. "Six of them, maybe seven, I've lost track."

"I wonder if Lady Marchfield will turn up," Weston said. He did not know his aunt well, but she was in the habit of sending a card over Christmas, which was more than the duke had ever done.

"Hard to say," Lord Ledderbey said. "I am told by my sister that the duke and Lady Marchfield do not care for each other in another one of her letters full of gossip I did not ask for."

Weston looked around. Now that he was here, he did feel a bit fish out of water. What was he supposed to do? Where was he supposed to go? He did not know anybody here.

The porter came into the room. "My lords, here is the correspondence that has arrived to the house since I was employed."

Weston looked at the tall stack of letters the porter carried. "Correspondence? From who?"

"Invitations, likely," Lord Ledderbey said.

"Invitations from who and to what?" Weston asked. "I do not know anybody."

Lord Ledderbey laughed. "That does not matter. You are the heir presumptive to a dukedom and it seems that word has gotten out that you are here. Mamas all over Town will wish you on their guest list."

People he did not know wished for him to turn up at their house, all because he might someday become a duke. It seemed extraordinary.

"Prepare yourself, my boy," Lord Ledderbey said. "You are on the verge of having every young lady in Town thrown in your direction. Careful who you catch."

"What a situation," Weston muttered.

Both he and Lord Ledderbey retired to the drawing room while the staff got their rooms ready. There had been some question as to which rooms would suit, but neither of them cared about it. Weston's opinion was a bed was a bed. Lord Ledderbey claimed he'd be comfortable in a closet, as long as he had an interesting book and a decent glass of claret. They'd left it up to Stockton's good sense to sort it out.

Stockton did use his good sense. Both gentlemen had rooms overlooking the square and its greenery. If one squinted, one could almost imagine oneself back in the countryside.

Weston flipped through the stack of letters. "I've got to reply to all of these. How am I supposed to choose where I will go? How am I to keep track of where I am supposed to be?"

Lord Ledderbey considered the matter. "You'll need a diary to keep your calendar. Perhaps you ought to hire a secretary to manage it. It might be beneficial to write to your aunt and ask for her assistance. I'd say ask the duke, but well…"

Weston smiled. Lord Ledderbey would trust the duke with nothing, not even a party invitation. He had a good idea, though, about writing to Lady Marchfield. "You do not suppose Stockton could do it? Act as my secretary?"

Lord Ledderbey snorted. "Stockton arranging your musical evening or attendance at a card party? I do not think he would thank you for it."

"Musical evening? Good God, what is that?"

"Young ladies display their musical talent, everybody rises up in applause even if they are dreadful, and then outrageous compliments are handed out to those same ladies at a small reception. I seem to remember they are tedious but somehow necessary."

"Tedious? It sounds tortuous," Weston said. "Is it similar to what we experienced when we got bamboozled into attending Lord Waterstone?" Waterstone was not five miles off but rarely at home. Last year, he had been at home and had brought his niece, Miss Bing. After dinner, they'd been forced to sit for an hour while Miss Bing banged determinedly on the pianoforte.

"Imagine ten Miss Bings, all at the ready to delight your ears," Lord Ledderbey said with a snort.

One Miss Bing had been quite sufficient. Weston rummaged through a desk for some writing things. He must contact Lady Marchfield and hope the lady was amenable to helping him sort through this pile of invitations he'd not asked for. And would help him avoid any musical evenings that were included in the stack.

Though, he supposed the pile of invitations did answer the question of what he was supposed to do with himself while he was stuck here.

CHAPTER THREE

D AMIANO ENTERED THE inn's dining room to find the duke and his daughter already there. Confirming the endless eccentricity of the English, the housekeeper and the fat dog were there too.

"Come sit by me, Count," the duke said.

This seemed painfully obvious, as the housekeeper had her charge settled on the other side of the table. "Yes, Your Grace, most considerate. A fine evening."

"Do you enjoy our weather?" Lady Valor asked.

Damiano had to pinch his leg to stop from laughing. Who on earth enjoyed English weather? Mother Nature seemed to glare down at this spot of the world and order more rain, and then more rain again. That rain was reliably cold. The sun appeared very reluctant to ever make an appearance.

"Oh yes," he said. "It is so…forceful."

"Hah! Not like your Sardinian weak-willed sunshine. Surprised you don't get tired of it, day after day," the duke said.

"What brings you to our shores?" the housekeeper asked.

Now he was to paint a picture that did not at all say why he was here. "Ah, my family has deep roots in England. I was educated at Eton and I have cousins here. After I check on our estate in Hertfordshire, I will spend time enjoying the London societal season."

"Do you spend much time at your estate in Hertfordshire?"

Lady Valor asked.

"Naturally," Damiano said. "A fine estate just north of St. Albans. If I have to criticize it in any way, it is that it is in a very quiet neighborhood. But then, I find I can appreciate quiet. I have been considering settling there permanently so that I might enjoy the peace of the bucolic English countryside."

There was no confusion about how that idea landed with Lady Valor. She was most approving of it. His suspicions were confirmed that she was a rather timid lady who would not care for anything too exciting. Another type of lady might thrill to hear of a swordfight. Lady Valor Nicolet would rather hear of cows grazing.

"Do you collect anything, Count?" Lady Valor asked.

He was not certain what she was fishing for, but he collected knives and was relatively certain she would not see the beauty of them. "Ah, I carry on the family tradition—we collect art. Is there anything so satisfying as going to a museum and walking the hushed corridors amidst the works of great masters?"

"That does sound rather marvelous," Lady Valor said.

"Could there be anything more wonderful than the Capitoline in the Palazzo dei Conservatori?"

"I'm sure I do not know," Lady Valor said. "I've never been to the Continent."

Of course she hadn't. These young English ladies never went anywhere. "But then," he said, "you have your own storied institutions. The British Museum is very fine—what do you think of it?"

Lady Valor blushed up to her ears. "Goodness, I've never been."

Mio Dio, she had not even bothered to go to a museum so nearby. "No! I cannot believe it. You must allow me to escort you there."

"Papa?"

"Fine, fine, as long as Mrs. Right or one of your sisters accompanies you. Now, I did not wish to put a damper on the evening, but we ought to look sharp these days. I am certain there is a French spy in this neighborhood."

One of the innkeeper's waiters set a platter down with a crash. The other spun round and stared at the windows. Then he hurriedly closed the curtains.

Damiano set his glass down slowly. What did the duke say? Did he somehow know that Damiano spied for the French? He must do, why else would he say it? Was it a warning of some kind? But then why allow his daughter to be escorted to a museum by him?

The duke suddenly roared with laughter. "Works every time! The look on your faces!"

"Count, my papa likes to invent a ruse to amuse himself," Lady Valor said.

The housekeeper nodded in agreement. "He's very clever about it. Last year, he had everybody celebrating Captain Cook Day, a holiday that does not exist."

"Good fun," the duke said, "that's what's needed to ease these interminable journeys."

A ruse for the fun of it? About a French spy in the area? Damiano did not see the humor in it.

And what was he talking about to name a trip to London an interminable journey? These people were not even traveling outside of their own country. "Ah now I see," Damiano said, though he did not see in the least, "Your Grace enjoys a jest."

"Yes, why not," the duke said. "Passes the time."

As this conversation was unfolding, the waiters' looks were getting very dark. Damiano presumed they'd been the previous victims of Captain Cook Day.

"Eh, boys?" the duke said to them. "Remember Grassington Hambac?"

Damiano did not have the first idea of what Grassington Hambac might be, but noting the ever darkening looks of the waitstaff, he presumed they did. It did not seem as if they had fond memories of it.

To move the conversation past the duke's eccentricities, and frankly annoying jests, he said, "I rather like traveling in England. There are so many quiet and peaceful byways." He was certain that Lady Valor was perhaps less than valorous and would find favor in the idea.

Which she did. He spent the next half hour hearing all about the peace of the Dales and pretending to be charmed by it. Apparently, one could see for miles. As the view described was one of farmer's fields divided by stone walls, he was rather at a loss as to why anybody would want to. Nevertheless, he took the proverbial stage at Drury Lane and playacted that he was mightily intrigued.

All in all, he'd made a good effort. He was to locate and woo a duke's daughter and he'd found a very likely candidate. She seemed to like him, her father was a fool, she was well-funded, she was pretty, and she would certainly be easy to manage. He did not suppose he could do better than that.

WESTON HAD JUST returned to the house. He'd decided that morning that since he was forced into attending a London season he might as well do some things he actually liked. He'd gone to Lackington & Allen and acquired a pile of books for Lord Ledderbey's library. He would not necessarily have known which books to choose but Mr. Lackington had been very helpful in assisting him. Then he went on to Tattersall's to have a look at the horseflesh on offer, which was something he understood far better.

Now he sat in the drawing room with his boots up on a table. Lord Ledderbey was examining the books he'd returned with, clearly delighted with the unexpected additions to his collection and wondering how he'd known just what to choose.

Malberry entered with a letter on a salver.

"If it's more invitations," Weston said, "just add them to the pile in the hall. I'm hoping Lady Marchfield will come and sort through them."

"My lord, this appears to be a letter from that very lady."

"See, she responds promptly," Lord Ledderbey said. "Must be a good sign."

Weston took the letter and unfolded it.

My dear Tramondeley—

I will admit to being surprised at hearing from you and finding the wording of your letter so pleasant. I have always constrained myself to only sending a Christmas card on account of the duke claiming you did not wish to hear from us. (I now wonder if that was ever true.)

In any case, I would be delighted to assist you in navigating the treacherous landscape of London society. I will attend you at two o'clock this very day.

Your Aunt Penelope,
Countess of Marchfield

Weston passed the note to Lord Ledderbey. "That duke really is a devil," he said. "It was not enough that he never gets in touch, but he goes so far as to trick my own aunt into ignoring me."

"Why has he done it, though," Lord Ledderbey said thoughtfully. "He might be eleven eggs short of a dozen, but I suspect he had a reason." The lord paused. "Gad, she says two o'clock, that is in five minutes time!"

Both of their gazes drifted to the clock. It was even less than five minutes. Weston heard the distinctive sound of carriage wheels rolling to a stop.

He got his boots off the table and brushed off the dried mud that had been deposited there. "Malberry, meet Lady Marchfield and escort her in and then get something from the kitchens. What should we have for a lady? Not brandy, I imagine."

"A tea tray, my lord," Malberry said gravely.

"Yes, yes, you'll know what to do," Weston said.

Malberry turned and stalked out. Weston could see out the drawing room windows a very prepossessing matron descending from her carriage. So that was his aunt.

The butler had the door open and the lady was inside in a trice. He led her into the drawing room.

"Lady Marchfield," Weston said, bowing.

She took his measure and said, "I did think, from the tone of your letter, that we were not to be so formal. You may call me Aunt, Tramondeley."

"Very kind," he said. "Might I introduce Lord Ledderbey."

Lady Marchfield nodded. "Lord Ledderbey, I suppose we owe you great thanks for watching over Tramondeley during his formative years."

"He has been excellent company, Lady Marchfield, and so I think most of the advantage has been to myself. Do sit, a tea tray will be up shortly."

Lady Marchfield took a chair. She said, "Might I clarify one matter before we go further. Tramondeley, did you tell the duke that you did not wish to hear from any of us, on account of the rift between the duke and your father?"

"I did not," Weston said. "I have never said anything at all to the duke. I have never laid eyes on him, met him, or corresponded with him."

"That devil," Lady Marchfield said.

"Do you have any idea why he invented such a story?" Lord Ledderbey asked. "We did wonder, over the years, why he did not get in touch. At least, I wondered."

"I do not know why he's done it. At least, not precisely," Lady Marchfield admitted. "But I can tell you, if there is a right way to do something, my brother will about-face and go in the opposite direction."

"He rented this house for me," Weston said. "I am not clear why."

"Nor am I," Lady Marchfield said, clearly surprised by that

information. "I would say perhaps his conscience catches up with him, but that seems too unlikely."

"We are to dine there on the thirteenth," Lord Ledderbey said. "I suppose he's issued you the same invitation."

"He has not," Lady Marchfield said grimly. "But rest assured, I will attend. You will not face him alone. It will not be the first time I have been forced to invite myself. In any case, I have recently installed a butler on the premises and would like to see how he gets on."

Weston had initially imagined that the duke had asked Lady Marchfield to hire a butler for him. But then the tea tray came in and she poured out the cups and described what happened to the other six butlers she'd sent into the duke's house, one of which was still writing her letters from America. This new one, she claimed, would stick no matter what the duke's deranged housekeeper tried—he was a regular barnacle on a boat.

The duke was beginning to seem even more bizarre than he'd imagined.

"Now, I've already sent a note to Lady Westmoreland alerting her that you are in Town," Lady Marchfield said. "She will see to it that you are given vouchers and tickets to Almack's. The opening ball is in a week, it is critical you show yourself there. Bring me the invitations you have received so far and let us see what we have to work with."

Weston nodded to Malberry to fetch the stack. Though, he remained silent on the idea of a ball. He certainly would not attend Almack's as he did not dance. Were there any other balls in those invitations, he would not attend them either.

For all that, he was rather glad he'd handed over the task of sorting through that correspondence to Lady Marchfield. With the efficiency of a general, she put the piles into yes and no, explaining to him why. Some were routs thrown by what his aunt considered to be "climbers of the worst sort." Others were in the yes pile, such as Lady Jellerbey's candlelight picnic, only because the attendees were rather rarified, though the event itself was absurd. Yet others were in the yes pile as being dignified evenings where he would mingle with the right sort of people. Two of those were the dreaded musical evenings. Still, she'd left him to write out the acceptances and he felt he had a much better idea of what was what in this town. He did not necessarily need to accept everything she'd given the stamp of approval.

After she had the invitations squared away, she went down to the kitchens to alert the Cook as to the most reliable grocers and explained to Malberry that he could contact her own wine merchant and use her name. Should they wish for the best tea, Mr. Twining was their man. She would send over her own butler for a consultation on anything else that was needed.

She'd glanced at Weston's clothes and asked about the state of his wardrobe. Discovering it was much the same as what she currently viewed, it was deemed insufficient. "I will contact Mr. Rigleur myself and have him call on you. He will know what's needed—Lord Marchfield depends upon him."

She left with his assurance that he and Lord Ledderbey were to come to her house to dine on the morrow and that Lord Marchfield would be happy to see them.

After she departed, Lord Ledderbey said, "She is a helpful sort of lady."

"Rather," Weston said. "I believe we have found the captain of our London ship."

"And from what I can gather, the duke will not like it."

"All the better," Weston said.

Mrs. Agnes Right found herself in an almost melancholy sort of mood. The carriages had entered the environs of London and the future she'd always dreaded marched inexorably closer. Her last girl would marry and leave the house.

Over the years, it had been so difficult to watch them go, one by one, but she'd soothed herself with the idea that there were still some of them in the house. Then after Winsome had wed, it was just Valor left to her.

That interesting poppet had done her level best to remain at home forever. Mrs. Right had almost hoped she'd succeed in it too. She had not, and the housekeeper had seen those inevitable signs of maturity coming over her. Like all the rest, she would wish for her own family.

And now here it was. The beginning of the end. Her only hope was that it might take more than one season to settle her.

Valor peered out the window at the bustling streets. "What do you think, Mrs. Right? My aunt says the new butler will be a barnacle on a boat."

"Aye, so she says. Mr. Hubert Huberville is his name. But what I say is that any harbormaster worth their salt can scrape a barnacle off a boat with very little trouble."

"So you will be the harbormaster?"

"I always have been, love."

The carriages had entered the square and slowed to a stop.

Mrs. Right kept her eyes on the front doors, and she was glad she did. They were flung open and a short and round individual flew outside and promptly tripped. He fell on the road and rolled a few feet before coming to a stop.

The duke and his valet, Reynolds, had descended from their carriage. The duke stared down at the prone butler.

Charlie opened their carriage door and snorted. "Well Mrs. Right, there's Lady Marchfield's latest man lying on the ground looking like a dug-up potato."

They were helped out, along with Sir Galahad who had, for the past hours, been snoring on his blanket. Valor took him in her arms and the little pug seemed very surprised that they'd turned up in a new place while he napped.

Meanwhile, Mr. Reynolds helped Mr. Huberville to his feet, his coat now severely muddied. Thomas ran ahead to get the door open for the duke, who stepped around Lady Marchfield's latest project.

Really, where did the lady find these men?

Mrs. Right held up her head and did not deign to even glance at the muddy butler.

In the great hall, Valor said, "Goodness, this would be a moment when all my sisters would race above stairs to fight over the rooms. Now there is no need to run as nobody will compete with me."

"Cheer up, Poppet," Mrs. Right said, "you'll finally have the best room."

Valor nodded. "But I will be alone in that corridor. I'm going to ask Papa if you can take the room next to me."

Mrs. Right nodded and presumed the duke would sanction it. They already did so in the Dales. Valor had ever been harassed with nightmares and they still came upon her from time to time. She was especially prone when left alone with only her imagination for company. Mrs. Right had long moved out of the servants' quarters on account of it after Winsome had gone.

"And we must be sure that Sir Galahad's bed is put back together again by his bedtime. He's been a very good soldier about roughing it over the past days."

Mrs. Right nodded. Sir Galahad, unlike most canines, reposed in a miniature four-poster bed with a canopy of silk and a knit blanket it had taken Valor several years to complete. The pieces of that very fancy dog bed were currently packed in the coach, but Charlie had disassembled and reassembled it so often that he would have it back together in no time. Whether or not this bed was necessary was an ongoing question, as Sir Galahad more often ended up sleeping in Valor's own bed, but Valor thought he preferred it for daytime naps.

"You go up and I will go down," the housekeeper advised. "I would like to have a word with Cook regarding our new inhabitant."

Valor carried Sir Galahad to his new bedchamber and Mrs. Right made her way down to the kitchens. She found Cook waiting for her as he would have heard the ruckus of their arrival over his head. As they'd always done, he'd traveled ahead and had been in the house for some days already to get the place in shape for the arrival of the duke.

"Well?" she said. "What do we have on our hands?"

"I hardly know how to explain it, Mrs. Right."

"Do take a stab at it, though."

Cook nodded. "You know how all these butler fellas think they're above everybody else, as if they ain't made from the same cloth?"

Mrs. Right nodded, as that was the primary thing she had against butlers.

"This one don't. He's as jumpy as a jackrabbit and forever apologizing over I do not know what. This morning, he claimed he was sorry he'd finished his breakfast plate as he thought I might want some of it. Why should I want something from his plate when I have my own? I am the cook, can I not be trusted to make myself enough food? That's the way of him, sorry over everything."

Mrs. Right tapped her chin. This was new. She'd made a habit of taking a butler down a peg but it did not seem as if this one had any pegs to take down. "He ran out to greet the duke and fell on the road," she said.

"Oh yes, that's him all over. He's always in such a state he's forever falling over. He's fallen off his chair twice already."

Mrs. Right heard the familiar sound of footsteps on the stairs. Mr. Hubert Huberville came round the bend in a rush, bounced off a wall, and steadied himself with the back of a chair.

"Mrs. Right, an honor to meet you, my lady."

My lady?

Mr. Huberville raised his hands as if she were on the verge of saying something, which she was not. "Now, I know you are the ruler of this roost! Rest assured, good lady, I do not intend on getting in your way!"

What in the world was she to do with this specimen? She'd

never encountered the like of it.

Mr. Huberville mopped his brow with a handkerchief. "What next? Think, Huberville! What is to be done next? Don't fall apart on the first day!"

"Mr. Huberville," Mrs. Right said, wondering if the fellow was on the verge of expiring, "nothing must be done this minute. Charlie and Thomas will see to the trunks—"

"Charlie and Thomas," Mr. Huberville said. "Just saw them, seemed like good sorts, those two."

"Yes, very good sorts. Do sit for a moment. Cook, might we get a tea tray?"

"The water is on the boil, Mrs. Right," Cook said.

Mr. Huberville collapsed on a chair. He pointed at Cook. "He knows what's what, on the ball, as it were."

Mrs. Right took her place at the head of the table, which she noticed Mr. Huberville had not challenged her on. "Mr. Huberville, in the general way of becoming acquainted, might you relay to me how you ended up losing your place, twice? Lady Marchfield did note it in her letter to the duke."

This seemed to undo Mr. Huberville entirely. He covered his face with his hands. "You're bound to find out the truth anyway."

"Which is?"

"I'm not very good at it," he whispered. "I try to be, but it's just one thing after another. And then, people are so particular! One dinner party missing some forks and wine glasses and suddenly it's 'pack your bags, Huberville!' One dropped saucière of gravy on somebody's lap and it's 'pack your bags, Huberville!'"

Extraordinary. Mrs. Right wondered if Lady Marchfield had done this on purpose. Had she sought out the worst butler in London as a jest?

Cook brought over the tea tray, glancing at Mrs. Right with raised brows as if to say, *You see what I was talking about.*

Thomas and Charlie came down the stairs. They would have got the trunks in the house and would have their tea before hauling it all above stairs. With only one of the duke's daughters left, it was a far less onerous job than it had been in years past.

Both footmen looked enquiringly at Mrs. Right. She nodded and said, "Sit down, boys. We have an interesting situation here."

Their eyes drifted to the interesting situation, just now staring morosely into his tea.

"It's me, she's talking about me," Mr. Huberville said. "I'm terrible at my job, that's what. Oh I know, you two fellas must be burning with hatred. Probably want to punch me right in the face. Why should Huberville be the butler instead of one of us when he's not even good at it? I don't blame you for despising me, how could it be otherwise? I'm sorry! Don't punch me if you can manage it, I believe I suffer from very weak face bones."

Charlie and Thomas looked wide-eyed at Mrs. Right. She sighed. "I can at least clear one thing up, Mr. Huberville. Neither Charlie nor Thomas want to be a butler. They've long cooked up a plan between them to open a tavern. They've since made a deal with the duke to take over an old baker's premises in our village and pay the duke the handsome sum of one pound a year and free ale for life. It's all to proceed at the end of this season."

"That gives us enough money in our pockets to turn the place into something nice and buy all the supplies. It's a better deal than it looks—the duke hardly ever drinks ale," Charlie said.

Thomas nodded. "He's to stock his own private reserve of claret out of his own pocket and that's what he'll want to drink when he comes."

"He says it's important that he show his face there so his tenants know they can talk to him if they want."

"Personally," Thomas said, "I think they'll all need a few drinks in them before they approach the duke—good for business, I reckon."

Mr. Huberville took up his tea in a shaking hand. "A tavern. That's a relief, I can tell you. I've had nightmares about it. What will those poor boys think! How hard will they punch? And me, with weak face bones!"

"P'raps take in some deep breaths," Charlie advised.

"I'll get a brush from Reynolds to get the mud off your clothes and you'll be right as rain," Thomas said encouragingly.

Mr. Huberville took that moment to cry, "Such kindness!" and then weep into his tea.

What in the world was she to do with this person? How was one to go about doing battle with a bowl of sobbing jelly?

CHAPTER FOUR

V ALOR STOPPED IN her tracks. The afternoon had gone by so joyfully. Three of her youngest nieces and nephews had come for a visit. Serenity's girl Daisy, Verity's boy Henry, and Winsome's boy Leland had made happy chaos in the drawing room.

Valor had heard all about them in letters of course, but what jolly little people they were. At least, mostly. Young Henry Foster could not be mistaken for anybody's son other than Lord Wembly, as he came with a shock of red hair. While Verity assured her that Henry could be in a temper on occasion, he'd spent the hour very creditably by laughing at everything that caught his notice and Sir Galahad in particular. Isabelle had more wildly swinging emotions, so was sometimes laughing and sometimes red in the face. Leland was really still a baby and spent most of the time examining how the other two were up on their feet and trying to accomplish the same.

Now this evening was to be a family party and she would see all her sisters and her dear nieces and nephews after a long parting. She'd just risen to go above stairs to change her dress when the duke had said, "By the by, did I mention that Tramondeley is coming?"

"Tramondeley?" Valor asked, turning round. "Your heir? The terrible fellow who might make me a governess to his children if I end a spinster?"

"Ah yes, as to that, perhaps I outlined the worst case. Perhaps he's not as bad as that. In any event, he is living just across the square. Seemed like it wouldn't be the thing to ignore him. We'll take him as we find him, I suppose."

Her father's heir. They'd never laid eyes on him. All Valor knew about him was that the duke and Tramondeley's father had never seen eye to eye. His father had been a very serious sort of person and the duke…was not. His father thought the winds of fate had been blowing in the wrong direction to have made her papa the heir and not himself.

They'd had a final falling out about something or other and never spoke again.

"Cheer up, remember that all my grandchildren are coming too. We'll see them before dinner and then they will be entertained by the housemaids below stairs. That is the end of the good news, I'm afraid," the duke said. "We will also see your aunt. Apparently, Lady Misery has got her claws into Tramondeley, though I do not know how she even discovered he was in Town. She's sent me a note that she was coming whether I liked it or not."

Goodness, Tramondeley was coming and so was Lady Marchfield. It was not to be the carefree dinner she'd imagined.

Valor hurried out of the room and up the stairs. She was relieved to find Mrs. Right already waiting for her. She examined the rather simple dress that lay on the bed.

"I think I will wear something different," she said. "I thought this dinner was to be just my sisters and their husbands, but did you know that Lord Tramondeley is coming?"

"Tramondeley?" Mrs. Right said in evident surprise. "The duke's heir? I thought he was holed up in Cornwall somewhere."

"Now he's here and living just across the square," Valor said. "And Lady Marchfield comes too."

"Does she now?" Mrs. Right said. "I suppose she'll want to have a look at how Mr. Huberville gets on."

"How *does* he get on?" Valor asked. "Every time I see him he looks as if he's seen a ghost."

"Aye, that's his natural condition. He is nervous and apologetic and falling down every time a person turns round."

"Goodness."

"Goodness is one word for it. Now, what do you think about that dark-blue silk with the velvet edging on the bodice and cuffs?"

Valor nodded, as it was a very good choice. Just then, the door was flung open and her oldest sister, Felicity, burst into the room with a case under her arm. "There you are, Val. Gracious, you have grown into a proper lady!"

"Felicity!" Valor said, flinging herself into her sister's arms.

"Now, I do not arrive so early for no reason," Felicity said, laying the case on the bed. "I have conducted a sisterly conference of sorts about what we ought to do about your jewelry, or lack of it."

Valor had long been aware that she'd got the short end of the stick regarding her mother's jewelry. Their father had allowed them to take what pieces they liked, but Valor had been far too young for the task. She'd picked out the worst sort of paste and anything loud and colorful that had caught her eye. For years, she'd been dogged about wearing a particularly awful, enameled parrot pin.

"We've all contributed pieces that we thought would suit," Felicity said, opening the case.

Inside were all manner of necklaces, earrings, bracelets, and even a tiara.

"We all pitched in for the tiara as nobody could be convinced to give up their own," Felicity said, laughing. "Poor Stratton was taken aback to get a bill from Rundell & Bridge for one-sixth of a tiara. He wished to know what I planned to do about the other five-sixths."

"I could wear it tonight, even though I am not engaged," Valor said, marveling at the platinum and diamond piece. "Papa will not mind it."

Mrs. Right had fetched the dark-blue silk. Felicity looked it over and said, "Perhaps add the delicate diamond necklace, that came from Grace and will suit the dress very well—it's not too showy."

Her sisters were very dear to compose a jewelry case for her. She really had not known what she was to do about that.

"Felicity, did you know Lord Tramondeley was coming to-night?"

"Our papa's heir?"

"Yes, and our aunt too."

"Gracious, this might be more exciting than I had imagined. Is that why the new butler looks on the verge of collapse?"

"No, he's always like that," Mrs. Right said. "He's not one of Lady Marchfield's sturdier specimens."

"Well, I will give our aunt credit for dogged determination with her butlers. I'm sure however you manage him, Mrs. Right, this certainly must be her last effort. Val, get dressed and don your new tiara," Felicity said. "I cannot wait until we are all together again. For now, Isabelle is in the drawing room giving her sage seven-year-old advice to Papa on what he ought to do if he finds himself in a temper, which she has vast experience with. Closeting oneself in one's room and stomping on the floor is highly recommended."

With that, Felicity left the room.

Weston held his arms up and Stockton put on his coat. Lady Marchfield had been as good as her word and sent a very skilled tailor. The man was almost a magician, he'd returned days later with an entire wardrobe. Stockton said he employed an army of tailors working night and day to execute his designs. Considering the bill, it might have been several armies.

Despite the enormous expense, both Weston and his valet

approved of the result. Weston had been forceful in his view that he did not want to be turned out as a prancing dandy and he'd not been. The clothes were elegant and simple, with a precise cut, just what he would prefer.

It had probably been time he did something with his clothes in any case. It was just that there did not seem to ever be an extra moment when he was in Cornwall. He was awake most nights sailing and asleep most days, which did not make for an opportunity to accomplish mundane tasks.

Stockton brushed his coat and made some small adjustments to his neckcloth. "I don't like it, my lord."

His valet was a man of few words, but as they'd known one another and worked in close quarters for years, Weston understood his meaning. It was not a comment on the clothes. In answer, he said, "I will go to the dinner and meet this duke and then I suppose that will be that. We are not likely to become friends. He might rent me a house but that does not buy my approval."

"Careful of that last daughter he has hanging about the place."

Weston laughed. "I imagine you have not met many duke's daughters. She'll be insipid and fanning herself and fishing for admiration. She will find, though, that she fishes in an empty lake and will not find any compliments on her hook. It is always the way with a duke's daughter."

Stockton snorted. "How many duke's daughters have you met?"

"Just Lady Letitia when she visited Lady Monroe and they turned up at the house. That was quite enough for one lifetime. Lady Monroe was most approving of Lady Letitia, so I presume she was a very usual sort of duke's daughter."

Weston had not comprehended it at the time, but he now suspected that Lady Monroe's visit to the house with Lady Letitia in tow had been for the sole purpose of throwing that lady in front of him. They had arrived unannounced and pretended they'd thought it was Lord Ledderbey's at-home day. The lord did not host an at-home day, which Lady Monroe would know very well. He and Lord Ledderbey went on very much as hermits and nobody would imagine they would fling open their doors to all and sundry. On occasion, a card had been dropped off but they generally looked at it and shrugged, never thinking about it again.

Nevertheless, Lady Monroe and Lady Letitia were persistent at the door and Ledderbey was forced to let them in. Then he had to explain how it was that Weston was still asleep at two in the afternoon. He'd made up some story about Weston just returning from a trip. After Lady Monroe put up an endless fuss over not seeing him, Lord Ledderbey was cornered into asking them to come back for dinner.

What a night that was. Lady Letitia was a tall and razor-thin lady with an oddly pinched face, rather bulging eyes, and a painful shriek of a laugh. She had apparently bathed in powerfully scented water and was a walking flower garden, the scent lingering in any room she'd been in. He'd been surprised she had not attracted bees.

The lady had encased these charms in a sickly green taffeta concoction with ruffles going in every direction. She had whipped her fan around like a sword and in fact hit him several times with it in some sort of bizarre flirtation.

None of that would have put him off a friendship, but the lady had nothing of note to say. She was all shrieky giggles and spent the evening accusing him of staring. If he *had* stared, it was only out of stupefied wonder—nothing could have prepared him for the assault on his senses. By the time those two ladies should have been on their way home, Lady Letitia had threatened to play the pianoforte. Fortunately it had not been tuned in years. Both Weston and Lord Ledderbey had been exhausted by the time they'd maneuvered those two ladies out the door. He did not expect anything different from the Duke of Pelham's daughters.

He went downstairs and found Lord Ledderbey in the drawing room. "Now my boy," he said, "are you certain we ought to bother with the carriage?"

It was true the duke's house was only across the square, but it was also true that it would be just a bit too far for Lord Ledderbey to walk, especially to have to come back again later when he would be tired.

"I do think it best," Weston said. "It is muddy outside and we should not like to turn up looking disheveled."

Ledderbey said, "All right, I'll pretend to believe you on that. Well, these old bones won't mind a ride, I suppose. We'd best be off for our thirty seconds of carriage ride to the other side of the square."

They set off and were indeed there in under a minute. It looked as if quite a few other people had arrived too, the duke's endless supply of daughters, Weston imagined. How on earth did he have so many of them? Had anybody ever had so many without running into a son at some point? Seven. It was bound to be a trying evening surrounded by seven versions of Lady Letitia. If they all had fans, he might come out of it badly bruised.

He helped Lord Ledderbey to the pavement and the doors flew open. "My lords! Step inside and I will announce you. Yes, announce, that is what I'm to do. Got to get it right!"

The butler was a short and squat individual whose voice shook as if he were on the verge of panic. He also seemed to be unaware that he was saying his thoughts aloud. Weston ought not be surprised. He imagined anybody working for a duke who was eleven eggs short of a dozen was bound to be a wreck.

The fellow attempted to lead them in but ended up running himself into the doorframe and clutching at his forehead.

"Are you quite all right?" Lord Ledderbey asked.

The man hit the emerging lump on his forehead as if he could make it go away. "Fine, fine, don't tell anybody!"

"No, of course not," Lord Ledderbey said in a soothing tone. "Let's get you inside."

"Thank you, yes, that would be helpful."

"No trouble at all, allow me to give you an arm—you've had a nasty encounter with that door."

"I did hit it rather hard."

It was extraordinary. Somehow the roles were reversed and they were escorting the butler into the house. They were not even inside the doors yet and the eccentricity of the household was pouring out of it like an overflowing basin. Lady Marchfield had told him that nothing the duke did was usual. He could well believe it. Though, it just occurred to him that Lady Marchfield had also told them that she herself hired this interesting individual who had just now assaulted himself on a door. He wondered where she'd found such a person. Malberry would take one look at him and send him packing.

They finally did get inside despite the butler. That fellow, who they now knew to be a certain Mr. Huberville, explained that it was of the utmost importance that the duke never discover that anything untoward had happened at the door, as he'd already been dismissed twice with no reference. He even let them in on what was said at those distressing moments—"Pack your bags, Huberville!"

Lord Ledderbey finally convinced him to stop mopping his brow and announce them after assuring him that the growing lump on his forehead was not too noticeable. As they entered the drawing room, Lady Marchfield was by their side in a moment and took them round for introductions.

Lady Felicity and Mr. Stratton, Lady Grace and Lord Dashlend, Lady Patience and Lord Stanford, Lord and Lady Thorpe, Lady Verity and Lord Wembly, and Lord and Lady Manderbey. None of them particularly resembled Lady Letitia, which surprised him. The youngest was not yet present so he assumed they saved the worst for last.

At the far side of the drawing room, a bunker of sorts had been set up using cushions and pillows pulled from the sofas. As far as Weston could tell, this was to box in some very young individuals who could be presumed to be the cousins once removed the duke had mentioned in the letter he'd left at the house. Six of them were behind the barrier, seemingly led by a young man of nine or ten. The duke stood by them, arms folded and nodding approvingly.

Lady Marchfield led Weston there and finally, after all these years, Weston was introduced to the duke. He was a middle-aged fellow with a bit of a paunch, the sort who looked as if he'd enjoyed life. Why would he not? A duke was never troubled by much.

"There you are, Tramondeley," the duke said in a jolly tone. "Ledderbey, well met. Also, I'm not as bad as you've been told."

Lord Ledderbey wobbled a little over that comment. Lady Marchfield muttered, "He most certainly is."

The duke waved his arm. "All my grandchildren together, just as I like to see them. Young Miles is just now mustering the troops. Carry on, Captain."

The captain nodded gravely and said, "Yes, General."

One of the youngest of the troops had made a staggering effort to stand and promptly fell down. Another of the troops, likely just a year older, had observed this operation disdainfully and stood to show how it was done.

Young Miles, or Captain as he was called, said, "Daisy, do stop teasing Leland. Remember, we are all cousins and must stick together against the world. Now, as this is our first meeting—Lily, do stop making faces! As I said, this is our first meeting. I am the oldest, so I am the leader. Isabelle is my second-in-command."

"And nobody should forget that," a young lady of seven or so said in a rather threatening tone. "When Miles is not around, I am in complete, total charge."

These pronouncements seemed to have little effect on the youngest of the party, as they were more interested in pulling out strands of carpet or seeing if they could fit their fist in their mouth.

"We will begin corresponding between our houses," Miles said. "I realize some of you cannot write yet. Simply dictate your letters until you can."

Weston was fascinated by this directive, as clearly some of them could not speak with any cogency yet either. The youngest of them confirmed the idea by commenting, "Bahbahbahbah."

"And we will have a name for ourselves," Isabelle said, "besides our regular names."

"Yes," Miles said. "We are to be—"

"You said I could say it!" Isabelle said, getting very red in the face.

Miles nodded to her. It was a bit of an exasperated nod.

"We are to be Pelham's Pirates," she said. "You see? Grandpapa is the Duke of Pelham."

"And it sounded the best," Miles added. "Though on no account will we act like pirates. In most cases."

"And because we are pirates, we can use pirate talk when we want. The only one I know so far is if we want to talk we call it a parlay."

"Pirates!" Lily shouted.

"Well, Grandpapa? I've done what I can," Miles said.

"Well done, Captain," the duke said. "Remember, these are early days."

Miles nodded gravely.

"Now I know it is a burden to keep this army in order while your elders dine," the duke said. "You are of an age, and Isabelle too, to dine with us. However I am counting on you two to manage it for me below stairs."

"We will do our duty, Your Grace," Miles said, adding a salute to it.

"Good lad."

"And I'm in charge if Miles goes anywhere," Isabelle said.

"Excellent news." The duke turned to Weston. "It was Miles' idea to keep the cousins all in close contact. My Gracie's son, he's a clever boy."

Weston did not comment that the duke had not bothered to stay in close contact with *him* though that might also have been clever. He got the sense that the duke was not prone to that sort of self-reflection.

The second-in-command, Isabelle, did not seem to take kindly to hearing the duke compliment young Miles. She was getting very red in the face.

"Isabelle, I count on you to use your sharp eyes, I quite depend upon them," the duke said in an effort to mollify.

"Sharpest, Grandpapa," Isabelle said cheerfully.

"Ah, and here is my youngest daughter just coming in," the duke said.

Weston turned and suddenly felt a bit wobbly. My God, she looked nothing like Lady Letitia. She was dark haired with round hazel eyes and rather perfect lips. Her dress was entirely elegant. *She* was elegant and there was not a waving fan in sight.

"Val, you already know all your sisters and my collection of sons-in-law, come and meet Tramondeley," the duke called.

She approached and delivered a smart little bob. "Lord Tramondeley," she said.

"And that fellow is Lord Ledderbey," the duke said jovially. "Friend of my brother's. I already told him I am not as bad as he might have heard."

"And I said he most certainly was," Lady Marchfield said.

"Aunt, you know you love Papa. Deep down. Lord Ledderbey," Lady Valor said. "My father likes to jest, but if you have heard that he is bad, then I am afraid you *are* mistaken. So many people do not understand my father."

"Oh I see, yes of course," a rather dumbfounded Lord Ledderbey said.

Weston was not precisely dumbfounded, but he was something else. Lady Valor's voice was soft, but it had a rich tone. It had none of the high-pitched squalling of Lady Letitia. As well, he could not say he was convinced she was right about her father, he probably *was* as bad as they thought, but he could admire her willingness to defend him. And those eyes...those pretty hazel eyes.

"We're very glad to know you, Lord Tramondeley," Lady Valor said. "I hope you do not mind it if I climb the ramparts and say hello to all my nieces and nephews."

"Certainly not," Weston said.

Lady Valor proceeded to lift her skirt, which revealed a pretty little ankle, and climbed into the fray. She was instantly overcome by said nieces and nephews, but for young Miles, who at his age looked for more dignity for himself.

The hapless butler suddenly caught Weston's eye. Actually, he caught almost everybody's eye. He was at the drawing room doors making all sorts of hand motions at the duke—he raised his arms over his head like a drowning man waving for a life ring, then pointed determinedly in the direction of the hall, then he ended the dramatic performance by waving his arms in that direction as if he were a constable waving a cart forward in an effort to clear a road.

The duke heaved a sigh. "Lord help us, I think that man is trying to tell me we can go through. Miles, Mrs. Right and some of the maids will be in shortly to lead this circus below stairs. Tramondeley, take Valor in. Ledderbey, I'm sure Lady Misery would not mind an arm."

CHAPTER FIVE

A S WESTON HELD out his arm to help Lady Valor over the cushion wall, he wondered if he'd really just heard the duke refer to his sister, a countess and respected matron, as Lady Misery. Lady Valor had not blinked over it. Noting Lady Marchfield's expression, though, he rather thought he had heard that correctly.

They proceeded into the dining room and the duke steered him to his location. Lady Valor was to his left and Lady Marchfield to his right at the top of the table. He'd been warned by both Lord Ledderbey and Stockton that the duke might have a matchmaking plan up his sleeve. He'd laughed off the idea, imagining he would encounter a version of Lady Letitia. Now he wondered if it really was such an outlandish idea.

After all, a lady like this coming to Town for her first season was not likely to require a second season.

"You see how it is, Misery," the duke said. "I've given you the head of the table, else I'd have to seat you next to me. This way, you are as far away as possible, which will suit us both."

Lord Ledderbey, who was to Lady Marchfield's right, seemed very shaken over these sentiments. Lady Marchfield had thoroughly warned them of the duke's rudeness and taunts, but it was another thing to see it in person. Especially for Lord Ledderbey, who never put a foot out of place when it came to manners.

When they'd dined at Lady Marchfield's house, she'd out-lined all of the duke's crimes, which Lord Ledderbey had found almost hard to believe. Lord Marchfield, on the other hand, had all sorts of conciliatory things to say. According to the lord, one could develop a fondness for the duke if one did not take him seriously and hardly ever saw him. These seemed to be two things beyond Lady Marchfield's reach. She was still burning over the time, some years ago, that the duke had left her at a cyprian's party. Apparently, the diabolical housekeeper on the premises had arranged it all.

Everyone had been seated and the two footmen, who seemed far more on the ball than the butler, brought round the wine. Mr. Huberville watched them as if it were the first time he'd seen it done. Weston watched the butler reach for a crystal decanter and then pull his hand away from it as if he was afraid of it.

The duke said, "All my girls together again. Well! We've had some jolly times in this room."

"Val used to give some terrific speeches to start us off," Lady Felicity said.

"Ah yes," Mr. Stratton said, "Lady Valor engaged in a spirited and endless war to keep her sisters at home and unmarried."

"Perhaps those speeches are best forgotten," Lady Marchfield said through pursed lips. "Among other things."

Weston turned to Lady Valor. "I do not have brothers and sisters, so I do not know what it is to have them leave the house."

"It was devastating," Lady Valor said. "We all were so happy together in the Dales and then we came to London that first time and Felicity left. I was so young I did not even realize it was permanent."

"That must have come as a shock."

Lady Valor nodded. "Once I found it out, I became deter-mined to keep the rest of my sisters at home."

"How though?" Weston asked, rather interested to hear it.

"Oh, I would make a speech pointing out certain things. If that did not work, I might send a letter of some sort. The last was sent to Lord Manderbey. I pretended to be Winsome and broke it off with him. It was not the first time I tried it, either."

Weston laughed. There was a certain amount of daring to such a scheme. "I presume Lord Manderbey figured it out."

She nodded. "I made the mistake of signing as Winny instead of Winsome. He'd already heard me call her by her nickname."

"Undone by a nickname. That is bad luck."

"What do you do all day in Cornwall? Do you collect anything?"

He was momentarily put on the back foot. Lady Letitia had not asked him a single thing outside of if he was staring at her again. "Collect? No, not really. I buy books for Lord Ledderbey for his library when I get the chance."

"You do not read them yourself, though?"

"Not many of them," Weston admitted. "I have other things that take up my time."

As soon as the idea that they must leave for Town had been broached, he'd wondered how much he should say about his nighttime activities. But then, he reasoned that he would be away from Cornwall and the French would no longer be looking for the Mosquito as they were no longer bothered by him. He'd had the boat moved and he'd already decided that when he took up the operation again he would relocate himself well away from Lord Ledderbey's house. In any case, the last place one would run into a Frenchman was London.

"Other things take up your time? What things?" Lady Valor asked. "You live near the sea, I understand. I suppose you go looking for shells?"

Shells. He could not say he did. He was not certain if Lady Valor would be all that approving of what he did get up to. Though, he did not suppose that once she asked a question she could be easily brushed off. There was a certain intensity to her. "Well, mostly, me and my valet, Stockton, take out my sloop at night and harass any French frigates we are able to find. It is well to know their locations and our turning up unsettles their crews."

"Sailing at night? In the sea? Away from land?"

Weston nodded. "Yes, we really can only do it at night so that we can get away into the darkness without being run down."

Lady Valor looked alarmed to hear it. "I see," she said softly.

He thought it might be well to change the subject of the conversation. "You mentioned collections—do you collect anything?"

She shook her head. "I have my dog," she said. "He's a pug and really is tremendous. His name is Sir Galahad and I've been told he has exceptional form by a Sardinian count who seems to know the breed."

Weston was mystified. "I see, so you have been to Sardinia? I suppose it was long ago, as it is impossible to safely travel there just now."

"Oh no, I've never been. Count di Compressio is here in England. We met him on the road, at an inn, where he generously gave over his private dining room. He stays with Lady Tallifer in Town."

A Sardinian count? What was he doing in England? One might have thought he'd be either in Napoleon's custody or hiding from him. Perhaps he'd decided to hide in England? The other explanation was that Napoleon was using the count for his own purposes.

That was probably unlikely though. He did not know Lady Tallifer, but it seemed a stretch to believe an English noblewoman would be involved in any sort of espionage.

"What do you suppose brings him here?" Weston asked.

"The count? He has an estate in Hertfordshire. He's thinking of settling there as he likes the peace and quiet of it. He's a very gentle individual and it would suit him."

A gentle individual? Weston supposed he was a dandy down to his shoes, waving a handkerchief and requiring a vinaigrette at the slightest upset. Or if not that, perhaps he just posed as one. Nobody would expect a dandy to get up to anything, good or bad.

A Sardinian count that suddenly turns up and claims he would like to emigrate and live in Hertfordshire? He supposed it was possible, considering the state of the count's own homeland at this moment.

Weston realized that all his chasing the French around had made him far more suspicious than might be right. He did not suppose he would discover the truth from Lady Valor. And he must admit, her seeming admiration of this Sardinian dandy rankled him a bit. He would put his wondering on a shelf for the time being, he was bound to encounter the fellow somewhere and would make his judgments then.

"How else do you occupy your time?" he asked.

"I keep my dear papa company and act as his hostess at home. We have a terrific time. Sometimes we invent things to say to the vicar that will send him into a fit."

Weston laughed. He could not say he minded anybody harassing a vicar. Their own neighborhood was in possession of a very sour individual who disapproved of everybody who did not fawn over him. Or attend him every Sunday, which he and Lord Ledderbey were often remiss about. The fellow did not dare scold them over it, so he relied on his frown to send the message.

"I hope you will tell me some of what you've said to your vicar," Weston said, "as I have my own vicar to tease. I had not thought of it, but I think I'd be happy to do it."

"Oh well if that is the case, the easiest thing in the world is to claim the Ten Commandments are too strict. I have made the case that sometimes stealing is necessary and have never bothered to clarify that I spoke of biscuits from the kitchens. Every time I am anywhere near the altar he looks nervous and keeps checking that he's still got everything on it. It's very amusing."

And so they went on, speculating on what could be said to drive a vicar mad. She was so animated and pretty. There was nothing stiff about her. He would have assumed a duke's daughter would be circumspect regarding her vicar but that clearly was not the case. It seemed she'd also accused that vicar of being involved in a plot to murder women in the middle of the night, even though she now knew those screams she sometimes heard at night were from a fox. He was further enlightened that the duke had a white domino with painted flames on the bottom of it that appeared to be a vicar going to the devil that they all found terribly amusing.

However eccentric this family might be, they were not stiff. Weston did not know what he expected, but Lady Valor had not been it.

VALOR DID NOT know precisely what she had expected of Lord Tramondeley, but she'd not conjured the reality of him. He was a regular confluence of contradictions.

On the one hand, he was the most handsome gentleman she'd ever laid eyes on. He was tall and seemed muscular under his coat. His hair was a marvelous caramel color and his eyes a deep blue. He had the sort of features that were perfectly balanced, not too sharp and not too round. He was also easy to talk to, she certainly had not imagined that. He was not stern and reserved and thought her harassment of the vicar was amusing. He was not as delicate as Count di Compressio, not at all. And yet, there was a calm assurance about him, as if not much ruffled his feathers.

But on the other hand, it could not be ignored that his mode of living was positively bizarre. He took a sloop out to sea at night to chase French boats? With his valet? Was he mad?

If he'd come to Town to find a wife, he'd better give up the habit at once. How on earth was a lady to sit alone at night, shivering from the fox's screams out of doors and wondering if her husband was drowning at that very moment? The poor lady would be a wreck. What a life.

And yet, she thought he would probably convince somebody to put up with it. He was very hard to look away from. Somebody sturdier than herself would take the chance.

It really was too bad, as in every other respect she liked him very much. Yes, she really did. However, he was not exactly her picture of a retiring baron who collected rare books or coins. He did not even collect shells though he must be surrounded by them. He was not a collecting sort of person. She was not either, but it seemed to be the most likely way to judge how a man lived. Count di Compressio was far closer to that type of man—he liked the peace of Hertfordshire and collected art.

"Has anybody told him yet?" her father said from the other end of the table.

Of course, Valor knew very well that the duke spoke of Fact or Fib. Though, they usually trotted out that game when there was a budding romance in the offing. She suspected her father just wished to put Lord Tramondeley on the back foot. Her papa was rather adoring of putting people on the back foot.

Lord Tramondeley looked round the table to see her sisters' smiling faces interspersed with her brothers-in-laws' rather downcast expressions.

"The game is on," the duke said.

"Gracious," Lord Ledderbey said. "We are so isolated in Cornwall that we've not kept up with London games. Is it cards?"

"In a manner of speaking," the duke said.

"No it isn't," Mr. Stratton said. "It's diabolical."

"They invented it," Lord Stanford said.

"Drink a lot of port and keep your head down, that's my strategy," Lord Wembly said.

Lord Manderbey nodded. "The port is essential."

"What my rascally sons-in-laws are getting at," the duke said, "is that I don't go in for the men sitting here with their port and the ladies relegated to tea in the drawing room. I'll bring in the bottles." The duke looked round the table. "Unless anybody opposes the scheme because they wish to bore me about a horse they're thinking of buying. Or worse, politics."

"My brother considers all of our fine traditions to be primed for upset. If a thing is done, he must undo it," Lady Marchfield said austerely. "If it is accepted, it must be rejected. Furthermore, Roland, that game is a deplorable scheme to embarrass people."

"Maybe, but it's also fun," the duke said. "Oh, that's right, I forgot. Lady Misery over there likes to stomp on fun wherever she finds it. Fun is against her religion."

Valor gave Felicity a glance, as Lady Marchfield was getting very heated. Things never went well when their aunt got heated.

"It is just a harmless little game, Aunt," Felicity said soothingly.

"It is the devil's work, in my view," Lady Marchfield said.

At mention of the devil, Mr. Huberville dropped the cheese and fruit he'd been just moments from setting down on the table. In his scramble to pick up an array of cheeses, rolling grapes, and candied cherries scattering on the floor, Sir Galahad made an appearance from under the table. Valor had been well aware that he'd been there patiently waiting for something to drop and now a whole tray had. He wasted no time in hurrying there to investigate. The pug got under Mr. Huberville's feet, he staggered back and stepped on a generous wedge of stilton. That particular leg went flying toward the ceiling and he landed on the floor like a pile of bricks.

Sir Galahad glanced over at the sound but speedily put his attention back on what was to be had from the spilled tray.

The duke peered down at his butler. Then he said to Lady Marchfield, "That right there, on my floor, is the real devil's work, in my opinion."

"Just say it!" Mr. Huberville cried, rolling over and kneeling on the ground with a handful of Stilton in one hand and a wedge of cheddar in the other. "Pack your bags, Huberville! It always comes to that. But nobody stops to think—I had to choose, step on the dog or the cheese! Stilton is slippery!"

Sir Galahad took that moment to relieve Mr. Huberville of

the cheddar wedge in his hand and trotted out of the room.

The duke gave a look to Charlie. The footman nodded. He helped Mr. Huberville to his feet and whispered some soothing words in his ear, leading him out of the dining room.

"Thomas," the duke said, "you'll bring the bottles into the drawing room. After that, see if Cook can be convinced to compose another cheese tray and send that in too. And send that lunatic to his bed."

They all rose and gingerly stepped round the cornucopia of cheeses and fruit on the floor.

Though Valor was always eager to play Fact or Fib, especially now that she was older and did not need to excuse herself on account of feeling tired, she did experience some hesitation. She hoped she was not the subject of any embarrassing inquiries. She had always been the inquisitor; nobody had ever asked her anything of note. Would things be different now that she was grown? She did not see how it could be so, she had just arrived and not been anywhere yet—what was there to ask? However, with Fact or Fib anything could happen.

"If you are bound and determined to play that ridiculous game, I will depart," Lady Marchfield said.

"You know where the door is," the duke said, laughing.

She turned to Lord Ledderbey and said, "I would advise you to do the same."

The lord shrugged. "I do find my interest piqued, though, Lady Marchfield."

Lady Marchfield sniffed. Thomas hurried over to her with her pelisse. In a low tone, she said, "Remind Mr. Huberville of our conversation. He is a barnacle on a boat, regardless of what happens. No need to fetch my coachman, he will be outside at the ready, as he knows very well that I might find the need to leave at any moment when I come to my brother's house."

Valor was surprised to see the look of astonishment on Lord Tramondeley's expression, until she remembered that while Lady Marchfield's departure had been done in a very usual fashion for that lady, it was perhaps surprising to an outsider.

He did not seem to see anything alarming in floating around in a dinghy in the dark, looking for French frigates, and yet he seemed alarmed at Lady Marchfield's stomping off. Very odd.

WESTON WAS NOT at all clear on what this game was. Only that it was so offensive to Lady Marchfield's sensibilities that she'd departed.

Then it was explained to him. It was called, very aptly as it turned out, Fact or Fib. They would be asked questions and then the answers would be determined to be a fact or a fib. He did not understand how it could be so. They knew next to nothing about him—how could they judge whether he was truthful or lying?

He supposed he'd find it out. All he knew for now was that one received a yellow ticket for the truth and a blue ticket for a lie, a blue ticket canceled a yellow, and it took three yellows to win. At least it was not complicated.

The footman brought round the port and he could at least be grateful for that.

"Val," the duke said, "you've always insisted on going first."

"Oh no, Papa, not this time," Lady Valor said. "That was only when I was too young to stay up late." She appeared embarrassed to be asked.

"I'll start us off, Papa," Lady Felicity said. "Lord Tramondeley, I understand from my aunt that you have received a voucher for Almack's. Who shall you request the patronesses to put you down for?"

From that, Weston presumed that one had to ask the patronesses to be put down on a lady's card, rather than the lady herself. It seemed an unnecessary palaver, but it was none of his concern. He'd still not got around to telling Lady Marchfield he would not attend, but now he felt backed into it.

"Nobody," he said. "I will not attend as I do not dance."

The sisters all stared at one another. Lady Felicity picked up a blue ticket. "Fib," she said. "It must be. Everybody dances."

"I am afraid it is my fault," Lord Ledderbey said. "I was remiss in neglecting that part of the boy's education."

"Now hold on," the duke said. "Tramondeley says he does not dance and Ledderebey says he never learnt. Two different things, to my mind."

"I've never learned," Weston said. "It has never seemed a priority."

Lady Felicity slowly switched the colored tickets in her hand.

"Easily remedied," the duke said. "Val can teach you. I'll send her over with Mrs. Right and I'm sure her sisters will pitch in as they can."

"Oh yes, certainly," Lady Serenity said. "I am just a few doors down."

"Yes, Serenity will be the best to go. She is so nearby and, in any case, I might not be the very best teacher," Lady Grace said. "I sometimes wobble."

"She's adorable when she does wobbles, though," Lord Dashlend said. "And it's not nearly as much as it was."

Lord Dashlend's caveat to Lady Grace's wobbling was met with nods of approval from her sisters.

Weston was dumbfounded. They would come to his house and make him dance? He was not at all certain how Lady Valor viewed the idea of being volunteered for the task. Her cheeks were a rather fiery color. He would not be surprised if she were furious. Why should she not be? It was an imposition.

"What an admirable solution," Lord Ledderbey said. "Look at that, my boy, you can attend Almack's after all."

Wonderful.

The game continued and Lord Ledderbey was asked just how badly he thought of the duke, considering he had been a friend of his departed brother. Lord Ledderbey hemmed and hawed and claimed it was not so bad and was instantly named a fibber.

The crowning moment came when Lady Patience inquired what Weston had first noticed about Lady Valor. The real answer was how different she looked from Lady Letitia, but he thought it unwise to say so. He claimed it was her elegance. There was some whispering between the sisters over it, and then it was deemed true.

Nobody was getting anywhere near three yellow tickets, but fortunately Lord Ledderbey mentioned he was tired. There was nothing for it but to conclude without a winner. Weston could not help but notice the various looks of relief and joy on the other gentlemen's expressions.

They were led out by a footman. It seemed that Mr. Huberville had been sent off to recover from his violent encounters with a doorframe and a cheese tray.

The carriage set off. Lord Ledderbey said, "Well that was something."

"It was something, but what?" Weston said with a laugh.

"It was not what I expected. Yes, the duke is entirely bizarre and his treatment of Lady Marchfield is abhorrent. On the other hand, she seems to give as good as she gets. I did find him likable in a very odd way. What did you think of him?"

"He's a strange fellow, there is no doubt about it. And very presumptuous too. He never even bothered to inquire if I wished to know how to dance. I am not sure I do."

"Ah well, too late now, I suppose. He's arranged to send Lady Valor, Lady Serenity, and their housekeeper over tomorrow afternoon. I will be interested in getting a look at this housekeeper—Lady Marchfield is convinced she is the devil in disguise."

"At least they do not send Mr. Huberville," Weston said laughing.

"That poor fellow. He is very excitable. But tell me, what did you think of Lady Valor? I found her very pretty and composed. Very much a lady, I thought."

Weston shrugged. "She seems to admire some Sardinian count with an estate in Hertfordshire who likes peace and quiet."

It was true, she did seem to admire that Sardinian fellow. It was also true that Weston seemed to admire *her*. However, if that was what the duke had in mind, he was not amenable to cooperating. There were a hundred ladies in London he might wed. There was no reason why he must go for the duke's daughter.

Though, she was exceedingly pretty and he liked her manner very much.

"Well, we'll see what the future holds. Excellent news that they will teach you to dance, in my view. I feel I have been given a reprieve from my laxity on the subject."

Weston nodded. He could not say he wished to know how to dance as it seemed the sort of frivolous activity a dandy spent his day on. But on the other hand, he had noted the ladies' expressions this evening when he said he did not dance. They were incredulous and assumed he was lying. Clearly, a lady expected a gentleman to dance.

Therefore, he ought to learn how to do it whether he liked it or not.

CHAPTER SIX

DAMIANO HAD INSTALLED himself in Lady Tallifer's house on Brook Street. The lady was as he recalled—a small and fluttery woman who became nervous of silences and filled them with nonsense. Nevertheless, she was exceedingly indulgent. He had a very fine room, reasonably good dinners for England, and drinkable wine. It was not up to his marquis's standards but then, he did not expect it would be. He'd informed her at once that he was here on his father's business and would travel to their estate in Hertfordshire. She'd spent days composing what ought to be in a picnic basket to take in the carriage and made a list of preferred inns.

Of course, he'd had no intention of traveling to Hertford-shire. Their steward at that estate did not require any supervision from him. Rather, he'd taken himself off to Cornwall to deal with the second reason for his trip. Locate the Mosquito and eliminate the operation.

He'd not been given a lot to go on. Just where the pier was that the sloop used for docking and the direction the carriage departing the pier traveled before disappearing behind hills.

It would have been helpful if somebody had told him what he could expect from the people of Cornwall. His experience so far was that they were surly, inscrutable, gave away nothing, did not like his questions, and did not trust foreigners.

The pier where the infamous sloop was meant to be was

empty of sloops and only housed some very rickety-looking fishing vessels. He'd inquired about the sloop from a fellow who looked after the small shack associated with it and got an earful.

Why did he want to know? Why was some foreigner to come snooping around the neighborhood? Who did he know in this neighborhood? Could anybody vouch for him? Where did he stay?

Then, the fellow had squinted his eyes and asked him if he worked for Napoleon. Which was hitting a bit close to home. While London was cosmopolitan and encountering people from other countries was not unusual, it appeared to engender deep suspicion here.

He'd given up inquiring as he began to worry that he'd be attacked by a crowd of these local people. He'd already been forced to move to another inn to escape the dark looks he got at the first one. He satisfied himself with riding his horse in every conceivable direction leading away from the pier, searching for the abode that housed the Mosquito operation.

It did him no good. He passed by no end of houses and structures in various styles and sizes but there was nothing to give away the Mosquito. Further, where was the sloop?

He supposed that would be the report—the boat was gone and the man who sailed it could not be identified. He imagined the good news was that perhaps the fleet would not be further harassed by the sloop. Perhaps the Mosquito had been spooked or had a close call and decided to take cover.

It really felt like a pointless trip and he could not get back to London soon enough. If he could do nothing about the Mosquito, he could at least find a bride. Lady Tallifer had pulled on some connections and got a voucher to Almack's for him. He was certain Lady Valor would be there, among every other eligible lady in Town. As the marquis was insistent on a duke's daughter, his targets must be Lady Valor, Lady Letitia, and Lady Elizabeth. Lady Tallifer said that Lady Elizabeth was expected to engage herself shortly, so he might be down to two choices. One was at least acceptable and the other would be a lifelong trial.

In any case, while Lady Valor's company was not scintillating, it was far more preferable to these surly Cornwall people who all looked as if they were on the verge of shooting him. Further, he was tiring of waitstaff who slammed his plate in front of him, watered down his wine, and then smirked when he noticed it. These uncultured beasts clearly wished to drive him out and he was perfectly amenable to being driven out. If he never saw Cornwall again it would too soon.

VALOR HAD DONNED her coat with Serenity, Mrs. Right, and Thomas and they set off across the square. It was decided that Thomas must come with his pocket violin, else how could they properly dance with no music?

Really, Valor did not understand why her father had arranged it at all. If Lord Tramondeley required instruction on dancing, he ought to hire a dancing master. That's what the duke had done, and then he ensured that they all received the booklets each year from renowned dancing masters showing the new dances of the season so they would have ample time to practice. The early years had been filled with seven sisters taking turns acting as the gentleman. Then one by one, their numbers dwindled. Mrs. Right had been her partner in preparing for this season.

As much as she was against it, the duke *had* committed his youngest daughter as the lord's dancing instructress and there was nothing for it. As he had, she had been heads together with Serenity and had come to some conclusions. They would teach Lord Tramondeley the various steps for the cotillion, Scottish reel, and quadrille, and leave him two booklets from Mr. Wilson—*The Supplement to the Treasures of Terpsichore* and *An Analysis of Country Dances*. She would also provide him with some cards she had written out, showing the likeliest dances and steps.

The waltz would not be danced at Almack's so if Lord Tramondeley wished to know anything about it, he could inquire elsewhere. Valor knew perfectly well how it was done but did not choose to find herself in such close quarters with the gentleman.

He was a beautiful specimen of a man, but it could not be overlooked that he was not right in the head. Nobody with any sense went sailing into danger in the dark.

It was a very fine day by London standards. There was a brisk breeze that blew away the noxious fumes and fog that often hovered over the town.

As they walked across the square, Serenity said, "I know these paths better than I know my own name. Remember, Valor, it was on these paths that Thorpe and I fell in love while walking our dogs."

Of course, Valor did remember perfectly well. She'd spent those walks attempting to break them apart. They would walk ahead, Serenity walking Nelson on one side and Thorpe walking Havoc on the other side and their hands brushing. It had been like a large wave rolling toward shore—no matter what outrageous thing she said or did there'd been no way to turn it round.

"I could just cry to think of it," Serenity said.

"Oh do not cry now, Serenity," Valor said. "Not when I need you to help me with this ridiculous project."

Serenity mopped her eyes. "I know you are very against it, but do you not think Lord Tramondeley very handsome?"

"I think he is exceptionally handsome, but I do not see how that signifies."

"It is generally the beginning of the thing, is what I think Serenity says," Mrs. Right put in.

"But Serenity," Valor said, "you know that for me I look for something else. Something else that is more important."

Serenity nodded. "Safety, as you always have."

"That's right, and did you know that Lord Tramondeley goes out in a sailboat, at night, in the sea, to look for the French and harass them?"

"Goodness, no," Serenity said. "I had wondered what he was doing with himself in Cornwall as he's never bothered to learn how to dance. I thought he might be fishing all day."

"Chasing the French on a boat at night. Have you ever heard of anything more outlandish and as likely to lead to death?" Valor asked. "To think, a person looks out upon a vast and dark sea and knows the enemy lurks out there somewhere and thinks he ought to raise the sails and go find them?"

"Perhaps he's not the right gentleman for you, then," Mrs. Right said. "Anyway, Poppet, such an important decision on how you are to spend the rest of your life does not need to be made in one season. You have all the time in the world."

"That's right, I really do. I do not have to rush into anything, no matter who I meet," Valor said. She had thought the very same more than a few times. Her papa would not mind it if she were to require a second season to be really certain of the gentleman who would suit.

"Well, I find it a shame. When I first saw him, I was certain you would be struck."

Valor did not answer. The truth was, she had been struck. He was devilishly handsome and she'd enjoyed talking to him quite a bit. Except for the part of the conversation where he revealed himself to be a madman intent on personal destruction.

They had reached Lord Tramondeley's doorstep all too soon. The butler had clearly been keeping an eye out as the door swung open before they used the knocker. That gentleman was at first at a loss over what to do with Thomas, but he concluded that he would lead him to the ballroom and fetch him some ale while he waited. Thomas appeared enormously agreeable to the plan, as he was not at all used to being led to a ballroom and given ale in the middle of the afternoon.

Valor, Serenity, and Mrs. Right were led into the drawing room to find Lord Tramondeley and Lord Ledderbey waiting for them.

Lord Tramondeley said, "I fear this has been an imposition,

Lady Valor."

She shook her head no, but she did not have any words in response because it *was* very much an imposition. As she thought that, though, she could not help noticing how well he looked in his morning coat. She suspected he'd look even more spectacular in riding clothes. Most gentlemen looked very well in their riding clothes.

"Now," Lord Ledderbey said, "as this current imposition has really been all my fault, I have done my very best to inform Lord Tramondeley of some of the basic steps."

From the expression on Lord Tramondeley's face, it did not seem as if he had enjoyed the experience of dancing with the older gentleman.

"I showed him as many of the steps as I could recall. I am afraid, though, that I did not make a very convincing lady," Lord Ledderebey said.

"You are not to fret over it, Lord Ledderbey," Serenity said. "Dancing is very natural and I'm certain Lord Tramondeley shall take to it in a trice."

"A trice might be rather too hopeful," Lord Tramondeley said.

They proceeded to the ballroom to find Thomas sitting on a stool with a half empty glass of ale. He jumped up and set it down on a windowsill.

"We should probably begin with a simple country dance," Valor said. "Lord Tramondeley, I am sure Lord Ledderbey has already explained that the top couple will dance the steps and then everyone else only need copy them. At Almack's, I would suggest you put yourself very far down the line. That way, you can see it demonstrated more than once."

Serenity looked critically at the group. "I wish we had more people. We ought to have thought of it and made all our sisters bring their husbands. Why did I not even think of bringing Thorpe? He would have been delighted to assist."

Valor was not certain of Lord Thorpe's delight, but he certainly would have done whatever Serenity asked of him. She was not aware of a single time that lord had not indulged his wife. He'd even gone so far as to build a crypt for the dead bees she'd been collecting all her life though he likely did not understand the need for it.

Valor determined that while it would be nice to have more people, they had to work with what they'd got. "Let's begin with a curtsy and bow, then a righthand star, then a two hand turn to return to our places," Valor said. She was not certain what she could do with Lord Tramondeley, but at least he was listening closely. He seemed rather intent, actually.

He nodded and Thomas struck up his little violin. She curtsied and Lord Tramondeley bowed. They began the righthand star, both arriving to the opposite side of where they started and then the two hand turn to their original places. It was the first time their hands touched. It might be the first time she'd touched any man's hand outside of her own father. Valor found herself stupidly flustered over it.

"That was very well done, Lord Tramondeley," Serenity said.

Outside in the corridor came suddenly a lady's voice. A very hearty woman's voice. "I heard he was in Town. Lord Tramondeley was very naughty in not letting us know!"

"He will be delighted to see us, I can assure you," another lady said.

Lord Tramondeley and Lord Ledderbey stared at each other. Valor thought they appeared almost panicked. "Lady Monroe and Lady Letitia," Lord Ledderbey whispered.

"Will Malberry let them in?" Lord Tramondeley whispered.

Lord Ledderbey shrugged. "I do not know—I never thought to instruct him."

"Engaged in the ballroom?" the woman Valor presumed was Lady Letitia shrieked. "Lead us there, we must discover what Lord Tramondeley is up to in that room at this time of day."

Valor did not know who these two ladies were, but from the expressions of both lords upon hearing their demands to be shown in, she thought both gentlemen could not be eager to encounter either of them. Perhaps they were people from Cornwall who they'd hoped to avoid?

She was not so sure she was eager to encounter them either. They sounded very loud and forceful. Valor glanced at Serenity and found her wide-eyed. Mrs. Right, on the other hand, seemed to find the whole thing amusing. As did Thomas, who had picked up his ale and drained it in the interlude.

Two ladies sailed into the ballroom with a very contrite-looking butler following them. One was a very usual-looking middle-aged matron, the other was something else entirely. She was very tall and decorated from head to toe in all manner of ruffles, bits, and bobs. Her bonnet had more accoutrements than Valor had imagined possible, most startling being a sequined butterfly looking as if it were ready to take flight. Despite one lady being older, it was the younger with the fantastical hat who took the lead.

"Lord Tramondeley," she fairly shrieked. "Could anybody be as naughty?" She punctuated that scolding with a further scolding from her fan, which she whipped around rather menacingly.

The lord flinched away from her as her fan landed on his arm.

"Lord Tramondeley," Lady Monroe said, "we presume it was a mere oversight that you did not alert us to your arrival in Town. We were bowled over when he heard of it, I can tell you. I said to Lady Ludwig, 'Tramondeley is in Town? He will ache to see us.'"

"Lady Monroe," Lord Tramondeley said, "I had no notion I was meant to alert anybody to my arrival. I do not even know Lady Ludwig and have contacted nobody about my arrival."

"Do you hear him?" Lady Letitia cried. "He had no notion to alert *us*? Such very good friends and we were not to be informed? You are outrageous, Tramondeley."

"We really only recently arrived," Lord Ledderbey said in a conciliatory tone.

"Well, we will forgive you, as friends do," Lady Letitia said, once more smacking Lord Tramondeley. "Now, what do we have here?"

"Ah, Lady Monroe, Lady Letitia," Lord Ledderbey said, "allow me to present Lady Thorpe, Lady Valor Nicolet, and Mrs. Right."

"Ah," Lady Monroe said, "Lady Valor is the Duke of Pelham's daughter, I think? And Lady Thorpe too, recently wed to the marquess."

Both Valor and Serenity nodded.

"And Mrs. Right?"

"I'm the housekeeper," Mrs. Right said.

"I see!" Lady Letitia said. "Tramondeley, you are very modern to have your housekeeper comingling with your guests."

"I'm the Duke of Pelham's housekeeper," Mrs. Right said in a tone that brought both ladies up short. Not for long, though.

"I understand, yes I see, you act as a duenna," Lady Monroe said. "Of course, I would not send Lady Letitia out with my housekeeper. Her father, the duke, would expect more from me than that! Lady Letitia stays with me for the season, you understand, her duke being rather poorly. But then, people do things differently, one never really knows."

"Yes, I suspect we *are* different," Mrs. Right said, staring the lady down.

Lady Monroe could not hold up against the determined look of the housekeeper and turned to Lord Tramondeley. "Might I inquire what the activity is that you are currently engaged in?" she asked, looking round the ballroom, her eyes settling on Thomas.

"Lady Valor has very kindly agreed to give me dance instruction," Lord Tramondeley said. "I have never got around to learning the steps."

"It was my fault," Lord Ledderbey said, sadly shaking his head.

"Dancing!" Lady Letitia shrieked, as if it were the first time she'd ever heard of the activity. "Lady Monroe, can you believe

Tramondeley did not come straight to us? Heavens, we might have taught him when we visited last year!" Before Lady Monroe could weigh in with equal shock, Lady Letitia said, "Never mind, we are here now. How far have we got?"

And so went the next hour. Lady Letitia took complete control, called out the steps, and insisted on partnering with Lord Tramondeley. Valor partnered with Lord Ledderbey, who appeared apologetic for every minute of it. The old lord also did not last long at the activity, as he clearly became tired and Valor insisted he stop. As there were not chairs in the ballroom, she walked him to one of the low and wide windowsills, and he watched from there.

Finally, Serenity could take no more. Though Valor's sister was generally the sort of person who would go along with anything, she apparently did have her limits. She very pleasantly said, "I wonder if that is not enough for one day?"

"Yes!" Lord Tramondeley almost shouted. His tone was filled with the desperation of one who was waiting for a life ring to be thrown after falling overboard in high seas. "We cannot impose on Lady Valor and Lady Thorpe any further."

"Now, that does not mean we need to stop," Lady Letitia said. "I am well able to carry on."

"Very kind," Lord Tramondeley said, "but I am engaged to escort the ladies across the square. Allow me to see you to your carriage."

Lady Letitia appeared to be mulling in her mind some way round that idea. Fortunately for Lord Tramondeley, she did not find one. Instead, she said, "Very well, I suppose we will see you at Almack's, Lord Tramondeley." She held up her hand and cried, "You need not even ask, *of course* you must put yourself down on my card."

They were finally able to get to the street, though Lady Letitia poked her head in all the rooms along the corridor and made comment on them. They were to know that she would change the carpet in the drawing room and order new drapes for the library.

Lady Monroe's carriage was duly loaded with its passengers, though Lady Letitia took the opportunity to open the window and shout, "Almack's! Don't forget, it's on Wednesday."

Lord Tramondeley nodded at this directive, though he did not seem overjoyed. The ladies' carriage jerked forward with Lady Letitia waving her handkerchief out the window as if she were setting off on a long sea voyage.

"I will escort you home, Lady Valor."

"There is no need, I have my sister and Mrs. Right with me and it is just across the square," Valor said.

"I did tell Lady Letitia I would, though. I do not like to be a liar."

"Oh I see," Valor said.

They bid adieu to Lord Ledderbey, who looked as if he was relieved to get them all out of the house.

As they walked along the paths lined with shrubberies, Valor said, "I presume Lady Letitia is from your neighborhood."

"Lady Monroe is not five miles off," Lord Tramondeley said. "Lady Letitia visited her last year."

"She's very lively," Serenity said.

Lord Tramondeley laughed and Valor could not tell if he agreed, or thought it was funny that Serenity should say so.

"Lively is one word for it," Mrs. Right said.

Lord Tramondeley's brows raised and Valor was certain he was not used to a housekeeper joining in on a conversation. Of course, he could not know that their dear Mrs. Right was not just a housekeeper. She was a mother of sorts, especially to Valor, who had never known her own mother. She was very much part of the family though other people might think it odd.

"Look!" Serenity cried. "There is Thorpe coming out with Havoc and Nelson."

Valor looked in that direction to see Lord Thorpe just coming out of his house leading Havoc on one side and their little Nelson on the other.

"You won't mind, Val?" Serenity said.

"No, go to your husband," Valor said, laughing.

Serenity picked up her skirts and sprinted down the path.

Lord Tramondeley squinted. "Is that…does that dog, is he missing a leg?"

"That is darling Nelson," Valor said. "We found him on one of our trips to Town. He was begging for scraps outside an inn and of course we had to have him. He's blind in one eye as well, so you can imagine what sort of hard life he had. We've spoiled him terribly to make up for it."

"I see. Well I do not suppose your own dog, a pug I think, has suffered too very much."

"Sir Galahad?" Valor said. "He is lucky to be alive! He was the runt of the litter and a terrible old lord was going to drown him."

Lord Tramondeley looked at her quizzically, and Valor realized there was quite a large gap in information between Sir Galahad on the verge of being drowned and his now more comfortable situation.

"Lord Thorpe convinced the old gentleman who wished to drown him to hear what I would say about it, and I took the little dog from him and sent him on his way."

"With a terrible scolding too," Mrs. Right added.

"Lord Thorpe brought the man and the dog to your house?" Lord Tramondeley asked.

Valor nodded. Though, as she'd got older she'd wondered about it herself. Why hadn't Lord Thorpe simply taken the dog? How was that earl convinced to come to the house with Sir Galahad? If he really was so cruel hearted to wish the dog drowned, why was he setting off in a carriage to do it himself? Or why would not he not have done it already? Why had he agreed to hear about it from a young girl he did not even know?

She generally dismissed those questions from her mind, as whatever it was that had happened, it had seemed very real at the time. In those early days when she did not have any questions about it, she'd liberally embellished the encounter. At one point, she even claimed that she'd fetched her father's gun to drive the fellow off. She had not, but when she'd thought over the encounter later, she had dearly wished she had. She did not claim so anymore, but she did remember her outrage over Sir Galahad's situation and knew very well she would have been willing to do it if she'd thought of it. When it came to that precious little dog, she could be very brave.

They had come out of the square and crossed over the street. Valor waved to Serenity and Lord Thorpe, who were walking together and laughing with their very enthusiastic dogs.

"Lady Valor, I thank you for the dancing lesson and apologize for Lady Letitia's interruption."

"I do not see why you are to apologize," Valor said. "I do not imagine you could have stopped her."

Lord Tramondeley laughed. "No, I do not think I could have."

"Well, she will find you again at Almack's I suspect."

"Do you really think I have to go?" Lord Tramondeley asked.

Valor laughed. "My aunt has got you the voucher and tickets, I rather think you do have to. Or if you do not, I would suggest hiding from her for a very long time. She is a very determined lady."

"I had not taken that into consideration. I suppose I will go, then."

"Come, love," Mrs. Right said, "let us get you inside. Sir Galahad will wonder where you are."

Valor nodded and then bobbed a curtsy to Lord Tramondeley. They left him standing on the pavement.

Once inside, she threw off her pelisse and peeked out the drawing room windows. Lord Tramondeley stood there for a half a minute looking pensive and then turned and walked back through the square.

He really was very handsome. It was too bad he liked to chase French boats in the dark. If only he would think about collecting rare books or snuff boxes instead!

CHAPTER SEVEN

M RS. RIGHT HAD followed Valor into the drawing room and noted her watching Lord Tramondeley make his way home. She should not be surprised, as the lord was handsome and seemed a pleasant and reasonable sort of person. She supposed the duke would be pleased if there were to be a match. She, herself, would be pleased too. If she had to lose her last girl to matrimony, he would be the best choice. After all, he was the duke's heir and would eventually take over in the Dales. They might all go on very comfortably together, assuming the lord did not insist on a butler. Anyway, if he were in the Dales, he could not go off sailing in the middle of the night which, as far as she could see, was the only thing Valor held against him.

There was a sudden crash coming from the dining room across the corridor. She and Valor looked at each other.

"Do you suppose it is Mr. Huberville again?" Valor asked.

"Probably," she said. "That fellow will not leave us with one unbroken piece of crockery in the house if he has his way. I'd best go see what he's smashed this time."

She hurried from the room and crossed the hall. She found Mr. Huberville staring forlornly at the remnants of a porcelain dish that usually held potatoes.

"It just flew right out of my hands, Mrs. Right," he said.

"Quite a lot flies out of your hands," Mrs. Right pointed out.

"Very true, very true," Mr. Huberville said, his head bobbing up and down.

"Mr. Huberville, have you considered that butlering is perhaps…not for you?"

"Of course I've considered it! What do you take me for, a dullard? The idea haunts me night and day."

"Well then, why not find another line of work? Find something you'd be more suited for."

"Like what? That's the question, Mrs. Right. Like. What."

Mrs. Right tapped her chin, attempting to come up with something Mr. Huberville might be suited for. He was a short and round individual, so she imagined any sort of physical labor was out. He had not demonstrated any sort of special knowledge or skill. Any skill he attempted to demonstrate ended badly. He was the clumsiest person living.

His mind was not much better. He'd made a complete mess of the household accounts when he'd decided to "modernize" them. It had taken Mrs. Right hours to straighten it out. He seemed to be fond of adding zeros everywhere, so suddenly nine shillings for butter was recorded as ninety shillings. He'd tried to defend it until she asked him how one pound of butter could cost four pounds and ten. Then he admitted it "seemed like a lot."

He'd enraged the cook when he'd thought to be helpful and unbox the groceries, which would have been perfectly fine if he had not got the flour and sugar bins mixed up. That misstep had been discovered when Cook had tasted a gravy and found it sweet.

Reynolds, the duke's stern valet, was quietly steaming because Mr. Huberville had tripped and dropped his toast, which had been dripping with jam. That item had landed on some of the duke's newly laundered neckcloths and then Mr. Huberville had attempted to *rub* out the stain. Any person over the age of five understood that rubbing out a stain was in fact rubbing in a stain. It was presumed Mr. Huberville now knew it too, considering the tongue lashing he'd heard from Reynolds.

Mrs. Right briefly thought Mr. Huberville could perhaps be a waiter in an establishment, until she recalled the broken china at her feet.

"You see?" Mr. Huberville said. "You cannot think of a single thing! Anyway, I cannot leave the house. Lady Marchfield told me I must be a barnacle on a boat and a barnacle I will be!

Mrs. Right sighed. She really did not know how she was to drive Mr. Huberville out. If she could not, the duke would eventually send him packing. However, there were two problems with that solution. One, she would have been defeated and she did not like to contemplate that. Two, she suspected Mr. Huberville might starve on the road. Unlike the other butlers who had landed firmly on their feet, he would not. He was one part enraging and another part pitiable. As much as she resisted it, she'd begun to feel sorry for this particular barnacle.

WESTON HAD BEEN pensive as he returned from escorting Lady Valor to her house. If there had been anything in the world that might show that lady's worth, it was viewing her side by side with Lady Letitia.

Lady Valor had arrived in a simple white muslin dress with only a blue ribbon round the waist for decoration. Her manner was...not reserved, not demure, she was rather frank actually. But she was not a chatterer. She had a particular wit about her and he was certain she was as put off by Lady Letitia's manner as he was himself.

And then, she seemed to be a rescuer of dogs, which was admirable. Really, when he'd spotted the three-legged and half-blind Nelson, he was surprised the duke had allowed it. A highly unattractive and deformed dog did not seem as if it would be a duke's choice for his daughters.

The story about the pug was unusual, to be sure. Why would Lord Thorpe leave it up to Lady Valor, who was apparently very young at the time, to rescue the dog?

He did not know and supposed it did not signify. What did signify is that Lady Valor had pointed out that Lady Marchfield would expect him at Almack's. She'd said the matron would hunt him down if he did not turn up and upon thinking about it, he did not doubt it. Therefore, he and Lord Ledderbey came up with a plan.

While it had been nice that Lord Ledderbey had done his best in showing him steps and very nice of Lady Valor to come and help him practice, he could not fool himself that it was enough. They sent Malberry to make inquiries at an employment office and he'd returned successful. For the next two days, Mr. Riley and his wife were with them night and day, putting him through his paces. Weston had paid dear to hire a dancing master who was willing to work twelve hours a day, but it had been worth the price. His legs ached, but at least he knew what he was doing. He could not say it was something he wished to spend endless amounts of time doing, but if he must do it he would prefer not to appear the fool.

It was well he did put the time into it, as Lady Marchfield had sent a note saying she would come for them in her carriage. Apparently, she was not willing to wait and see if he would turn up but would escort him herself.

She had just sailed into the drawing room and looked him over. "I see you took my advice on a tailor, excellent. Lord Ledderbey, how do you do?"

After the introductions, they made their way to the carriage. "Lord Marchfield does not attend?" Weston asked.

"He will be deep in cards at his club by now. He convinced me long ago that he ought not attend balls—he does not care for dancing and makes himself a nuisance with complaints until the carriage is called."

"I will be sorry we do not see him," Weston said.

"It cannot be helped. One realizes, in a marriage, that one ought to carefully choose one's battlefields. I do not complain about his cards and he does not complain about the new furniture in my writing parlor."

"Very sensible," Lord Ledderbey said.

Weston had not considered the matter, but it did sound sensible.

"Now, Lord Tramondeley, I do not suppose anybody has explained to you how things are done at Almack's."

"Not specifically, no."

"One of the patronesses will arrange who you dance with. It will likely be Lady Westmoreland as she will know you are the duke's heir presumptive and she has always taken a particular interest in the Nicolets. Though how she tolerates my brother, I am sure I do not know. Maybe I should ask her for tips. In any case, if she asks, feel free to inform her if you have any specific preferences on which ladies you might like to be paired with."

"I've only met Lady Valor and Lady Letitia," Weston pointed out.

"Two dukes' daughters, very good choices."

"Can I tell Lady Westmoreland who I'd like to avoid?" Weston asked. "I really do not care for Lady Letitia."

Lady Marchfield frowned. "Certainly not."

Weston sighed. He was afraid that would be the case. A gentleman could never offend a lady, even if the lady was offensive. Upon being apprised of this some years ago by Lord Ledderbey, he'd decried it as unfair. Lord Ledderbey had gone on to outline all the advantages in the world that gentlemen had and ladies did not. Then it began to seem a deal more fair.

"I hope you have eaten a good dinner," Lady Marchfield said. "I did outline in my note that you will not find much there."

"We took that advice to heart, Lady Marchfield," Lord Ledderbey said.

"Why is that, though?" Weston asked. "If this place is supposed to be a pinnacle of some sort, why do they allow their guests to starve?"

"Because it *is* the pinnacle and they will dare you to complain about it," Lady Marchfield said. "I suggest you wait until you are a duke to do so."

Weston suppressed a snort. "I presume the Duke of Pelham does a lot of complaining."

"And worse," Lady Marchfield said. "Do not follow his habits in anything."

Rather than answer, Weston looked out the carriage window at the lights from various windows shining down on the wet streets. He might never get over how closely packed together everything was in this town. As for Lady Marchfield's warning regarding the duke, he did not know what it was about, but as he was not likely to begin following the duke's lead in anything, he did not suppose it mattered much.

He did find himself looking forward to seeing Lady Valor again. The last he'd seen her, she'd been dressed in a simple muslin. She would look far different tonight.

"Here we are," Lady Marchfield said.

They proceeded in and Weston did not know what he was expecting, but it was not a particularly prepossessing sort of place. He supposed that had to do with being the pinnacle and not having to try very hard to impress the fortunate people who were let in the doors. He found the idea in some way tedious.

Lord Ledderbey patted his arm and said softly, "All your hard work will pay off now."

An elegant woman drifted over to them. "Lady Marchfield, I suspect I know who you have brought us."

Lady Marchfield nodded graciously. "Lord Tramondeley, the Duke of Pelham's heir presumptive, and his companion and guardian in his youth, Lord Ledderbey. Gentlemen, may I present Lady Westmoreland."

"You are new to Town, is my understanding," Lady Westmoreland said. "But if I understand Lady Marchfield at all, I imagine you have been well-briefed on how we do things."

"Indeed, Lady Westmoreland," Weston said. Though, he was tempted to say he'd been briefed on the utter lack of food and had a question about it.

"Excellent, do you have any preferences for which young ladies making their debut you ought to be put down for?"

"I am acquainted with Lady Valor Nicolet," Weston said, refusing to say the name of Lady Letitia.

"Ah yes, Lady Valor, that will suit very well. I will put you down for the first. I must also tell you I have had a preference told me by one of our fairer guests. You will escort Lady Letitia into supper. She tells me she is acquainted with you from Cornwall."

Weston gritted his teeth and worked to show no particular feelings about it. He did not even know there was to be a supper. Had not Lady Marchfield said not to expect much in that department? He'd expected a lonely sideboard set up somewhere to minister to people who were on the verge of a faint from lack of food.

Now he was to take Lady Letitia into this supper? If it was anything like when she came to dine he might be better off hanging himself from the highest tree. It might well be a more pleasant experience.

"I will inform you of the other dances after I've arranged them," Lady Westmoreland said, turning to greet some newer arrivals.

"Come," Lady Marchfield said, "let us proceed to the ball-room."

They set forth and found the room to be again nothing particularly impressive. Weston had been very practiced about keeping himself out of ballrooms up to now so he could only compare it to Lord Ledderbey's ballroom. It was larger, to be sure, but their own had better windows.

He scanned the room, ignoring the idea that he looked for Lady Valor.

And there she was. She was looking far different than she had at his house. She was looking rather magnificent actually.

Her hair was elegantly composed. She wore a cream silk dress with an overlay of the same color and a pearl necklace. There was something sophisticated in the simplicity of the color and restraint in decoration.

She was positively lovely.

She was also surrounded by her sisters as if they guarded a delicate flower.

He made his way over.

VALOR COULD NOT help but to feel her stomach lurch at the thought of Almack's. Year after year, her sisters had set off for that place, looking a bit sick as they got in the carriage.

It was not so much that there would be dancing with as-yet-unknown gentlemen. It was not even that it would be a first foray out into society. It was that Almack's was the place a lady would be examined, closely, and for the first time. An opinion would be formed, cementing perceptions of that lady. Some of the patronesses would stand in the upper gallery, looking down with falcon eyes on all that transpired.

Nevertheless, all her sisters had gone and survived it, even Grace who might have fallen on the floor at any moment. Tonight, they would all be there to support her. She must find her courage in that.

She would also find courage in her dress. Madame LaFray had explained that her dark hair and hazel eyes could stand up to a light color and had designed a lovely cream silk dress with gently puffed sleeves and a chiffon overlay of the same color. There was a subtle chain of cream-colored flowers embroidered around the waist and hem, otherwise it was unadorned. The dressmaker had told her that it could be a temptation to keep going with decoration, but it only resulted in something that was over-wrought.

As she already felt a bit overwrought, she did not care to look overwrought. Serenity had advised that the string of pearls

Winsome had given her last season would set the whole thing off. According to her sister, the aim was to avoid looking as if one tried too hard. One should appear as if one had grabbed the first dress within reach with hardly a thought about it. Elegant, but unstudied.

She could not say she appeared quite that nonchalant, but she did feel confident she wore the right dress for Almack's.

There had been some debate over her slippers, a matching cream color and of delicate construction, as it had rained heavily and the streets were wet. Mr. Huberville had offered to carry her out to the carriage.

On top of not wishing to find herself in the arms of their current butler, the risk of him dropping her on the pavement was deemed far too high, considering what else he'd dropped in the past days.

The problem was getting to the carriage in Grosvenor Square. Almack's had a covered portico so getting out again was not a danger. Mrs. Right finally came up with the practical solution of wearing her boots into the carriage and then changing to slippers once inside.

Valor had been sure her father would inquire into her dancing lessons with Lord Tramondeley. She'd expected he would, but over the past days he'd said nothing about it.

As for herself, she had perhaps looked out her bedchamber window from time to time and peered across the square to his house. She could just see the front door through a break in the trees. The only thing of note she spotted was a couple dropped off by a hackney in the early morning and then setting off again at the end of the day, two days in a row. They must be very close friends to spend so much time there.

Now, she and the duke had positively arrived to Almack's after a rousing talk from her father in the carriage. He reminded her that she was a duke's daughter and need not concern herself with anybody's approval. He'd patted his flask in his pocket. "Do you think those patronesses don't know I make free with my brandy in their establishment? They do, a few of them will be predictably outraged over it, and yet they do nothing about it because I am a duke."

He'd managed to make her laugh, which was always good for settling nerves.

Her father had presented her to Lady Westmoreland who turned out to be a very pleasant woman. Valor did not know who the lady would choose for her card, but she did hope that Lord Tramondeley was on it.

She reasoned that it was not so much because she admired his person, but more that he was new to dancing and would require support to keep his spirits up about it. After all, he'd only had a brief lesson. He must be nervous even if he would not show it.

As she thought of that, she had begun to wonder if a gentleman who went out sailing at night, looking for trouble of the French variety, might give it up eventually. After all, did not a young gentleman mature? She did not know of a single older gentleman who would try out such a thing. Lord Tramondeley might just decide he'd had enough of it and give it up for rare book collecting. Perhaps he'd just not yet thought of collecting something.

"I've had one request relating to you already, Lady Valor," Lady Westmoreland said.

Valor felt her heart speed up the littlest bit. It must be Lord Tramondeley.

"Conte di Conpressio, he is the eldest son of the Marquis de Rossi."

"The Sardinian fellow we met at an inn," the duke said.

Lady Westmoreland nodded. "He is very well connected in England and maintains an estate here. They are an exceedingly cosmopolitan family—I find his father, the marquis, an absolute delight."

"Pleasant enough fellow, I suppose," the duke said.

Valor was disappointed that it was not Lord Tramondeley, but she was happy to see the count again. She also found herself gratified to hear Lady Westmoreland express her approbation. The count had made a very good impression on Valor and it seemed her estimation was correct.

"Oh, and Lord Tramondeley mentioned he was acquainted with you."

Was that all he said? Just that they were acquainted?

"Tramondeley, excellent," the duke said.

Valor felt someway insulted by that. Mentioned they were acquainted, indeed.

They proceeded into the ballroom and found her sisters all together.

"Where are your husbands?" Valor asked, thinking surely they'd not all come alone.

"Huddled in a corner with Lord James," Felicity said, laughing. "There is to be a carriage race from here to Brighton on the morrow. Speculations abound and the bets are being laid. I hope they are being subtle about it, else the patronesses will not like it."

From out of the corner of her eye, Valor saw Lord Tramondeley come into the ballroom with Lord Ledderbey. He was looking very dashing indeed and his caramel-colored hair shone in the candlelight. His eyes settled on her, which gave her a bit of a shiver. Then he strode purposefully in her direction, which gave her another little shiver. He really was a glorious sort of man, excepting his dangerous habits. And only being *acquainted* with her.

"Goodness," Patience said softly, "here he comes."

CHAPTER EIGHT

"LADY VALOR," LORD Tramondeley said.

Lord Ledderbey had been trailing behind and now caught up to him.

"Lord Tramondeley, Lord Ledderbey," Valor said. "You will know my sisters and of course my father."

"Tramondeley," the duke said, "how do you get on?"

"Very well, Your Grace. Lady Valor, Lady Westmoreland indicated she would put me on your card," Lord Tramondeley said. "I did not even realize there would be a supper."

"Oh, I am afraid Lady Westmoreland has arranged for me to go into supper with Count di Compressio."

"The Sardinian fellow," the duke said, in case anyone wondered about it.

"I see," the lord said, a flash of irritation crossing his features. "I believe I may be engaged to take in Lady Letitia. But then I suppose nobody needs to strictly only talk to their assigned partner at this supper."

"No I suppose not," Valor said.

"You are not to be fooled by the term 'supper,' Lord Tramondeley," Grace said.

"Heavens no," Verity said.

"Dry cake, weak tea, sour lemonade, and stale bread," Winsome said, laughing.

The look of consternation on the lord's expression was almost amusing.

"It's the worst sort of trickery, in my view," the duke said. He pulled his flask from his pocket, opened it and took a swig. "Brandy," he said, handing it to Lord Tramondeley. "Help yourself, there will be nothing better to be had."

The lord did help himself to it. "Thank you, Your Grace."

"How about you, Ledderbey?" the duke said, laughing.

"No, I thank you all the same," Lord Ledderbey said.

"Your Grace, Lady Valor."

Valor turned to find Count di Compressio. As she had seen him last time, his clothes were very regular, but cut just the smallest bit different. He looked very elegant.

"It's the Sardinian," the duke said.

"Your Grace, I have the honor of a dance with Lady Valor and then escorting her into supper."

The duke laughed. "Wait until you see what it is. You won't think it much of an honor."

The count appeared perplexed, which did not particularly surprise Valor. The duke often perplexed people until they got to know him.

Lady Marchfield approached. "Roland," she said flatly. "Girls, you all look very well." She paused and stared at the count.

"Aunt," Valor said, "this is Count di Compressio. We encountered him on our trip to Town and he was kind enough to give over the only private dining room available. Count, this is my aunt, Lady Marchfield."

The count gave Lady Marchfield a rather elegant bow. "Charmed, Lady Marchfield," he said.

"He's a Sardinian, but we do not hold it against him," the duke said. For good measure, he patted the pocket that held his brandy flask in case Lady Marchfield had missed its presence.

"I presume my butler gets on very well," Lady Marchfield said to the duke.

"If by 'gets on,' you mean breaks everything in the house," the duke said, "then your barnacle on a boat does splendidly."

Lady Marchfield sniffed.

Lady Westmoreland brought Valor's card to her and then listed for Lord Tramondeley who he was to escort through the dances. Valor glanced at her card and was gratified to see that Lord Tramondeley was marked down for the opening set.

The orchestra, which had been tuning for some time, suddenly stopped. Lady Salisbury would open the ball and she gave the signal that the dancing was set to begin. The first was to be a cotillion and she called the changes and the figure.

Valor was very afraid Lord Tramondeley would not be able to keep track of it all.

"Tramondeley! Count!"

Valor turned to find Lady Letitia bounding toward them. She did not wish to think unkind thoughts, but the lady was very loud and dressed in such a manner that would make Madame LaFray frown. She wore a salmon-colored taffeta with large ruffles on the sleeves and a complicated swirling decoration of silver embroidery at the hem. She looked a bit like a cake.

"Tramondeley," Lady Letitia said, waving round a like-colored silk fan, "I will see *you* at supper. Lady Valor, how do you do? Count? Are we ready?"

"Ah, yes," the count said. "I escort Lady Letitia for the opening of the ball." He held his arm out and led the lady away.

"My God, she's loud," the duke said.

Lord Tramondeley laughed and led Valor to their places.

Thinking to put him at ease as they joined a square of three other couples, she said softly, "I will remind you of the steps as we get to them, Lord Tramondeley."

"I thank you, but I believe I understand them."

Valor was surprised by that. How could he? She'd seen how little he knew when she was at his house. She hoped the claim was not some sort of misplaced manly pride. One could say one was confident, but the dance would soon start and the truth would be there for all to see.

The music struck up. After the requisite bow and curtsy, Lord

Tramondeley led her through the steps. Much to her surprise, he executed them perfectly and with an ease that suggested he was well-practiced.

Seeming to note her confusion, he bent his head and whispered, "I hired a dancing master who has been with me night and day. It was exhausting, but I would hardly allow myself to arrive here in the shape you last saw me."

Valor laughed, as it occurred to her that the hackney she'd seen arriving for two days in a row had been the dancing master. That gentleman *had* been there for strangely extended periods. She could not say so, of course, else she admit to peering at his house from her window.

"I admire your preparation, Lord Tramondeley," Valor said. "I am not sure another gentleman would have done the same."

"Then that other gentleman would be rather foolish," he said. "I've never had so many matrons staring at me in my life. They are even overhead in the gallery, peering down like hawks on the lookout for a mouse."

Valor nodded. "You are a duke's heir, they will be interested in you."

"Why? It is not as if I am a prospect for any of them."

"My sister Serenity would say they are queen bees. They like to have their hand in everything even if it has little to do with them."

"Cornwall is a much simpler place."

"As are the Dales. How strange that you will inherit the place and yet have never seen it."

Lord Tramondeley led her through the figure and they returned to their place. "I've never been that far north so do not have the first idea. In any case, the duke seems a hale and hearty individual, so I do not think the question of inheritance will come up any time soon and I am only the presumptive. He could remarry tomorrow and produce a son and then I am out."

Valor laughed at the idea. "I think it highly unlikely that my father will wed again. If he would do it, I suspect he would have done it long ago."

Lord Tramondeley shrugged by way of reply and Valor got the idea he did not particularly care one way or the other.

"Perhaps it was unfair that he did not take you in," Valor said. "Then you would have grown up there and it would be your natural home."

"Which makes me think he might remarry at some point. Deuced awkward to have to push out the presumptive to make room for an heir apparent."

Their turn came round again and the lord led her forward. It was really extraordinary how skilled he'd gotten. Nobody would ever know that just days ago he'd known next to nothing.

When they returned to their place, Valor said, "I suppose you would like to get back to Cornwall…back to taking your boat out at night."

She longed for him to say he would not like it. She wished for him to say he'd given it up and was planning to take up rare book collecting.

He seemed pensive about it. "I would like to get back to harrowing the French, it seems a duty, you know. But I must think carefully on how and where to do it. I would not like to put Lord Ledderbey in danger."

"In danger? Lord Ledderbey? I had not known he went out with you on the boat. Is that safe? He is an older gentleman."

Lord Tramondeley laughed. "He does not go out with me, that is for me and my valet alone. However, I have been warned that the French are looking for my house and it is not clear if they wish to destroy my boat or me. I would not like Lord Ledderbey to be a casualty when he has been so kind to me."

Valor felt almost frozen upon hearing that information. She had thought the danger was sailing out into the dark. She had never contemplated the idea that people staying safely on land would be in danger too.

"What are you to do, then? You cannot go back there."

"Not for now. But there would be other places I could base

myself. I just do not know what to do with Lord Ledderbey—he's very fond of his home, but it is not safe for the time being."

Valor was not forced to answer as it was their time to take a turn. That was well, as she did not have an answer. She'd hoped that Lord Tramondeley would think better of putting his life in danger in such a bizarre manner. But he had not. He was thinking about where else he might base the operation.

They went on in silence from then on and Valor found herself very shaken. She realized that all thought of Lord Tramondeley was to be dismissed. Even if she were to put her bravest face on, she could not possibly sleep at night if there was always the lingering idea of the doors being broken down by the French. It was impossible. She would be positively terrorized.

She also realized that perhaps she had been thinking about him more than she ought. She discovered herself let down that she should not think of him further.

DAMIANO KEPT A smile on his face, but he was not in the best of spirits. He'd come to London imagining he might have his choice of duke's daughters, as there were just now three of them available. As Lady Tallifer had predicted, Lady Elizabeth had just engaged herself. Another was not at all what he was looking for. Lady Letitia was a most unpleasant lady. Why did she talk so loudly, as if everybody in her vicinity required an ear trumpet that they'd forgotten at home? Why did she ask prying questions and then answer them herself?

He'd been quite offended when she'd inquired into his mother's jewelry collection and then proceeded to speculate on its quality and that the next marchessa would inherit it all. She was already talking about his mother's death! He was not sure he could bear Lady Letitia's company for years on end.

That left Lady Valor, which he was perfectly agreeable to, but he sensed there was something between her and Lord Tramondeley. It would make perfect sense; he was the duke's heir. She really was the only tolerable possibility though. His father would approve of her, while the marquis would not know what to make of Lady Letitia. Or worse, he might become entirely fed up with that loud lady and order poison for her drink. The marquis had got impatient, intolerant, and reckless in his late years and Damiano already had his hands full trying to keep Monsieur Bernard alive.

His sisters would positively despise Lady Letitia, though those girls with their noses up in the air would likely be more satisfied with Lady Valor. They would still look down on her, but without the viciousness they would bestow on Lady Letitia.

Now, he led Lady Valor into this supper the duke had made some sort of joke about. He imagined the food was very bad, but then it was England and all the food was very bad. He did not suppose he'd notice a further drop in quality. Over his shoulder, he heard Tramondeley call out to Lady Valor.

"We can join you," the lord said.

"I would positively refuse to share Tramondeley's company," Lady Letitia said, "but as it's the count, I must make an exception. What say you, Lady Valor? Are we to be surrounded by handsome gentlemen?"

Lady Valor, to her credit, did not answer this tasteless question. Why was Tramondeley pushing in? It might be that he found Lady Letitia as tiresome as he did. Or it might be that he was particularly interested in Lady Valor. Or it might be both.

Whatever he was, Damiano was not interested in his company though there was no polite way to get rid of him.

They entered the supper room and he'd hoped there would not be four chairs together, forcing a necessary parting.

That was not to be.

"Right there," Tramondeley said, "to the right. We can all sit together."

"You see how masterful he is, Lady Valor," Lady Letitia said.

"Indeed," Lady Valor said softly.

They were seated with the two ladies between them. It was just as well that Tramondeley was not beside him as he did not have an interest in talking to that fellow. It was not as well that Tramondeley leaned forward to avoid being captured entirely by Lady Letitia.

A footman approached and asked them if they cared for lemonade or tea.

Damiano stared at the young man uncomprehendingly. "I would prefer to hear the wine list," he said.

This set Lady Letitia into a roaring and unpleasant laughter. "Wine? Do you hear him? Count, there is no wine here!"

What could she mean? Why on earth would there be no wine? "What is available, then?" he asked the young man, presuming he would be forced to put up with a sherry.

That young man was beginning to look terrified. "Lemonade, tea, dry cake, and buttered bread, everybody knows it."

Damiano had not known it. It seemed the sort of thing Lady Tallifer might have mentioned. What sort of place was this? The English really were so uncivilized, one never knew what they'd take it into their heads to do next.

"My sisters all advise the tea and dry cake," Lady Valor said, "as the lesser of the evils."

Damiano nodded. "We will bow to Lady Valor's prior knowledge of the matter," he said.

The young man hurried off, likely glad to be away from them. But really, he could not be the first person to be annoyed by this alleged supper. Why call it a supper when it was only a few crusts that any self-respecting servant would turn in their notice over?

"Now Tramondeley," Lady Letitia said, "you must tell me all about your life in Cornwall. I long to visit that county once more. I was positively struck when I was there."

As the lord gave the lady some nondescript answer of the weather being as expected, Damiano said, "Lady Valor, do you also long to visit Cornwall? I have not been there myself."

"I hadn't thought, I have not been there either," Lady Valor said. "Lord Tramondeley lives with Lord Ledderbey by the sea."

She said it in a very pensive manner. He said, "You do not prefer to locate yourself by the sea?"

"Not right now, no. There are French frigates, I understand. At least, nearby Cornwall there are."

"I see," Damiano said. What was Napoleon doing? Was he thinking of a landing? It really would be ill-advised. He was not well-acquainted with the Frenchman's plans as his primary contact was Monsieur Bernard and that fellow either knew nothing or pretended to know nothing.

"Lord Tramondeley goes out to sea in the night, which I really cannot like. He sails around in the dark to harass the French."

The young waiter and another one arrived with a cart holding a large and heavy teapot and plates of dry cake. Damiano was glad for the distraction as he did not wish to give himself away. Tramondeley was in the habit of sailing out at night to harass the French. My God, could he be the Mosquito? It seemed preposterous.

But on the other hand, the sloop was missing from the pier and he'd received a report that it had not been positively seen out at night for some time. Tramondeley lived in Cornwall, by the sea. There was still the odd unconfirmed report of a sailor seeing a flash of light here and there, but that was probably just a sailor's active imagination. Nobody had seen the boat itself. Could it possibly be true? Was Tramondeley the Mosquito?

If it were true, how was he to confirm it? If he confirmed it, what was he to do about it? It was one thing to dispose of a Cornwall fisherman, which he had presumed he was looking for. It was quite another to murder a lord. A duke's heir, no less.

Could he murder the duke's heir and marry his daughter? It seemed a bit much, even for him.

Lady Valor broke apart her dry cake with a fork. She really

did seem unhappy about Tramondeley getting up to such activity. She would not be so unhappy if she were not interested in him. After all, why should she care who the duke's heir was? If she were interested in somebody else, she would marry out of the family and it would not matter to her who was sitting in her father's place in the Dales.

Her concern or disapproval was perhaps an angle he could work with. Now was not the time though, as that lord was within earshot.

Tramondeley had just leaned forward. "Lady Valor, I forgot to inquire, did you receive an invitation to the prince's fête?"

Lady Valor nodded. "Yes, indeed we did."

"Do we have to go?" Lord Tramondeley asked. "Is it the kind of thing that's required?"

"I expect so," Lady Valor said.

"Do you hear him?" Lady Letitia cried. "Does he have to go?"

Damiano wished to cut off the conversation before there was any mention of an idea of Tramondeley and Lady Valor going together. "Lady Valor, you did promise to allow me to escort you to the British Museum. Would tomorrow be convenient?"

"Oh yes, I suppose so," she said.

"Excellent. I will come at one o'clock. I will ride my horse but can send my carriage."

"I imagine my father will prefer me in his own carriage," Lady Valor said.

"Ah, quite right. Or perhaps your own horse? Do you ride?"

Lady Valor seemed unsure of whether she rode or did not.

"I do, a little. It's just that I really prefer to walk my horse and sometimes Tulip seems fed up with it and wants to go faster than I'd like. She's a Dales pony and very much has her own mind."

She rode a horse but only walked it. It was perhaps emblematic of what he understood of Lady Valor's temperament. She was naturally cautious.

"I see," Damiano said. "So horse and rider must be brought to an agreement. What I would do if I were to oversee such a horse would be to send a groom to gallop Tulip, and then when she has rid herself of pent-up energy she will be happy to walk."

"That is a clever idea," Lady Valor said. "Why argue with her when we can both have what we want?"

"Just so. That way, you may always feel safe when you mount her."

Lady Valor nodded in hearty agreement.

"What say you, Val?"

The duke had appeared behind them.

"My flask is empty and my patience is empty too. Have you had enough of the place?"

Lady Valor smiled indulgently at her father. The duke was strange, but his daughter seemed fond of him. Perhaps that was well. His own father was strange. It would be well for a bride of his to be prepared for some eccentricity. His marquis had lately begun to believe he was untouchable and might do anything at all that sprang to mind, including poisoning Monsieur Bernard.

"We can go, Papa," she said. "I know you have had to put up with this for six prior seasons so I am not surprised your patience has run out."

She rose and Damiano rose too. The duke called to Tramondeley, who was looking like a cornered hare in the clutches of Lady Letitia. "Come by the house in the afternoon if you like, we can go for a drive in the park."

"Thank you, Your Grace."

"Oh no, Papa," Lady Valor said. "I have just committed myself to going to the British Museum. You did say that I could if Mrs. Right would come with me."

"I did say that," the duke said, looking a bit resigned.

"Never fear, Tramondeley," Lady Letitia said, "Lady Monroe and I would be delighted to take you to the park. Consider the matter settled. One o'clock."

Damiano had been considering what to do about Tramondeley, but Lady Letitia was helping out quite a lot in that effort. Tramondeley had an expression that could only be described as deep sadness.

Too bad for Tramondeley.

CHAPTER NINE

WESTON HAD BEEN handed a letter as soon as he walked through the doors arriving home from Almack's. Malberry said, "The fellow said he'd come a long way and it was imperative that you receive this letter instantly. He wished to go to Almack's and find you until I was able to convince him he would not get through the doors."

"Gracious," Lord Ledderbey said. "I hope nobody has died. We know so few people, I cannot imagine who it would be."

Weston asked Malberry for two large glasses of brandy for he and Lord Ledderbey, as they'd got nothing of substance at Almack's. They proceeded into the drawing room and Weston tore open the letter. He glanced down at the signature. It was from Mr. Lawrence Cadwalker, the former secretary to Admiral Peter Parker.

Lord Tramondeley—

It is with urgency that I send this missive. As you may imagine, Admiral Parker had sources of information ranged all along the southern coastline. Some of these sources still send me information as we wait for a new admiral. I received an alarming report of a man, a foreigner, poking around your neighborhood. He was particularly looking for the sloop (which I gather he did not find) and asking questions about its owner and where that owner lived. As far as I know it, your good Cornwall neighbors gave away nothing and made his stay most uncomfortable.

The description of the man is that he is tall, dark-haired, angular features, and has an accent, though it was not a French accent. The fellow who looks after your pier claims the man is from the continent somewhere and that he was very well-dressed. (Or as the man describes it, "A fancy type what don't have no business here.") It could be possible that the man was from Florence or Turin. Napoleon has pressed many citizens of the countries he's invaded to cooperate or lose everything. On the other hand, your pier man might be mistaken, as he won't have heard many accents in the course of his life. When I think about it, what strikes me is wondering who can travel round England so freely? He stayed at inns and did not hide himself. Does he perhaps have connections here?

I really do not know if that is the end of it or not. I cannot be certain if this foreigner was able to glean any information. I write to you to put you on your guard as the man has left the environs of Cornwall but did not comment on where he was going.

The only thing that relieves me at this moment is knowing you are far away in London. I will write again if I discover more about this man.

Lawrence Cadwalker, Former Secretary to Admiral Peter Parker.

He handed the letter to Lord Ledderbey, who read it with dismay. Weston rose and closed the curtains on the windows overlooking the square. He had the sudden feeling of being watched, though he knew it was his imagination.

Malberry brought in two glasses and the decanter of brandy and poured out generous amounts. Weston took his and drained it.

"Thank heavens we relocated when we did," Lord Ledderbey said with a shiver.

"Yes, but I think it wise that we keep our eyes open. Malberry, arrange for some men to guard the house on a rotation, day and night. They can take shifts and share a room in the stables."

"Yes, my lord."

"That's a good notion," Lord Ledderbey said. "Gracious, a foreigner poking his nose round our neighborhood in Cornwall. It is upsetting if I'm honest. He would have stuck out very noticeably too so he must not have cared about that. Can you imagine if… that is, the only foreigner we have encountered…"

"Is Count di Compressio," Weston said. He'd already been thinking in that direction. Would it be too absurd to imagine it might be the count? He seemed a bit of a delicate flower to be employed by the French for such a thing. On the other hand, perhaps he just playacted to seem so. His family must be in a very uncomfortable spot with Napoleon just now…

"But certainly, he would not have—"

Weston shrugged. "We have to find it out, though."

"I do not suppose he would tell you. In any case, it is far more likely he's got nothing to do with it and you will have offended him for nothing. For one thing, he is here, not there."

"But he might have been there and come back," Weston pointed out. He tapped his chin, considering a way to confirm whether it was or was not the count poking around Cornwall. "I know what we will do. Malberry, find me some artists for hire. Artists that can sketch portraits. Do not bother with those that sketch landscapes."

"Yes, my lord."

"My dear boy, I hardly think you'll be able to hire an artist who is willing to spy on the count to capture a likeness."

"No spying required. We will host a party and the artists will be there to sketch likenesses as part of the entertainment. A small party, we will say it is very usual for Cornwall and we will keep all the sketches to have them framed. Then the artist can make copies of the sketch of the count. We can send some of those copies to Cornwall to discover if that is our man. I suspect the count will come to our party if he knows Lady Valor has been invited."

"Very original notion. Yes, I suppose it could be done. Malberry, what say you? Are you up to locating several artists and preparing for a party?"

"Of course, my lord."

"And just think, my boy, it might be very pleasant to have a sketch of Lady Valor. You might make a copy of her sketch too."

Weston did not answer but rather poured himself a second brandy. It would be pleasant, though he found himself loath to admit it. He'd all along sworn he'd keep the duke at arm's length, and yet he did not wish to keep his daughter at arm's length.

He'd found himself exceedingly irritated by the count's attentions to that lady. Though, his common sense told him he must be careful in his thinking when it came to the count. He could not condemn him on little evidence because he was unduly swayed by his personal annoyance.

Nevertheless, that fellow ought to steer clear of her. A match between them would not even make sense. The count might say he wished to settle in Hertfordshire and make himself a regular Englishman, but that was just for now. Napolean would be defeated eventually and then Weston had no doubt the fellow would hightail it back to Sardinia to lounge in the sunshine. Lady Valor could not like to be ripped from her homeland in such a manner.

And what was this visiting the museum business? How had that happened? Why did the duke allow it?

"Now my boy," Lord Ledderbey said, "you know I am always eager to support you in everything. However, I might have to cast you adrift regarding tomorrow afternoon's jaunt to the park. Lady Letitia gives me a headache."

"Lady Letitia *is* a headache."

"You do not mind that I bow out of that particular experience?"

"No, I'd bow out too if I could figure out how to do it."

"Very pleasant of the duke to invite you to the park, though. A shame Lady Valor was already engaged. And then Lady Letitia made clear she was not."

It *was* a shame Lady Valor was engaged. Especially considering who she was engaged to see.

"I find myself surprised that duke somehow grows on me," Lord Ledderbey said. "Mind, I see what your father complained of. Lord Robert was a serious and thoughtful man and the duke is…well, he is not that. Nevertheless, he somehow grows on me. Or perhaps wears me down."

Weston thought back over the evening. The duke grew on him a little too. Weston could not entirely make him out. He supposed the duke was a bit of a deep character.

VALOR WAS OF course eager to see the museum. It was perhaps a lack in their family that they never got around to visiting such places. On the other hand, she could not ignore a lingering disappointment that she would not visit the park with Lord Tramondeley, and even an irritation that Lady Letitia would.

She had peered out her bedchamber window across the square to Lord Tramondeley's house, which she very well knew she ought not be doing. But then, there was that very convenient break in the trees that made it almost impossible not to look. A footman just now came out of Lord Tramondeley's doors. He held a paper in his hands and walked very determinedly through the square. Was he coming here? Was he bringing a letter?

Valor hurried downstairs to be on hand if a letter was coming to her. She heard the knock on the door and peeked round the doors to the drawing room. Charlie answered and took the folded paper.

After the door closed, Valor walked out and said, "Who is it addressed to? Me or the duke?"

"Both, Lady Valor," Charlie said, handing it to her.

Indeed it was. It was addressed to Lady Valor Nicolet and the Duke of Pelham. "My father will not mind if I open it without him," she said, hurrying into the drawing room with it.

She unfolded it.

Lady Valor and Your Grace—

Lord Ledderbey and I would like to invite you to a traditional Cornwall gathering. It will be small in size and have various entertainments, such as a sketch artist to make portraits. We will hold it on Tuesday next at seven o'clock and pray we will see your attendance.

Tramondeley

The invitation gave her a thrill. It was to be a small party and she must feel the compliment of being included. A sketch artist— that was so clever. She'd not expected Lord Tramondeley to host a party. She wondered if it were being done for her benefit? Ought she be so bold as to wonder that? What would she wear?

Then she brought herself down from the clouds and counseled herself very sternly on the matter. It was perfectly fine to find Lord Tramondeley handsome, and he really was. It was perfectly fine to consider him very genial, and he really was. It was even perfectly fine to feel drawn to him, which she must admit that she was.

However, from a practical standpoint it could go no further. She simply did not have the temperament to be able to sleep while keeping one ear out for French soldiers storming the house. Even when she was not asleep she would be jumping out of her shoes at every sound. She must remember that she was far more suited to a quiet life with a staid gentleman who collected something. It would not do to pretend she was other than she was. She was not some brave heroine who would risk every danger. She was a lady far more prone to hide under her blankets.

That brought to mind the count, as he was exceedingly handsome too, in a different sort of way. He seemed interested in her, he wished for a calm and quiet life, and he collected art. His estate was in Hertfordshire, with not a coastline or French ship in sight.

She had never conceived that she might find herself consorting with a Sardinian gentleman, but he really did have everything to recommend him. He had only the slightest accent, which lent a certain charm to his perfect English. His clothes had small differences, but they were so elegant they could be thought to be improvements.

He was considerate too. That clever idea of his that a groom should gallop Tulip before she mounted showed he understood her. He'd not counseled that she get used to trotting and cantering or made fun over her only walking Tulip. If she wished to walk her horse, that was perfectly fine. There was something comforting about being accepted as she was and not expected to be anything different.

If she could only stop thinking of Lord Tramondeley. Or, if a miracle would occur, if Lord Tramondeley would stop thinking about chasing French boats in the dark. She felt that hope was probably futile but somehow she could not entirely give it up.

As she had expected, her father would never have allowed her into the count's carriage, even if Mrs. Right was with her and the count was on horseback. She and Mrs. Right would take one of the duke's carriages driven by the duke's most trusted coachman. Winkman had been in the duke's service long and could be trusted that nothing went amiss. If the count or any other gentleman thought he might hand over a guinea and get inside the coach himself, that gentleman would find himself on the ground, looking up and wondering what had happened.

Felicity often said that while their father seemed so devil-may-care, he put careful fences round his daughters.

The count had arrived to the house on a very fine black stallion. He sat a horse very well, and Valor could only admire it. Though, as soon as she got in the carriage, she slid over to the opposite side and peered out the window toward Lord Tramondeley's house. Lady Letitia's carriage was already there. Lord Ledderbey led the two ladies out of the house. She could not hear what was said, but Lady Letitia threw her head back and laughed and seemed very jolly. The ladies got in the carriage but Lord Ledderbey did not. He waved them off. Then there was Lord Tramondeley seated on a fine chestnut.

Valor's own carriage jerked forward and they set off, leaving the view behind. She was determined to put away what she'd just viewed and enjoy the day. The count led the way through the London streets to Montagu House on Great Russell Street. He helped Valor and Mrs. Right down from the carriage and led them to the entrance. They showed their tickets and were met by Mr. Reed, a curator of the museum.

"Count di Compressio," Mr. Reed said. "Welcome to the British Museum."

"Mr. Reed," the count said. "I escort Lady Valor Nicolet, daughter of the Duke of Pelham, and her esteemed friend, Mrs. Right."

Mr. Reed greeted them. Valor was really appreciative of how the count introduced Mrs. Right. There might be some who dismissed her as only the housekeeper or might say she was only a companion, but the count appeared to hold her in high regard and see her for what she was.

"I understand, Count," Mr. Reed said, "you have a particular interest in the Townley Collection."

The count nodded. "If Lady Valor is agreeable. Charles Townley spent much time on the Continent and brought back some magnificent sculptures."

Valor nodded. Of course she was agreeable. She had not the first idea what this impressive building held, but sculptures sounded as good as anything else. She gazed round the high ceiling painted with an angelic fresco and the murals on the walls reaching twenty feet high and depicting ancient pastoral scenes, and the wide, sweeping marble staircase. The building was so grand it made her feel small. Even though their house in the Dales was likely larger, it was somehow more cozy and built for people. Theirs was all comfortable nooks and overstuffed furniture, and this was all cold gleaming marble and iron rails edging the stairs.

They were led up those stairs and there Lady Valor Nicolet had her eyes opened to the wider world. She'd had no idea there was so much beauty in it! It seemed astonishing that an artist could take a block of marble and transform it into a figure that looked almost alive. She was particularly taken with the Townley Caryatid, an eight-foot-tall sculpture of a women in flowing robes. The robes were carved in such a way that they appeared as if they might move in a breeze. The count explained the Caryatid was made of Pentelic marble, the same that had been used in the Acropolis. Mr. Reed estimated that it had been produced somewhere between 140 and 160 AD. It was astonishing.

It seemed to Valor that the world was bigger and more expansive than she'd thought it. She seemed to know so little of it, while the count knew so much. He was so worldly and perhaps there was a safety in that. A knowing protection of some sort, as if nothing could take him by surprise.

And then, he collected art, she could not imagine what he had in his house in Hertfordshire. He must be surrounded by such beauty.

What a day. First an invitation from Lord Tramondeley to a Cornwall party and then viewing wondrous sculptures she'd never known had even existed.

MRS. RIGHT HAD been out all afternoon, acting as duenna for Valor while she toured the British Museum with the Sardinian count. It had been an impressive place, she supposed. She had found it rather stark. She was not an admirer of an overabundance of marble and the place had been full of it. She found the look of it too hard and cold to be comfortable. In any case, she did not care for people carved in stone who stood eight feet tall. It was alarming.

What was more concerning were the attentions of the count. What was he intending? He was a charming individual who sought to please, but if he was out to wed her poppet, she could only see disaster ahead. He claimed he wished to settle in Hertfordshire. That might be acceptable, though still a bit too far from the Dales for her own taste.

But that would not be the end of it. These people who lived in perpetual sunshine always tired of English weather. Suddenly, they became depressed and their bones hurt from the damp and they complained bitterly about the rain and fog. They never could appreciate the charm of rain pounding on the rooftops while sitting in front of a cozy fire.

Eventually, they longed to return to their sunny locale. The duke had made the mistake many years ago of hiring a gardener from Rome. That fellow never stopped complaining about the cold and how he thought it was making his bones brittle. Mrs. Right had been tempted to trip him and find out if it were true. He'd finally given up his post and returned home. They'd all been glad to see the back of him.

That was just what would happen with the count. Valor, who would have no business gallivanting off to foreign shores, would find herself in Sardinia. She would be friendless! She could not even speak the language. She could barely speak French. She would be far away from the support of her family. She would be on the Continent, which was a place where anything could happen. Napoleon had recently been making that point. She was so unsuited to any of it.

Mrs. Right was beginning to think she ought to come up with some plan to drive off this foreign count.

It was true she'd made some errors in that regard in the past. Mrs. Right was not one to turn away from her mistakes and there had been some unfortunate mistakes made. Perhaps she had attempted to ruin the life of a gentleman who would go on to become the husband of one of her girls. As she *was* rather steely eyed at staring at the facts, she could even go so far as to admit that she'd erroneously attempted to ruin the lives of *all* her girls' current husbands.

But this situation must be considered a different matter. She did not act on speculation. The Sardinian count was admittedly and definitely from Sardinia. Everybody returned to their homeland eventually, that was a well-known fact. Valor Nicolet was not the type of lady who would be happy settling in a foreign place where she did not understand the language or the customs. Another well-known fact. This time, there was no possibility of a mistake.

Mrs. Right was afraid that Valor was attracted to the count's unwavering courtesy and gentle manner. She was afraid Valor believed this nonsense about settling in Hertfordshire forevermore to enjoy the peace of the countryside. She was convinced her little poppet turned in the count's direction out of fear. She must do something. And then, if Valor's eyes were to turn to Lord Tramondeley? This habit of his to go out in the night and chase French boats might be given up. It was not ideal that he was the sort of man who would do such a ludicrous thing, but he would have no chance at sinking his boat if they could get him to the Dales. He could sail round the lake, and if he sank he could just swim to the banks.

Of course, deciding she must do something about the count was all well and good. What that something might be was a different matter. How did one drive off a foreign count?

As she was mulling that over, she heard a loud crash from the direction of the dining room. Then Thomas said, "Oh Mr. Huberville!"

Mr. Huberville, apparently expecting that denunciation, cried, "I know! Things just fly out of my hand!"

Mrs. Right began to wonder if there was a way to rid them of both a count and a hapless butler. Mr. Huberville might like Sardinia and did not all foreigners wish for an English butler? She had no information that they did, but it seemed like they must.

After all, the English did things so superiorly to the rest of the world.

CHAPTER TEN

Damiano had quite the time controlling his feelings and appearing pleasant at the British Museum. He had specifically wished to view the Townley collection to see personally what that knave had taken from the continent. It was outrageous how these English people thought the world owed them their artifacts.

Why did they imagine they were so superior? They must take things that were not their own. And then, the majority of the population never even bothered to look at the things that were taken. They just must have it to have it. Lady Valor, a duke's daughter, would never have set foot in the museum if he had not proposed it. It really was distasteful.

As enraging as it was, he'd kept a neutral expression and worked to please and impress Lady Valor, which he thought he had done. She was all but stupefied over the Caryatid, having never seen such a thing. He understood very well that as a pursuing gentleman of a highly placed English lady he had an extra fence to jump. He was Sardinian. A foreigner. *He* knew that was a superior state of affairs, but he also knew the English did not perceive it. In particular, Lady Valor was not a particularly cosmopolitan specimen. She wished to retire to the English countryside and watch the grass grow.

Therefore, she must be convinced that he wished for just the same. Of course, he would not mind spending some months in

Hertfordshire to meet his promises. He might not even mind placing himself there until Napoleon had been satisfactorily dealt with. Though, that would not be practicable as his father would have need of him. Monsieur Bernard would not stay away from the villa forever and when he returned there, the marquis was likely to poison him over the first irritation. A dead attaché was bound to cause very big trouble with the French. They might even seize the villa in a fit of pique unless the household could invent a convincing story about what happened.

So, if his plan succeeded, he would go to Hertfordshire. Then he would receive a missive from the marquis regarding some emergency. He would pretend he did not like it, that he would rather stay in Hertfordshire and stare at cows. But alas, he could not escape family duty. Lady Valor might wish to stay behind, and he would point out that a lady living alone might be attacked at any moment. She would be safer with him. In any case, his father, the marquis, longed to make her acquaintance. If pressed, he would insist she accompany him. Then off to the villa they would go. She'd be terrified of the journey, he could not imagine what he would deal with on the sea voyage. However, once she got to the villa, she would appreciate the luxury and sunshine, the superior food and superior manners.

In the meantime, though, what was he to do about Tramondeley? It seemed he might very well be the Mosquito. He would not mind disposing of the fellow if it were not for the potential consequences. Did he dare it? Had the Mosquito been some insignificant fellow, nobody would spend too much time attempting to determine what had happened to him. His plan, though vague, had been to track down the Mosquito in Cornwall, murder him, dump him in the sea, and set the sloop adrift. It would look as if his quarry had fallen overboard and drowned, which would seem very predictable for a person chasing French frigates at night.

A duke's heir murdered in London, though? That was likely a different matter. How clever were these people? Could they work it out?

If Tramondeley *was* his quarry, then Lord Ledderbey worried Damiano the most. That fellow would know all about the nighttime excursions of the sloop. As he did know it, if Tramondeley turned up dead, would he not connect the two? If he connected it, would not somebody think to wonder about the foreigner who visited Cornwall and asked questions about the sloop? He had not used his real name at the inns, but nevertheless it was a risk.

As he was pondering it, Lady Tallifer fluttered into the salon. "Count, this has just been delivered. I did not recognize the livery and there is no distinct seal so I could not say where it is from."

He took the paper and unfolded it. It was from Tramondeley, of all people. "It seems, Lady Tallifer, that we are invited to a traditional Cornwall party, put on by Lord Tramondeley and Lord Ledderbey. I cannot say I understand what it is, all it says here is that it will be a small party. He invites my hostess too."

"Goodness, me," Lady Tallifer said, fanning herself, "I hope it is not to be a troil. Those are always very rough affairs."

"A troil?" Damiano asked, bracing himself for more English eccentricity.

"It takes place at the end of the pilchard fishing. I've not seen one myself, but my dear departed lord was from Cornwall. He told me the fishermen and their families gather in dank basements to process the fish and make terrible noise dancing in wood shoes and singing." Lady Tallifer paused. "Though, it seems a strange party to have in Town, so perhaps not."

Damiano was well aware that pilchard was used extensively in the dishes he was accustomed to at home. He rather wished he'd not found out what the fish went through before arriving to his villa. He could not guess if they were to experience a troil or some other bizarre custom. What he did know was two things: One, Lady Valor would surely be there, and two, he'd not conceived he'd have an opportunity to penetrate Tramondeley's house and look around for clues and yet here it was.

"Certainly we must go and discover what it is," he said.

"Yes, of course, if you think so," Lady Tallifer said, ever agreeable.

"If it is anything untoward or uncomfortable, I will escort you out of it, Lady Tallifer."

"I can always depend upon you, my dear cousin, just as I always could the marquis. Yes, I place myself in your hands. Let us go and see what it is all about. Perhaps it will be charming, one never knows."

With Lady Tallifer thus assured, Damiano wrote out his acceptance of the invitation. In the meantime, he was determined to see Lady Valor at the improbably named candlelight picnic held by a certain Lady Jellerbey. According to Lady Tallifer, it was one of the events of the season as only the best people were admitted. According to Lady Valor, her sisters had all claimed it was great fun. It sounded quite absurd, but he would attend with a smile on his face. If Tramondeley were there, he would keep a close eye on him to see if he would somehow give himself away.

This visit to England was becoming more complicated than he'd imagined it would be. How he wished to be back in the arms of Mother Sardinia.

"Did I say, oh dear, I am not sure what you will think of it?" Lady Tallifer said, twisting her hands.

"Think of what, my dear madam," Damiano said, swallowing a sigh. The lady was a great one for starting in the middle of a conversation.

"Well of course you would have heard of the prince throwing a fête," Lady Tallifer said. "Rest assured, we are invited. The invitation came today. It is just, well it is just…that we do not sit at the prince's table."

Damiano perfectly understood why the lady thought he might be annoyed at the information. If the marquis were here, he was certain they would be at the prince's table. It was both an affront and a relief of sorts. It was an affront to his station, but on the other hand, he did not care for the prince. He was a fat dolt and it would have been real work to feign admiration for the fool for an entire evening.

"Never mind it, Lady Tallifer. We do not need the regent to confirm for us who we are. We know who we are."

What he really wondered about was whether Lady Valor would be at the prince's table. Would Tramondeley be at the prince's table? If they were there together, that would be far more irritating than discovering he was not wanted there.

WESTON HAD NEVER spent a more tedious afternoon in his life. He'd been boxed into escorting Lady Monroe and Lady Letitia to the park. His horse had got one look at the expanse of greenery and wished to gallop. However, it could not be done. Lady Letitia insisted he accompanied them on the carriage road. Every time he drifted anywhere away from her window, she called him back to it. She was also insistent that all and sundry understand she was being escorted through the park by a gentleman. She'd called out to no end of people. "Lady Richards, this is Tramondeley, the Duke of Pelham's heir." Or perhaps it was, "Lord James, do you know Tramondeley? He's new to Town, Duke of Pelham's heir, you know."

While he was being subjected to all of that, Lady Valor was off with the count to poke around the museum. It was irritating backwards and forwards.

Fortunately, no afternoon, no matter how tedious, could last forever. When they'd arrived home, he'd glanced across the square but did not see anybody outside of the duke's house. Was she home already? Or was she still out gallivanting with that count?

He'd sent an invitation to his party to that foreign fellow. Sending a portrait of him to Cornwall was the only way he could think of to discover if he were the man looking for him and the sloop.

Of course, if it were confirmed, he was not certain what to do about it. He imagined the most sensible course was to inform Cadwalder of it and let the navy decide what ought to be done. It would be a delicate matter, though. Di Compressio was not some lowly person slipping in and trying to spy unnoticed. He was a count with deep ties to England. Weston supposed they might just quietly deport him to his home country to avoid any embarrassment on either side. He imagined the Crown would reason that he had not positively done anything other than poke around Cornwall. People did not get convicted of what they might have planned on doing.

He'd be satisfied with the count's deportation as it would take the count far from Lady Valor.

His musings were interrupted by Lady Letitia. She'd got out of her carriage. Why? She was meant to stay in it, keep going, and return home. She could not possibly wish to come inside. He'd had enough of her company. How could he keep her out?

Then he saw a man he did not recognize next to her. The fellow had not been in view as he'd been standing on the other side of the carriage.

"Tramondeley," Lady Letitia said, "this man has come to interview with your butler about a party. You did not say you were having a party! He says he sketches portraits, how original!"

Weston inwardly groaned and wracked his mind for what to say about it that would not involve inviting her.

Lady Letitia held up her hand as if she would stop the words he had not yet found. "Say nothing about it! I understand it all! It is to be a surprise and I would not dream of ruining it. Lady Monroe and I will simply patiently wait for the invitation to arrive and then be delighted over it. What day, though?"

With a sigh that was unfortunately audible, he said, "Tuesday next."

Lady Letitia poked her head inside the carriage. "Did you hear, Lady Monroe? There is to be a party on Tuesday next. But we are to know nothing about it until we are surprised by the invitation."

Weston could not hear Lady Monroe's response to this

communication, but it appeared the lady had in the meantime done him a different service. Lady Letitia pulled her head back out. She said, "Tramondeley, as much as we would adore coming in for tea just now, nothing more we'd long for, Lady Monroe reminds me that we have an appointment with a dressmaker. A waiting dressmaker is a cross dressmaker. They can be very uppity, you know. We very sorrowfully must bid you adieu."

"Of course," Weston said, though he could not claim his tone was particularly sorrowful to hear it. He only felt sorry for the dressmaker as that person was bound to be directed to construct something bursting with ruffles and entirely tasteless.

Lady Letitia was positively diabolical. She was the real mosquito—as much as one swatted, she did not go away. He was all but certain she would press her portrait from his party on him so he might admire it when she was not in view.

He wondered if she'd ever find out if he burned it. He would not like her to find it out, but he'd very much like to burn it if she were to leave it behind. He did not suppose it would be ungentlemanly to burn it. It would only be ungentlemanly if she found out he'd burned it.

It gave him a certain sense of comfort to imagine her face going up in flames. A gentleman could never say or do anything ungentlemanly, but his thoughts were free to roam where they would.

VALOR'S THOUGHTS FELT very muddled at the moment. She'd come into the season with such firm ideas. They were sensible ideas, too. She understood her own temperament and if she were to put herself in a gentleman's power, which was what a marriage was, she must be confident that it was a man who would be suitable for her temperament.

She found herself wishing she was some bold lady, full of

derring-do and devil-may-care. If she were, she might laugh off Lord Tramondeley's forays into the dark sea to chase the French. She might even claim it was rather dashing and romantic.

It would be romantic, if it were in a book! If a story's hero were getting up to such things he would be guaranteed to come through it. But for a real flesh and blood person to do such a thing…it was just frightening.

She was so attracted to Lord Tramondeley, but she knew she could not consider him if he would not give it up. She also knew that he would not give it up. He'd said it was a duty.

Then there was the count. If she were to review her requirements, he met them all. Peace and quiet and collecting art in the safety of landlocked Hertfordshire.

"I suppose you are excited to have received the invitation to Carlton House for the prince's party," Mrs. Right said, fussing over Valor's hair. She was dressing for Lady Jellerbey's candlelight picnic, though it had been a challenge to pick a dress. The only advice from her sisters was to wear a light color, as the rooms were rather dim.

"Oh that, yes, I suppose so," Valor said.

"You seem very pensive, Poppet," Mrs. Right said, as she put the last pins in.

"Winny said something to me when I visited her in Torquay last year. She said she could not understand how her sisters had gone through so much trouble to get married, until she tried it herself. I did not put much stock in the idea, but now I think I do."

Mrs. Right sighed and Valor did not really know what she thought about things. The housekeeper said, "I expect you'll do what your sisters have all done. You'll see where your heart takes you. I suppose if Lord Tramondeley could be convinced to give up his unfortunate sailing in the dark habit, that might give him a leg up."

Valor nodded, as it certainly would do. She did not hold up much hope for it, though. The only other answer would be that she would gird herself and tolerate it. She would become brave. She did not hold up much hope for that either.

"Let us get you into your dress now," Mrs. Right said.

Valor nodded and rose. She'd settled on a pale-yellow silk. It was a charming dress with embroidered daisies round the bodice and sleeves. She added a simple diamond choker from the collection her sisters had given her and was done. She faithfully followed Madame LaFray's directive of knowing when to stop.

This evening, through the dim corridors of Lady Jellerbey's house, she would see both Lord Tramondeley and the Count di Compressio. Perhaps her feelings would settle one way or the other.

From below, they heard a large crash.

"Lord help us," Mrs. Right said. "There goes another one of the duke's belongings, smashed courtesy of Mr. Huberville."

In truth, the household was getting so used to hearing crashes and shatterings that they'd almost begun not to notice.

Then they heard Mr. Huberville shout, "It's all right! It was silver, it is not broken!"

Valor glanced at Mrs. Right, as she must imagine the lady had some plan in the works to drive him from the house. Surprisingly, the housekeeper looked a bit downtrodden over it.

VALOR HAD NOT been able to resist having a look across the square when she went out to the carriage. Lord Tramondeley's carriage was out and she supposed he would set off for Lady Jellerbey's candlelight picnic near the same time she and the duke did.

They set off and she peered out the window to see Lord Tramondeley and Lord Ledderbey hurrying to their own carriage. Goodness, they would be right behind her.

Did she flatter herself that he had been waiting for her? She did not know, but the idea was thrilling.

As the carriage trundled along to Lady Jellerbey's house, the duke said, "So Tramondeley hosts a traditional Cornwall party. I suppose we'll get a look at what he's been doing down there all these years."

"Papa," Valor said, determined to ask a question that had popped into her mind several times, "you seem so friendly to Lord Tramondeley these days. Why did you never contact him before now? Or even invite him to live with us? He is your heir, after all."

The duke drummed his fingers on his knees as if he needed a moment to compose his answer.

"Lord Tramondeley thinks it was not just because you and his father did not get along. He thinks it was because you might remarry and have a direct heir."

The duke laughed at the notion. "The very idea. I already had seven of you holding sway over my household. If I'd tried for more, I am confident I'd have ended with eight or nine girls. There must be something in the Dales' water that does it."

"Then why did you not ask him to come?"

"I'm tempted to give you some story about it, but I will not. All along, I considered the fact that he was just two years older than you are. I thought, ought I not see if anything might happen there? Had he lived in the Dales with us, he would be like a brother and all possibilities ended. So, I rolled the dice. I do not expect you to go for him out of family duty. I just wished to leave the door open for it in case you did."

Valor was entirely taken aback. He'd never hinted at such a thing.

"Only consider him if you like him, Val. It's not the end of the world if you don't."

"And what is your opinion on Count di Compressio?" she asked.

"Ah. The Sardinian. I have never stood in the way of one of my daughters' choices, though I wondered about Stratton for a while. But a Sardinian count? Do you suppose you would be happy living there?"

"Oh no," Valor said, waving her hands, "the count intends to settle on his estate in Hertfordshire."

"For how long?"

"Forever?"

The duke shook his head. "That, I doubt. Sooner or later, he'll wish to return to his real home. I am sure of it. So, before you positively lean that direction, do consider that point. You'd be very far away from all you know. Your children would certainly be brought up in the marquis's household and might never know us."

Those ideas struck a cold ice in Valor's heart. She did not wish to live on the Continent and have her children's first language be one she did not even know. She did not wish to go to a strange country.

The count had led her to believe that he preferred England and he wished for the peace of Hertfordshire. But then, her father could always be counted on for good advice. He was certain the count would eventually return to Sardinia…

And why would he not? Did not everybody long for their home?

Why could no gentleman manage to be safe? Where was the gentleman who posed no danger at all? She'd had in mind that baron who collected books. Did one even exist? Perhaps he did, but he was sitting at home, examining his books. She had certainly not seen him in London.

The duke patted her hand. "Just follow your heart, Val."

She'd like to take that advice, if her heart knew at all what it was doing.

CHAPTER ELEVEN

WESTON HAD THE carriage called but had it wait outside the house while he kept an eye on the duke's house from across the square. He intended to arrive at the same time that Lady Valor did. He wished to avoid being commandeered by Lady Letitia, and he wished to prevent Lady Valor from being commandeered by the count.

He saw her come out of the house in a pretty blue pelisse with flashes of pale-yellow silk underneath it. He helped Lord Ledderbey into the carriage and they set off behind the duke's coach.

"Now my boy," Lord Ledderbey said, after having observed the operation, "it is clear as day that you prefer Lady Valor to any other lady."

"Perhaps," he said.

"I wonder, do you hesitate because of the duke? If that is all, I would not consider it a hindrance. You need not move into the Dales with the fellow."

"But then perhaps when we can return to Cornwall, when it's safe to do so, she would not like it. I do not get the sense that she approves of my nighttime sails."

"No lady is going to approve of that," Lord Ledderbey pointed out.

Weston had not thought of it that way. He'd not mentioned it to any other lady so he could not say what their views on it might be.

"If you will wed, and I do think it is high time, you must seriously rethink how far you go to risk your person. A lady puts her life in the hands of a gentleman and as a bare minimum expects him to keep himself alive. Otherwise, she is a widow living on a jointure. Furthermore, if you are not to be the duke's heir and produce an issue to carry on the line, God only knows what will happen to it. You have duties other than spying for England, my boy. I am sure the admiral would agree if he were still with us."

Weston did not respond, as the admiral *had* agreed when he lived. He had several times urged Weston to give it up. The information he gathered was helpful, but not so helpful as to risk the life of a duke's heir. The admiral had counseled that he did not wish to have a tragedy laid at his door.

When Weston had begun the habit of trailing after frigates, it seemed impossible that any tragedy could occur. He'd been sixteen and no sixteen-year-old was capable of considering their own mortality. He would live forever it seemed. Of course, he was older now, and could consider it, but he'd continued with the night sails out of a sense of duty. Did not other men risk their lives in service to England? Why should he be exempt just because he was an heir presumptive to a duke?

"My boy, we are even now wondering if the count is the same person who was in Cornwall looking for you and the sloop. You cannot put a lady into a situation so dangerous. If you wish to wed, you must get out of this business."

He supposed it was something to think about if he were set on Lady Valor. Considering how darkly he looked upon the attentions of the count to that lady, perhaps he was set on her. He'd not expected it to be so, but there it was.

"My advice? Do not pass up a chance at a good life by continuing an effort that does not really need to be done. Our navy is well able to track the French. Furthermore, do not pass up a chance at happiness just to spite the duke," Lord Ledderbey said.

Weston was a bit stung by the idea that the navy could get on perfectly well without him. Was it true? If it *was* true, then had his forays into the night only been some sort of self-gratifying operation?

As for spiting the duke. Well, if he'd been asked that while he was still in Cornwall, he'd have gone all in for spite. Now though, he'd lost most of his rancor for the man. The Duke of Pelham really was too eccentric and odd for him to carry on with it.

They had pulled up behind the duke's carriage at Lady Jellerbey's front doors. He did not wait for the groom but leapt out of the carriage and put the step down for Lord Ledderbey. He gave him his arm to steady him and called over. "Your Grace. Lady Valor."

She was looking exceedingly pretty. She gave him one of her pretty smiles. Yes, he thought he must be set. He'd just chased her carriage to a party, what else could he be? He would just have to think about giving up his nighttime activities, which seemed rather hard, but probably necessary.

"Tramondeley, Ledderbey," the duke said. "We must have left at exactly the same time."

Weston got the feeling the duke was not particularly fooled by the coincidence. He was eccentric, but he did not miss much.

"It seems so," he said.

"I suspect we had the same idea of when we ought to leave," Lord Ledderbey said, attempting to offer cover.

"No doubt," the duke said with a smirk. "Well, here you are. I suppose you can lead my daughter inside?"

The duke was a master at throwing him toward Lady Valor. He did not mind being thrown. He held out his arm to Lady Valor. She laid her delicate gloved hand upon it.

"Have you ever been to a candlelight picnic held indoors, Lord Tramondeley?" she asked.

He laughed. "No, I did not imagine such a thing existed."

"Yes, I suppose it is a bit eccentric, though my father finds it amusing."

Weston supposed the duke would find anything eccentric

amusing. He might not even notice it was eccentric.

"We did get your party invitation and of course we will come. My father and I are very interested in discovering the nature of a Cornwall traditional party."

Ah, yes. He had said that was what it was. "It is nothing special really. Just a small party with sketch artists and a violinist and trays of food. Tables for cards and games if anyone wishes to play. Cornwall people are rather straightforward."

"Oh, the trays coming round. That is something Lady Darlington does at her annual masque. It is not a ball, nor a dinner. Just trays, quiet music, and admiring and voting on the costumes. At least, that is how it's been described to me, as my sisters go every year."

"Indeed, I do recall that invitation came to the house."

"How serendipitous that you should have rented a house on our very square."

He looked at Lady Valor in surprise. He was on the verge of informing her that he'd not done so, the duke had done it, when that very duke interrupted them.

"Lady Jellerbey," he said jovially. "Look who I've brought with me. My youngest, Lady Valor, the last of that endless string of daughters to be launched out of my house. And here is Lord Tramondeley, my heir, and his friend Lord Ledderbey."

"You are all very welcome," Lady Jellerbey said, looking fondly at the duke. "I do hope you will keep an eye on His Grace and ensure he does not set my curtains ablaze again."

To no surprise to Weston, this fairly staggered Lord Ledderbey. The duke found it hilarious. "You see, I was demonstrating how I once set Lady Vanderwake's curtains on fire and did it all over again. I probably do not have to say that Lady Jellerbey's claret is very good."

No, he probably did not have to say.

"Go on, you devil of a duke," Lady Jellerbey said merrily, "you will find an ample supply of that particular drink on my sideboards."

"God save the King and Queen, and God save Lady Jellerbey's curtains," the duke said, laughing, and strolled off.

He really was a strange fellow. People seemed either to find him amusing or enraging. Weston was not yet sure where he would end up landing on the question. Perhaps both, depending on the moment.

As the duke made straight for a sideboard, Weston debated picking up the conversation with Lady Valor regarding the house he currently resided in. He decided to leave it alone. At least for now. If her father had not told her, perhaps he had his reasons.

They made their way forward, Lord Ledderbey squinting at the gloom. None of Lady Jellerbey's chandeliers were lit. There were candelabras set on every surface and it reminded him of the house in Cornwall. He and Lord Ledderbey could never be bothered to ask a servant to go through the palaver of lowering a chandelier to light it and then hoist it back up again only to lower it again to put out the candles. It was easier to just carry the candelabras around, especially since Lord Ledderbey was in the habit of retiring to his bed with a book on the early side of things and Weston was out for most of the night.

"Lady Valor," he said, "what can I get for you from the sideboard?"

"I think a glass of hock. My sister Felicity says Lady Jellerbey's selection of them is very good quality."

He set off for the sideboard, keeping an eye out for both the count and Lady Letitia. Really, Weston could hardly decide which of them was the bigger annoyance.

For now, he did not see either. Only the duke pouring himself a very liberal glass of claret and talking to some other lord while he pointed at the curtains and laughed. Weston supposed he really ought to keep an eye on Lady Jellerbey's curtains, considering how proud the duke appeared to have set them alight in the past.

VALOR STOOD WITH Lord Ledderbey as Lord Tramondeley had gone off to fetch her a glass of wine.

Quite suddenly, and quite unexpectedly, Lord Ledderbey said, "I know you have only recently become acquainted with us, Lady Valor, but I hope you perceive the worth of Lord Tramondeley. He is a fine young man and it has been my honor to see him through his younger years and into his manhood."

She was surprisingly touched by that. Of course, she did perceive his worth. It was just that one thing about him, the danger about him, that worried her.

"Lord Ledderbey," she said boldly, "I am certain Lord Tramondeley is everything my father could have wished for in an heir. He will make a fine duke someday. Assuming he survives. But he does put himself in danger with this mad scheme to chase French frigates under cover of darkness."

Lord Ledderbey nodded. "I must admit, for many years I knew nothing about it. I like to retire very early, you see, unless there is a particular reason to stay awake. The boy began the project when he was but sixteen. Had I known it then, I might have put a stop to it. However, by the time I found it out he was already a man making his own decisions."

"Sixteen?" Valor said, though it really came out as a whisper.

Lord Ledderbey nodded. "I must say, I was very cross with his valet. That fellow should have told me, not gone with him and encouraged the business. But then, Stockton was a navy man and those two are as thick as thieves."

"It's such a risk," Valor said quietly. "I really do think that if a person takes a risk over and over again, then eventually…"

"Eventually they will run out of luck and it will end in disaster," Lord Ledderbey said. "I think the very same and I believe that idea has begun to occur to him. I hold every hope that he will give it up."

Valor felt her spirits soar. Lord Ledderbey thought Lord Tramondeley might give it up. Could it be true? Was it possible?

Lord Tramondeley returned with her glass. "I apologize for the delay. The duke was insistent on introducing me to Lord Gentian, as he witnessed the setting fire of Lady Jellerbey's curtains some years ago."

"Lady Valor!"

She turned to find the count approaching. Just now, she did not really wish to see him. Lord Ledderbey hoped that Lord Tramondeley would give up his nighttime sails. That idea somehow made the count seem far less important than he had been. Then her father's idea of her being dragged off to Sardinia threw even more cold water on the idea of him.

"Count," she said.

"Lord Ledderbey, Lord Tramondeley," the count said, "Lady Tallifer and I were delighted to receive your invitation to a Cornwall party. Neither of us have ever attended one."

"Have you ever been to Cornwall, though?" Lord Tramondeley asked.

It was such a usual question but for some reason it appeared to startle the count. He said, "Cornwall? No, indeed, my estate is in Hertfordshire."

"Yes, so you have said," Lord Tramondeley said. "But then, people do travel to other places beyond their estate. People often travel to Cornwall. They like the coast. I just wondered if you had yourself done so."

The count's looks darkened and Valor saw a flash of something she'd not seen before. Was he angry over the question? Why would he be angry over it?

"I have not, Lord Tramondeley," he said. "May I ask why people travel there? What do people do on this interesting coast? I suppose they sail quite a bit?"

Another very usual question and now Lord Tramondeley's looks darkened. "Some do and some do not," he said.

What on earth was happening between these two gentlemen?

"Do *you?*" the count asked.

He sounded as if he were challenging Lord Tramondeley to answer the question. Why? He already knew that the lord sailed. Valor had mentioned it herself when they'd sat down for the light supper at Almack's.

"Anybody worth their salt can sail a boat if they live on the coast," Lord Tramondeley said.

"I see," the count said. "What sort of boat do you sail?"

"I can sail any kind of boat," Lord Tramondeley said.

Valor looked back and forth between them. They were positively glaring at each other. Why? If they disliked one another, why had Lord Tramondeley invited the count to his Cornwall party?

"There they are!" a shrieking voice said from the gloom. Lady Letitia soon appeared, though nobody could have been in doubt as to who that voice belonged to. She really did speak exceedingly loudly.

The lady was trailed by Lady Monroe and both were soon in their midst.

After greetings all round, in which Valor worked very hard to appear delighted to see them, Lady Letitia smacked her fan on Lord Tramondeley's arm. "We received our invitation, my lord, and let me tell you we were ecstatic."

"A Cornwall party!" Lady Monroe said. "Who ever heard of it?"

"Cornwall people," Lord Tramondeley said.

Valor stifled a laugh. He really could be amusing.

The duke returned to the party with his glass of claret. Before he could say a word, Lady Letitia said, "I am certain His Grace is wild over the idea of a Cornwall party."

"Lady Letitia," the duke said, "I have been on this earth long enough to avoid going wild over anything. I presume you hint, though, that you will attend Tramondeley's party."

"We would not miss it for the world," Lady Monroe said.

"We simply long for it," Lady Letitia said.

The duke did not perhaps look as delighted by the news of their attendance as he might have.

Valor was not very delighted either. She'd not imagined that Lady Letitia would be on the guest list. Lord Tramondeley had clearly indicated that he did not care for the lady. Had it been Lord Ledderbey's idea? And then, why was the lady forever longing for things? It felt extreme.

"Count," Lady Letitia said, "do tell us we will see you there too. We would be devastated if we did not."

The count nodded. "I will most certainly be there."

Now the count seemed much more himself. He seemed more the calm and regulated individual Valor had become acquainted with than he had moments ago. She could not understand the exchange between him and Lord Tramondeley about Cornwall.

Valor felt there was something going on behind the scenes. There had been a feeling of real anger between the two gentlemen. She could not work out what it was, but it felt uncomfortable. It was like a tension waiting to break free.

Sometimes at their lake at home the surface would be absolutely still and then a sudden violent splash would occur, sending ripples in all directions. Something had gone on under the water that she could not perceive, and then the splash was the result of it. The something between Lord Tramondeley and the count felt like that.

But then, her mind drifted back to more pleasant thoughts. Lord Ledderbey hoped Lord Tramondeley might give up his nighttime sails.

What an idea. What if he would? Lord Ledderbey knew him better than anybody. If he thought Lord Tramondeley might give it up…

She gazed at him. He was so very handsome and had such a nice manner. He was a real gentleman in every respect. If he would only give it up…

He noticed her staring and smiled at her. It made her feel a bit wobbly on her feet.

If only he would give it up.

MRS. RIGHT WAS well and truly stumped by Mr. Huberville. He was absolutely incompetent and it was easy enough to see how he'd been dismissed twice. She assumed he'd left both of his prior places without a reference because his employers were enraged over losing so many belongings to a crash on the floor. Or perhaps it was just his all-round incompetence. Or perhaps it was both those things together that had finally driven those families over the edges of sanity.

The man could manage to fail at the simplest tasks! Who told him to polish the silver with bacon leavings? He'd had some idea that he'd heard somewhere that it made silver extra shiny. Which it did, but it also made it extra slippery and greasy. The kitchen maids had a time of it scrubbing it all off. They gave very dark looks to the butler while he apologized profusely.

It had become apparent that oftentimes Mr. Huberville's mind knew what to do, at least when he was not imagining some new way to polish silver. But then that mind became so discombobulated with nerves that he did something else. That something else often included dropping something.

Just now, Valor and the duke were out at that ludicrous candlelight party Lady Jellerbey held every year. The servants had gathered in their hall for a glass of whatever struck their fancy from the below stairs' supplies.

Mrs. Right sipped her sherry as Mr. Huberville raised his glass of brandy and then set it down again. Then he raised it and set it down. He'd been doing so for the past five minutes and it eventually occurred to her that he was practicing raising a glass and setting it down without breaking it.

"There," he whispered, "I can do it if I just stay calm."

Charlie cleared his throat. "Mr. Huberville," he said kindly, "this stress seems very hard on you."

"Very, very hard," Mr. Huberville said sadly.

"Have you always been so nervous?" Thomas asked.

Mr. Huberville raised his glass again and this time he drank it down. With a long sigh, he said, "Born with it, I'm afraid. My mother always said I was a fretful baby, forever looking wildly around like I was terrified to be in the world. I don't remember that, of course."

"Have you thought of doing something in the Church, Mr. Huberville?" Thomas asked. "It's quiet in the Church."

For some reason, Mr. Huberville took that suggestion rather hard. Then he cried, "That's where I started!"

The footmen stared at him. Thomas said, "But then, why are you not still in the Church? It was my understanding that it's a lifelong sort of employment."

Mr. Huberville chewed on his lip. "My mother somehow managed to get me a small living. Very small, in a lonely corner of Dorset. It was attached to an elderly baron and had only a handful of parishioners. It should have been perfect for me!"

Mrs. Right could not imagine how it had not been perfect, but from the butler's expression it seemed it had gone wrong somewhere.

"What happened?" Charlie asked, leaning forward.

Mr. Huberville stared over Charlie's head as if he were taking a stroll down a memory lane littered with tragedies. He downed the rest of his brandy and said, "I suppose it was a whole series of things. It began when I fell on elderly Mrs. Culpeper and broke her arm. That was not very well received, I can tell you. Then I thought I might smooth things over so I went to her house and brought a jug of apple cider but it had apparently fermented, caused the lady to become drunk that night. She fell on her other arm. Old people—their bones are so brittle!"

The servants round the table looked aghast.

"But in the end," he said, sadly shaking his head, "it was probably the fire that really sounded the death knell for me."

"Mr. Huberville," Thomas said wide-eyed, "you did not burn down Mrs. Culpeper's house?"

"No, no, just the church. But in my defense, there are a lot of candles that could be knocked over and a lot of old wood that could catch fire! An accident waiting to happen, to my mind."

"But Mr. Huberville," Mrs. Right said, rather bowled over by the havoc he'd managed to cause in such a peaceful setting, "it is my understanding that a lord cannot simply take away a living that's been given over. Even if they want to, they can't do it. The duke threatens our vicar with it all the time, but the fellow is never worried that it will come to pass."

"They can get rid of you if they get the bishop involved!" Mr. Huberville wiped his eyes. "As you might imagine, once it was explained that I was responsible for breaking both the arms of an elderly parishioner and then I burned down the church, it was 'pack your bags, Huberville!'"

Mrs. Right stared at him. What on earth was she to do with this person?

CHAPTER TWELVE

L ORD TRAMONDELEY MOTIONED to Valor. Lady Letitia had the count cornered on some subject and was making liberal use of her fan on his unsuspecting arms. The duke and Lord Ledderbey had gone off to a sideboard and then intended to find some chairs, as neither one of them cared for endlessly standing around.

Lord Tramondeley surreptitiously held his arm out. Valor laid her hand upon it, and they fairly tiptoed away. The lord led them toward some of the other rooms. Once out of earshot, he said, "Would it be ungentlemanly to say I wished to get away from Lady Letitia?"

"I expect so," Valor said with a laugh.

"Well I did. I will say something worse—I do not like her and if I never saw her again I could very happily go on with my life. She's too…everything."

"That is very severe, my lord," Valor said in a scolding tone. Really, she did not care, as she did not imagine her own life would be adversely affected by the absence of Lady Letitia. That was not to condemn the lady, but to only recognize that not every person suited every person. Or as Mrs. Right sometimes said, not every lid would fit every teapot.

"I think I'm too much a Cornwall man for all these delicate graces. I cannot go prancing through my life like your count."

Your count? What did that mean? Was Lord Tramondeley

jealous? It was a rather lovely prospect.

"I take no ownership of Count di Compressio," she said.

"Good."

Valor had to admit that gave her a thrill. He said it so forcefully too. They had just turned into a music room, lit with dim candles like every other room in Lady Jellerbey's house. A few people occupied the room and a lady desultorily picked out keys on the pianoforte.

"Where have they gone?" Lady Letitia's loud voice rang out.

Lord Tramondeley pulled Valor to the other side of a heavy oak cabinet. They pressed themselves against the wall.

"No, not in here," Lady Letitia said. "Come, Count. I cannot think how our party was separated but we must find Tramondeley—he will long to hear the anecdote about my horse."

Valor stood close to Lord Tramondeley as they hid on the other side of the cabinet. She could feel the heat of him and the scent of fresh-laundered linen. Her heart pounded over it.

Lord Tramondeley peered round the cabinet. "It's safe. She's gone."

They stepped back into the open and Valor thought it really was well that the room was so dim. Anybody observing them hiding would have wondered about it. They might have found it shocking.

"Lord Tramondeley," she said, "I really must inquire. If you are willing to hide from the lady, how did you come to invite her to your Cornwall party?"

Rather than answer, the lord just looked at her with his brows raised.

"Oh I see," Valor said. She presumed Lady Letitia had somehow invited herself.

"Exactly," Lord Tramondeley said. "Now, let us discover how long we can keep up this game of cat and mouse."

And so they did. It really turned into quite the entertaining game. Lady Letitia would come one way and they slip off the other way. Lady Letitia all but interrogated some of Lady

Jellerbey's guests regarding their location. The lady was told several times that they'd been recently seen but nobody knew what direction they went. Lady Letitia stalked the rooms like a hunter after a stag, getting more irate by the minute and beginning to blame the count for losing Lord Tramondeley. Valor at one point heard the count reply that he was not Tramondeley's governess.

At one point, they even hid behind a pair of curtains and Lord Tramondeley had made her laugh by his hope that the duke would not set them on fire.

Finally, they had returned to the duke and Lord Ledderbey. Lady Letitia and the count came upon them and Lady Letitia gave them a proper scolding. The count just looked annoyed.

Valor and Lord Tramondeley claimed they'd just been walking from room to room and could not imagine how they'd not encountered one another.

What a perfectly smashing evening.

As they made their way home from the candlelight picnic, Weston thought back on slipping from room to room, always just out of reach of the count and Lady Letitia. He'd been bold about his comments regarding his wish to avoid Lady Letitia. Lady Valor had scolded him over it but it had been a half-hearted sort of scold.

He'd avoided mentioning he wished to avoid the count too. Fortunately, Lady Valor did not seem as if she missed his company very much. She had been a willing accomplice in their cat and mouse game.

"Well, my boy, I sang your praises to Lady Valor this evening whether you wished me to or not. I must tell you, she was exceedingly approving of it. Of you. But for the night sailing. She is convinced your luck will run out one night and that will be the end of you. She specifically mentioned the habit so I think we can conclude it has been much on the lady's mind."

Weston had nodded but not responded. It was a very good sign that she was approving of whatever praise Lord Ledderbey had handed out. He supposed it was not surprising that she would express concern over his habit of harrying the French. Perhaps she was concerned she would end a widow, which would mean she'd considered a wedding.

He'd retired to his room when they arrived to the house. As Stockton undressed him, he said, "Do you think these forays we've done to harass the French…well, do you think they've been necessary? Or have they been me attempting to prove I've contributed something to the war effort?"

"Can't it be both?" Stockton answered.

"I don't know. Lord Ledderbey thinks it is more my own vanity that has caused it. He does not outright say so but I think that's what he means. He says the navy is well able to keep track of the French and harass them when they like."

Stockton shrugged. "I've never thought too deeply about it, my lord. I guess I just thought it was fun."

"It was fun, was it not?" Weston said. "Apparently, though, it is not a wise sort of fun for a duke's heir. Especially if that heir wishes to wed."

"Are you wishing to wed?" Stockton asked.

"Possibly."

"Not to the loud one, though?"

"No, not the loud one."

"Your duke's daughter, then."

"Yes."

"Even though some foreigner has been skulking around Cornwall, trying to track you down? I doubt he's looking for you only to have a polite conversation. I don't think a duke's daughter will like that very much."

"No, that matter must be resolved before anything can go forward. I am almost certain it was the Count di Compressio.

Once I get his portrait, it goes to Cornwall to be confirmed and then sent to the navy."

"Does he know it's *you*, though? What I say is, you may know it's him, but does he know you're the Mosquito?"

"I am not certain. He might. This evening, I asked him if he'd ever been to Cornwall. He looked surprised, and a bit rattled, as if I'd caught him out."

"Rattling the cage of somebody looking to do you harm is usually not a good idea," Stockton pointed out.

"Well perhaps not, but it's done now."

"Mr. Malberry and I have hired trained men to act as your waiters for the trays of food that are to go round at this Cornwall party. If there is any trouble, they'll be droppin' those trays and stepping into the fray."

"Let's hope there is no fray," Weston said. "Lady Valor is already spooked enough over my lifestyle."

"But you're gonna change the lifestyle."

"I think at this point I must. I must find another way to harry the French that does not involve such personal danger. It's been pointed out that I am irresponsible in doing it. I just do not know what we can do otherwise yet, but there must be something."

"Aye, we'll think of something," Stockton said. "It's become a regular hobby to be a thorn in their sides. We had 'em spooked. Spooked sailors are bad sailors."

Weston agreed. He hoped they could think of something that was both effective and not a risk to his person. It was going to be a delicate balance between ensuring that Lady Valor felt secure and ensuring the French felt insecure.

In the meantime, he reflected on the evening. He'd escorted Lady Valor round Lady Jellerbey's rooms, sweeping her away while the count was not looking. Lady Letitia had the count cornered and was firing off questions about his Sardinian villa when Weston suggested they take a turn.

Among other interesting things they'd talked about, Lady Valor mentioned that the duke considered his door open to his heir and he was to be free to walk over at any time. The duke thought that even though he'd been to dine, he ought to have a closer look at the house and poke around the rooms as he would be the master of it someday.

Weston said he'd nothing planned for the following day, so maybe he would. Lady Valor had nodded in approval.

So, that's what he would do. He should probably bring flowers of some sort. He had a vague idea that was done as a usual thing. Last evening, he'd asked her what colors she most favored. She'd said very dark blue and sunny orange. Lord Ledderbey had an abundance of marigolds around the estate in Cornwall and they were exceedingly orange. He left them in pots and claimed that pests were repelled by them.

Certainly, a florist must have them.

DAMIANO WAS RARELY in a state of being unsure what move to make. He did find himself in that attitude at the moment, though. He harbored not even a shred of a doubt now that Lord Tramondeley was the Mosquito.

Worse though, he now had the suspicion that Tramondeley might know or at least suspect that it had been him snooping round the coast, looking for the sloop.

He could not know how that lord had even heard of the foreigner looking around down there, but he supposed somebody had thought to alert him. Maybe they'd *all* thought to alert him. Damiano had not exactly been welcomed with open arms in that part of the country.

Tramondeley's questioning at the candlelight picnic had given away his suspicions. It was not just what he asked, but the tone he used in asking.

Had he expected a confession? Or perhaps he'd just wished to see Damiano's reaction to the questions. He thought he'd covered his alarm, but one never knew. He was a skilled card player, he could wear a mask of disinterest, but he'd not been expecting that question. He'd been taken by surprise.

If Tramondeley knew he was the man looking for the Mosquito, what would he do about it? Damiano thought he must be on his guard far more than he had been.

For a moment, he wondered if the party was a trap. But then he dismissed the idea. Lord Tramondeley would not allow Lady Valor to be brought into a dangerous situation.

He'd not had a chance to inquire of Lady Valor if she had suggested to Lord Tramondeley that he be invited, but he thought that must be the case. He doubted Tramondeley would have come up with the idea on his own.

Unless it was a trap.

Which it could not be on account of Lady Valor attending.

His thoughts were just going round in circles at this point.

To make matters worse, he had been plagued with Lady Letitia all evening. Tramondeley had stolen away with Lady Valor and no matter where they looked, those two people could not be located. They had finally caught up with them talking with the duke and Lord Ledderbey as if they'd not been missing for an hour. Most concerning, Damiano was near certain that they had purposefully avoided him and it had not been the work of Tramondeley alone.

This made him exceedingly unhappy. The Town was down to two dukes' daughters and one of them was Lady Letitia. He could not bring a less loftily titled lady to the marquis. His father would be offended to be presented with the daughter of an earl, or worse, a viscount. As for a baron, well, he might as well blow his brains out before his father did him the courtesy.

It must be Lady Valor or Lady Letitia. Lady Valor might be leaning in Tramondeley's direction. Tramondeley was certainly the Mosquito and might know he was the man poking around Cornwall. To kill him would kill two birds with one stone—rid himself of the Mosquito and an inconvenient suitor. He was not at all sure if he could get away with it, though. And then, did Tramondeley have any plans of his own to expose him?

He could not settle in any particular direction. For now, he just must stay on his guard. He would arrange for his trunks to be packed and only what was necessary at any moment to be taken out of them. There might come a moment when he was forced to flee to the continent. On no account could he be suspected of working for the French. Further, if he found he must dispose of Tramondeley, on no account could he be suspected of murder.

All this, as he attempted to woo a duke's daughter. While his friends would be lounging in sunshine and sipping prosecco, he was trapped in this dark and dank town full of fog and smoke. It was turning out to be a very trying time.

Then how to swing Lady Valor in his direction and away from Tramondeley? It was especially noticeable last evening. He had noticed her mooning in that lord's direction before they even slipped off together. They would not have had the opportunity had not Lady Letitia cornered him and demanded a description of his villa out of him. If that were not enraging enough, Lady Letitia had hinted that she might utilize the sketch artists at Tramondeley's Cornwall party to have one done for him.

Having her visage staring back at him when she was nowhere nearby was an unsettling prospect. He would not tolerate it and would be forced to accidentally drop it into a fire.

Where had Lady Valor gone with Tramondeley? What had they talked about?

He needed to pull ahead of that lord. He rubbed his chin and then thought he'd hit on something. He would visit the continental baker that kept Lady Tallifer's kitchens supplied with things he found tolerable. He would order a dozen Susamelle to be delivered to the duke's house. Nobody could dislike a biscotto flavored with honey, orange, cinnamon, clove, and nutmeg. Particularly, this baker's biscotto, which were light and crisp and dipped in a powdered sugar glaze.

Yes, that is what he would do. It would not be too forward.

The duke might not like flowers expressing love at this moment. Sending a bouquet of friendship was always stupid. Susamelle, though. That spoke of Sardinian sunshine. He would include a charming note. She was bound to like them. And, in any case, it would be well to acquaint her with Sardinian habits.

After all, Sardinian customs were far superior to whatever went on in Cornwall.

VALOR HAD BEEN greatly buoyed by the events of the candlelight picnic. First, Lord Ledderbey had made a point to tell her that Lord Tramondeley was a fine gentleman, which of course she already knew. But then…then…he'd said Lord Tramondeley might give up the nighttime sailing.

Had she not speculated that a gentleman might mature and leave behind his dangerous habits? She had, but she'd not dared to have the courage to believe in the idea.

It really might be true, though.

Perhaps he would not even wish to go back to Cornwall. Perhaps he'd wish to go to the Dales. Of all the things she had ever feared in the Dales, the French creeping around had not been one of them. He could build a boat and sail the lake if he liked and she would not at all worry over the danger of it. Though, perhaps she would not like it if he went out at night and she could not see that he remained afloat.

After that exhilarating idea, Lord Tramondeley had very naughtily stolen her away from under the nose of the count. She had not minded being stolen away one bit. They'd walked the dim rooms and spoke of this and that and then were positively terrible about hiding behind cabinets and curtains. When she was not thinking of him dying by drowning at sea, she was very relaxed in his presence.

And attracted too. She would never have believed it, but she had the urge to throw herself into his arms. As it was, their hands brushed several times.

In a fit of daring, she'd told the lord that her father wished his door to be always open to his heir and the duke thought he ought to have a closer look around since he *was* the heir. Lord Tramondeley seemed very appreciative of the idea and indicated he might take advantage of it this very day.

The duke had said no such thing, but she'd told him of it in the carriage on the way home and he named it a "grand idea."

This morning, she'd sent a note to Felicity so she would have sisterly reinforcements. She'd been glancing out the window ever since.

"Is this to be it, then?" Felicity asked, watching her pull aside the curtain once more.

"Is what to be it?" Valor asked, though she thought she understood the question.

"Tramondeley?" Felicity said. "I had for a while thought you might be leaning toward the count."

"Perhaps I was, on account of Lord Tramondeley's night sailing. You know I would never be able to stand up to the terror of it. But then, Lord Ledderbey claims that he might give it up. As well, Papa is convinced that, sooner or later, the count will wish to return to his homeland. Can you imagine? I'd end up in a foreign land, far away from my people."

"I see, so the pendulum swung the other way," Felicity said.

"I think I was leaning toward the count, just a little bit, only out of fear. Hertfordshire sounded so safe and Cornwall and Lord Tramondeley setting off in the middle of the night was terrorizing."

"But if not for that, you leaned toward Lord Tramondeley all along," Felicity said with a smile.

Valor nodded. "Well really, you can see for yourself how glorious he is."

"Positively glorious," Felicity said laughing.

Mrs. Right came in with a tea tray and sat down with them.

Valor peeked out the window again.

"Here he comes!" Valor said, smoothing her skirt. "He carries something, it must be flowers, it is wrapped in white paper."

"Shall I stay or go, Poppet?" Mrs. Right asked.

"You must stay, of course," Valor said. "You are a member of the family and Lord Tramondeley is Papa's heir. The sooner he understands you belong in here with us, the better."

"Quite right," Felicity said, nodding in approval.

Valor had dropped the curtain and picked up her sewing, which was the same sewing she'd been carrying around for months. It was embroidery and if she would make progress it would eventually be a charming pillow for Sir Galahad's bed. That darling dog was just now lounging on the sofa, as it was one of his usual naptimes.

Felicity picked up a book that was laying on the table. Mrs. Right occupied herself with the tea tray. Valor supposed they would appear very serene when Lord Tramondeley was led in.

CHAPTER THIRTEEN

THEY LISTENED FOR the door, and then Charlie brought him in. The footman had been well-briefed ahead of time. "It is Lord Tramondeley, Lady Valor. The duke has ordered that the doors are always open for Lord Tramondeley."

"Yes, indeed, Charlie," Valor said. "Lord Tramondeley, you know Lady Felicity, this is Mrs. Right, our dear housekeeper and member of the family."

Valor could see a flicker of surprise cross his features but he bowed and said, "Mrs. Right, glad to know you."

Mrs. Right nodded. "Charlie," she said, "you'd best bring in another cup. And will those be flowers, Lord Tramondeley? Will we need a vase?"

"Ah yes," Lord Tramondeley said.

Valor got the idea that he'd almost forgotten they were in his hand. He handed them over to the footman. She wished to see what they were, what message did they bring, but Charlie took them out with him in search of a vase.

"How does your Cornwall party preparation come along, Lord Tramondeley?" Felicity asked.

"It's no trouble," the lord said, "it's really a simple sort of party."

"Stratton is looking forward to it, though he says he only wishes for a sketch of me as nobody will want a sketch of him," Felicity said. "However, I want a sketch of him so I will cajole him into complying."

"Is it usual in Cornwall?" Valor asked. "That people want sketches at their parties?"

"No," Lord Tramondeley said. "I must admit that it's not. Most of the people in my neighborhood would assume I'd gone mad to suggest such a thing, but I thought it might be amusing."

"I think it's very original," Valor said.

"Why do not you come too, Mrs. Right?" Lord Tramondeley asked.

Valor beamed over the idea. How considerate!

"Gracious me, I do not suppose you want the housekeeper at your fancy party," Mrs. Right said.

"It is not particularly fancy," Lord Tramondeley said. "That is not the Cornwall way. In any case, I think you will know most of the guests, as there is a preponderance of the duke's daughters and their husbands coming."

Just then, Charlie slipped back into the room quietly, as if he did not wish to be noticed. He turned his back to the party and hurried to a small table by the window. Then he whipped around and stood in front of it.

"Charlie," Mrs. Right said. "Is that the vase of flowers you've just set down?"

He nodded sadly. "Yes, Mrs. Right." He slowly stepped away to reveal a vase containing marigolds.

"Goodness," Felicity said.

Marigolds? What did he mean by it? Why would he wish to communicate a message of sorrow and melancholy?

Lord Tramondeley seemed to notice that the ladies were staring at his flowers with various expressions of chagrin. He said, "Lady Valor did say orange was one of her preferred colors."

Valor and Felicity looked at one another. Then it occurred to Valor that if Lord Tramondeley had arrived to London without knowing how to dance, it would be unlikely that anybody had ever handed him a book on the meaning of flowers.

"Lord Tramondeley," she said, "I have a feeling that you are unaware that flowers, depending on the type you choose, send a particular message."

"Really?" Lord Tramondeley said, glancing over at the flowers. "What message does orange send?"

"Oh, it's not orange, it's marigolds," Valor said.

"Sadness and grief," Felicity said with a snort.

Mrs. Right held a napkin near her lips but it was evident that her shoulders shook.

"I most certainly did not mean to send sadness and grief," Lord Tramondeley said.

"No, we know," Valor said. She could not contain her laughter longer and neither could Felicity. Fortunately, this set Lord Tramondeley laughing too.

They eventually settled themselves and it was just in time for Thomas hurrying into the room with a very elaborate wrapped package.

"Lady Valor, this was just delivered. It is addressed to you."

Lord Tramondeley looked suspiciously at the box with its blue satin ribbon which confirmed in Valor's mind that whoever it was from, it was not from him. The count, perhaps?

"As Papa is not here," Felicity said, "and as a young lady ought not receive presents that have not been looked over and approved, perhaps I ought to open it."

"Do, Felicity," Valor said. She had not the first idea of what it was, and she could not say she much cared. Lord Tramondeley's irritation over it was far more interesting.

Felicity read aloud the note that had come tucked beneath the silk ribbon.

Lady Valor—

Enclosed are a biscotto called Susamelle. I hope you find this traditional item pleasing.

Count di Compressio

Lord Tramondeley's expression had grown very dark indeed.

"*Biscotto? Susamelle?*" he said. It was said in such a tone that one might have thought the count had sent a dead pigeon.

Felicity opened the box to reveal brown biscuits shaped in an *S* and coated with a sugar glaze.

"And look, it's shaped in an *S* in case anybody forgets what it is," Lord Tramondeley said derisively.

"It's a spiced biscuit, if I recall correctly," Mrs. Right said. "Cinnamon, honey, nutmeg, that sort of thing."

"It sounds terrible," Lord Tramondeley said. "It looks terrible too. It's very brown."

Valor was positively delighted with the lord's disdain over the count's gift. She determinedly picked up a biscotto and bit into it. Then she frowned and said, "Oh dear, I do not care for these."

"I knew it," Lord Tramondeley said, appearing supremely satisfied.

In truth, she liked it very much, but she would never, ever admit to it. It made Lord Tramondeley too happy that the count had not succeeded in impressing. He'd brought marigolds and despised the count's gift—it was exceedingly uplifting.

MRS. RIGHT DID not view herself as a lady prone to becoming a victim of flattery. She was well able to stand up to it when a tradesman trundled out some ridiculous compliment about her superior taste or hinted that she was a fine-looking woman.

If those fellows had anything more on their mind than selling their wares, it was to find a wife. Or more accurately called a cook, nurse, and housekeeper, for their household. They would name that person a wife and all sorts of nonsense would be said in the church, but that wife would be no better than a lowly servant of one. She had been lucky with her husband, but she'd seen time and time again what most men of that station expected.

Those gentlemen who occasionally tried it on were very

dense. Why on earth would she consider it when she had all the comforts of the duke's household? When the duke's girls were her girls? When she lived in grand houses and her duties were rather light? When she had such a comfortable relationship, more of a friendship these days, with the duke? To give all that up for a man who did not bathe as often as he should and could only provide her a small dwelling, no freedom, and onerous duties.

Of course, men generally thought very highly of themselves so it would not have occurred to them to think about what might be in it for her.

They might flatter until their last breath and get nowhere.

And yet, she could not help but to be flattered by Lord Tramondeley. To think, he'd invited her to the Cornwall party. That was a compliment that really struck home. Of course, there were a few other inducements that caused her to like him. He was the duke's heir and might come to live in the Dales. He had a certain charm about him, turning up to London without knowing how to dance or understanding the meaning of flowers. Heaven only knew what else he'd not heard of. There was something very endearing about it. He was not the suave and sophisticated London gentleman. Mrs. Right did not think that sort would suit Valor.

That sort might be summed up by the count. He was the suave and sophisticated type. Furthermore, the duke was right about him. This idea of living in Hertfordshire forevermore was nonsense. Sooner or later, he would wish to return to Sardinia. He would take his bride with him. The very idea of her poppet surrounded by foreigners…

Mrs. Right got the idea that the quiet of Hertfordshire had been the big draw for Valor. Now that idea had been upended.

She began to wonder if there could be a way to solidify the direction things seemed to be going. It would be well if she could drive that count back to Sardinia this instant.

How to do it though? She'd been thinking about it for days. What would drive a continental count to pack up and go home?

Just now, she peered into the dining room. Charlie was giving a last polish to the silver as Mr. Huberville looked on. She supposed all the bacon grease had been gotten off it. The ersatz butler reached for a crystal goblet and then pulled his hand back. Mrs. Right was fairly certain he worried about dropping it and breaking yet another item in the duke's household. He would be right to worry.

"Nothing broken today, Mrs. Right!" Mr. Huberville said.

The housekeeper swallowed a sigh. Mr. Huberville's standards, or lack of them, were such that not breaking something was the pinnacle of success.

"Mrs. Right," Charlie said, "why did that count send over those strange biscuits?"

"I imagine he meant to impress," she said. "It's probably a custom of some sort in his country."

Charlie snorted derisively. "I don't like these continental people with their strange biscuits and strange accents. Italian, French, German, they're all the same."

Mrs. Right smiled. She did not think they were quite all the same. The Italians and Germans had not produced a Napoleon, for one thing. It was the French that had inflicted the world with that despot.

Then she paused. Would not everybody hate a foreign count who was somehow aligned with the French? The count had not given any indication of it and she thought it highly unlikely, but that did not mean people could not start to believe it. If there was one thing the *ton* was good for, it was believing preposterous rumors. They did not have enough to occupy their days and so gloried in chewing over a story, the more unlikely the better.

What if a story were to go round that Napoleon's intimates were staying with that precious marquis in that villa the count seemed to be so proud of?

If society began to believe that the count was somehow sympathetic to the French, he'd have doors slammed in his face everywhere. He'd have to pack up and go.

Mrs. Agnes Right thought that if she knew anything at all, she knew how to get a story traveling round. The newspapers had been her right hand in the matter in years past and they could be again.

She would compose a tidbit to set tongues wagging. The Sardinian count was aligned with the French.

"Charlie, I must run out on an errand just now. Keep an eye on things and ensure that Mr. Huberville does not break anything."

Charlie nodded gravely and she hurried from the room.

"I haven't touch any of the glass!" Mr. Huberville cried out behind her.

Mrs. Right hoped he kept it that way.

TWO DAYS HAD passed and Damiano had no way to discover how Lady Valor had received the Susamelle he'd sent to the house. He must suppose she would be appreciative of it and that it would set him ahead of Tramondeley. Continental bakers were far superior to the stodgy English nonsense Lady Tallifer was always trotting out for tea. Deviled salmon sandwiches seemed to be a favorite. Lady Tallifer was always going on about the salmon from Scotland, another cold and dreary place. And then the mayonnaise she so loved. What a revolting thing to put on one's food. And of course the rolls at dinner were heavy enough to sink ships. He could just imagine the consequences if the marquis were presented with such a thing. Sardinians had a far more refined palate.

And in any case what could Tramondeley even produce from Cornwall? Rude people and a basket of fish?

His fluttering little hostess came fluttering into the drawing room appearing somehow more fluttering than she usually did.

"This is terrible," Lady Tallifer said, waving a newspaper.

"Just terrible, I cannot think what we are to do, too terrible, I cannot think, oh dear oh dear oh dear."

"Lady Tallifer, calm yourself," Damiano said. It would not be the first time he'd found himself asking the lady to calm herself. Every minor bump in the road assaulted the lady like a full-blown disaster of epic proportions.

"Calm!" the lady said, sinking into a chair. "How can one be calm at a time like this?"

"A time like what, if you would be so kind to enlighten me," Damiano said, preparing to hear that the lady's cook had threatened to quit again. That fellow was always throwing his apron to the ground and stomping off over something or other. Lady Tallifer generally chased after him and soothed him. If anything remotely like it ever occurred in his father's villa, that cook would not live to see the morning, nor would he expect to.

"This, this, this," Lady Tallifer said, opening up the newspaper and pointing to it. "Now, be assured count, I would not for the world believe it. The problem is, the world *will* believe it. I cannot think where this report has come from, with you being every bit the gentleman and the marquis, well, he is the marquis."

Damiano became more concerned than he had been, as this was clearly not about the lady's cook. He took the paper and read the section that was just now punctuated by her stabbing finger.

We have recently received a report that a certain Sardinian count just now making the rounds in Town arrives having concluded a more unsavory sort of business at home. This count is alleged to have long and close dealings with some who are members of Napoleon's trusted circle. Dare we speculate that the marquis may even be entertaining these devils in his villa? We wonder, if this is true, what brings the count to London?

Damiano dropped the newspaper. Who knew about Monsieur Bernard? He would not go so far as to say that buffoon was part of Napoleon's trusted circle, but certainly this report referred to him.

He'd come to do a bit of business in England, but was it possible that somebody loyal to the English was doing a bit of business in the environs of his father's villa? Damiano had sent Monsieur Bernard out of the villa while he was away so that the man did not end up poisoned. However, that had necessitated renting him rooms elsewhere. Was that where the information was coming from?

It would be just like that crass little man to get himself drunk at a taverna and take to bragging that he was usually to be found in the villa. He might well do. Monsieur Bernard was a very full-of-himself individual. He had long bored Damiano with reminisces of the conversations he'd had with Emperor Napoleon, most of which Damiano believed lived only in his imagination.

He could feel Lady Tallifer's eyes boring into the top of his head. He said, "What a bit of nonsense. Who imagines that my father, the marquis, would be so imposed upon? Naturally, the French do not dare it. Lady Tallifer, you know the marquis as your dear cousin. As one who knows him, you know this would be impossible."

"Of course I know it!" Lady Tallifer said. "But my dear count, this is England. The *ton* is all too willing to seize on a speculation and make it a fact."

Of course, that was true. These people did not have enough to do in a day and somehow could not devise more pleasant ways to spend their time than gossip. He supposed it was the weather that encouraged it. People were so miserable in the fog and rain that they looked for anything at all to take their minds off it.

"What do you advise?" he asked Lady Tallifer. He was not particularly interested in her advice, nor would he be dependent on it. However, it was polite to inquire.

"Perhaps, oh I do not like to say it," Lady Tallifer said, twisting her hands together, "but perhaps it would be best if you returned home before this goes any further. Then I can go round and dispute the report and it will all die down over time."

This, of course, was the very last thing he could do. Lady

Tallifer could not know the consequences of returning home empty-handed. Returning to the villa with the Mosquito going free and no duke's daughter on his arm? It would be a disaster on all sides. The marquis had become less and less able to look upon a disappointment with any sort of equanimity. His father had also become more and more intemperate with how he dealt with disappointment.

"Lady Tallifer, a di Compressio never, ever, runs from a fight. The only way to turn is to face it all down."

"Face it all down?" Lady Tallifer asked in her fluttery voice.

"Face it all down," Damiano said grimly. "This is a ridiculous rumor and must be faced down."

He was not precisely sure what facing it all down would entail, but the alternative was running and that he would not do. That, he *could* not do.

"But there is the matter of the prince's fête," Lady Tallifer said, her teeth chattering together.

"What of it?" Damiano asked. The prince had invited thousands to his birthday party so of course he had been included. It was not much of an honor, really. When one invites everybody in London, nobody could feel the honor of it. It was just like that fat fool to do it, though. Damiano presumed it would be a tedious display of English vulgarity.

"I am just afraid, well when somebody in the palace reads this, goodness I have never been disinvited to anything in my life, but it may happen…is what I say."

Damiano felt the insult down to his shoes. Disinvited? People clamored for him and the marquis to attend their soirees. Was he to be disinvited by that circus performer who called himself prince? Was he to be looked down upon by the likes of that precious Brummel who thought he was the epitome of style?

Who was at the bottom of this report in the newspaper? He must find out. If it was Tramondeley, then that lord would have proved himself more dangerous than he'd originally thought. Whoever was at the bottom of this seemed to have a network of some kind. How else could the information that Monsieur Bernard had installed himself in the villa have traveled here?

If Tramondeley was at the bottom of it, that would tip the scales that had been teetering in Damiano's mind. He'd been weighing the risk versus benefit of eliminating the Mosquito, but if this was a much bigger operation than had been previously understood…He must find it out. Once he found it out, he must not hesitate to act. His family's estates might depend on it.

In the meantime, Lady Valor would likely see this report in the newspapers. Would she believe it though? He supposed he would find out at that ridiculous Cornwall party.

"Never fear, Lady Tallifer, I will get to the bottom of this affront. I will expose the villain who maligns the marquis with these outrageous allegations. They will, when they are identified, be drummed out of London."

As he had expected, Lady Tallifer took great comfort in his assurances. He did not bother to mention that when he identified the culprit, that individual would leave London in a box. For now, he would go to the Cornwall party and see what he could find out. He needed irrefutable proof that Tramondeley was heading up some sort of network. Then he could act.

CHAPTER FOURTEEN

WESTON HAD SEEN the report in the newspaper hinting that di Compressio's family colluded with Napoleon. He did not doubt it. Though, he did wonder who was responsible for the report. There was some sort of game afoot that was opaque and could not be understood. Somehow, the report emanated from Sardinia and made its way to England. How else could it be known what went on in the marquis' villa? It hinted at a large operation.

Who was at the head of it? What would the count do in response? He'd not thought he could be of any use in the war effort if he were not on the coast. Perhaps that had been a mistake.

In the meantime, everything had been prepared for the Cornwall party. A violinist was in the corner of the room and had already begun to play soft music. The sketch artists had arrived and were placed with their easels in the four corners of the ballroom. The servers, who were in fact skilled fighters on the off chance they were needed, were in the kitchens with the cook. Malberry had orchestrated it all. He was a supremely competent butler and his worth had only been highlighted by the comparison to the bumbling butler the duke employed.

Since Weston's misstep with the marigolds, he and Lord Ledderbey had conducted a conference on what else he might have missed in his education. They had not come up with much, but for one thing. Lord Ledderbey explained that it was customary, should one propose marriage, to give the lady a token.

Weston had at first wondered if this was to be more flowers. It was not. It was to be jewelry of some sort. They'd made inquiries and discovered that Rundell & Bridge was the most likely place to purchase such a thing.

Weston had gone there and while he did not have vast experience regarding jewelry, he was able to describe what he'd seen Lady Valor wear so far. A tiara was ruled out, though he was not clear why. Mr. Rundell had said something about it being too big for a pocket. A sapphire necklace that was simple in its form was settled on.

Was he going to ask her? He thought he must be, as he kept doing things in that direction. But first, he must ensure she would be safe. She was worried about his night sailing, but that had become the least of it.

"Do you think he will come?" Lord Ledderbey said. They both sat in the drawing room, waiting for the first guests to arrive. The "he" in question was most certainly Count di Compressio.

"If he does, I imagine he will come with a story about how outrageous the report in the newspaper is and how he's going to track down the culprit."

"Put a good face on it," Lord Ledderbey said. "Yes, that is what I think he will do too. The count does not strike me as a gentleman who would wish to run away, thereby admitting guilt. He dare not. If it is believed that he conspires with the French, he would assuredly lose his estate in Hertfordshire and never be welcomed on these shores again."

Weston nodded. "Whatever is to occur tonight, the one thing that must happen is to get a sketch of the count. Then we will have a better idea of where we stand. If we can confirm it was him poking around Cornwall for the sloop and its owner, then it is much more likely that the report in the newspaper is true."

They heard a carriage roll to a stop outside the house. Weston pulled the curtain back. "Lord and Lady Marchfield. I am certain she comes early to check on us."

Lord Ledderbey laughed. "The lady is deeply suspicious of our abilities and does not understand how we get on without a mistress of the house."

They rose and Lady Marchfield was led in, followed by Lord Marchfield. The lady's discerning eye roved round the drawing room.

"The sketch artists are in the ballroom, Lady Marchfield, and the trays should be coming around shortly."

"Very fine idea, Tramondeley," Lord Marchfield said. "Very original."

"Perhaps, my lord," Lady Marchfield said to Lord Marchfield, "we ought to try out the artists' skills before it becomes crowded."

"My dear, I understood it to be a small party?" Lord Marchfield said hopefully.

"You promised you would not attempt to weasel out of it," Lady Marchfield said.

"Ah yes, so I did," Lord Marchfield said dejectedly. "I said I would not weasel out of the easel when I was feeling more jolly about it this morning."

"Indeed you did," Lady Marchfield said, "and I always do count upon your word." To Lord Ledderbey, she said, "I ask him these things after he's had his toast and coffee, he's always in a good frame of mind at that hour."

"Very sensible, I imagine," Lord Ledderbey said, appearing a little befuddled.

Their first guests made their way down the corridor as more carriages began to arrive. Weston peered out the window and saw Lady Felicity and Stratton disembark, followed by Lady Verity and Wembly. Past the carriages, he saw Lady Valor crossing the square and escorted by the duke, Mrs. Right, and Lord and Lady Thorpe.

It was dark so he could not see her clearly, but he recognized her charming outline. His stomach gave a bit of a lurch, which he supposed he could blame on his new condition of being struck by a lady.

She skipped ahead of her father. God, she was charming.

VALOR HAD HURRIED her father and Mrs. Right out of the house. Tonight was Lord Tramondeley's Cornwall party and she could not get there soon enough.

So many things had solidified in her mind. She was all but convinced that Lord Tramondeley would give up his night sailing. Perhaps he might give up Cornwall too. And then, in regards to the count, well, what she'd seen in the newspapers, coupled with the idea that the count would eventually force his bride to relocate to Sardinia.

Gracious, she began to wonder how she'd ever come to consider him. It occurred to her that her natural cautiousness, or fear as some would call it, was meant to keep her safe. Oddly, it seemed it would not always do so. She'd considered the count out of fear and it might have landed her in a frightening situation. Or as Mrs. Right would say, out of the frying pan and into the fire.

In any case, her father speculated that the count might not come tonight. He would likely be holed up in Lady Tallifer's house, waiting for the talk to die down. Valor hoped that was right. She really did not have any interest at all in seeing him.

Just as they set off across the park, Serenity and Lord Thorpe caught up to them. They were quite the party walking through the lighted paths and Valor was so gratified that Mrs. Right had been invited. Her father approved of it too, and Mrs. Right was looking very smart in her best dress. Really, if one did not know her and just saw her out and about somewhere, one would never guess she was the duke's housekeeper. She was a lady like any other.

As those thoughts crossed her mind, the old idea she'd held very secret in her heart when she was younger resurfaced. Long before she'd understood society, she'd harbored a hope that Mrs. Right would become her mother in name. Why did not Papa marry her when they seemed so fond of one another? She'd given it up when she got older and realized the difficulties, but looking at them walking side by side now…well they looked very natural together.

She had thought it as soon as she'd seen Mrs. Right dressed in her rather sophisticated blue silk dress and her hair done up more formally than it usually was. She was not alone in noticing the difference, Mr. Huberville had been bowled over by it.

Valor would give Mr. Huberville credit for one thing at least. When he'd become apprised that Mrs. Right was to go to the party with the duke and his daughter he'd cried, "Very well deserved, Mrs. Right, very well deserved indeed." Then when he'd seen her in her best dress, he'd cried, "A proper lady!"

He was entirely useless as a butler, but everyone agreed he would not harm a fly. He harmed his fair share of crockery and crystal, but other than that he was a very kind sort of person.

They reached Lord Tramondeley's house and she skipped up the steps. Lord Ledderbey's grave butler led them in.

Lord Tramondeley was looking very well. He smiled at her. Yes, he was looking directly at her and nobody else. It was as if he did not even notice that anybody else had come in.

Lord Ledderbey had of course noticed everybody else and welcomed their guests.

"Lady Valor," Lord Tramondeley said, "you look very well. The sketch artists will be delighted."

Valor was certain she blushed up to the roots of her hair, but who cared really?

He fetched her a glass of hock. "You prefer it, I think?" he said.

She did prefer it. He was paying close attention to her preferences.

"Tramondeley!" a shrill voice shouted.

Valor sipped her wine to cover the frown coming over her on account of hearing Lady Letitia had arrived. Lord Tramondeley was not as successful at covering his less than enthusiastic expression.

"This evening could not arrive soon enough," Lady Letitia said, "we have simply longed to be here."

Why did Lady Letitia *long* for everything? It must be uncomfortable to be always longing about this thing or that thing.

"Where are the artists?" Lady Letitia asked. "We do not want to miss our opportunity!"

"They are in the ballroom, Lady Letitia," Lord Tramondeley said.

Lady Letitia cried, "Do you hear that, Lady Monroe! I have longed to be sketched." The lady hurried out of the room and Valor presumed she would throw somebody out of a chair if there were not one free.

Lady Monroe was led to a chair across the room by Lord Ledderbey.

"If she tries to press her portrait on me I'm going to burn it," Lord Tramondeley said matter-of-factly. "I won't tell her, though. That would be rude."

"It certainly would be," Valor said, laughing.

Behind her, she heard a voice she knew all too well. Her papa had been mistaken, the count had come after all. She turned and noticed Mrs. Right staring at the count intently.

"Lord Tramondeley, Lady Valor," he said. "Lady Tallifer sends her regrets, she was struck down with a violent headache this afternoon."

"Oh dear," Valor said, "I hope she does not suffer from it long." It was the right thing to say, but her feelings were such that she would have been more satisfied if it had been the count struck down with a headache. Why had he come?

"It is a distress of feelings that has brought it on," the count said. "She is a cousin and has known my marquis long. Naturally she is devastated over this scurrilous report in the newspapers."

Goodness, Valor had not expected the count to mention it. Or if he would mention it, not so soon and directly.

"I presume you deny all knowledge of the French installing themselves in your father's villa, then?" Lord Tramondeley said.

"I hardly need to deny any knowledge as if they are there and I did not know it. They are not there. My father is powerful, as those French devils well know. They would not dare to approach his gates. Napoleon is already under immense pressure on account of imprisoning the pope, he will not complicate matters further by trying it with an influential marquis."

He said it so forcefully that Valor must assume it was true. It sounded true. In any case, the count's family had an estate in England. If their loyalty was to fall anywhere, it must be with the English.

"Then it seems our newspapers have devolved into more useless gossip than news," Lord Tramondeley said.

"Just so," the count said. "Now, I understand we are to have sketches done? Lady Valor, may I escort you to their location?"

"You will have your portrait taken too, Count?" Lord Tramondeley asked.

"Me? No, I have no need of it."

"But you are my guest at a Cornwall party," Lord Tramondeley said with brows wrinkled.

He very much gave off the impression that sitting for a sketch was expected at a Cornwall party, though Valor already knew that the people of Cornwall were not in the habit of hiring sketch artists.

"Ah, I see," the count said, "I had not understood it was expected. Very well, then."

Valor very much got the idea that Lord Tramondeley was pretending it was expected in order to tease the count.

"Come, I will lead you to the ballroom," Lord Tramondeley said. He put his arm out and Valor laid her hand upon it, even though the count frowned over it.

As they passed by the duke and Mrs. Right, who were both helping themselves to the trays of small bites coming round, the duke said, "The newspapers got you, eh Count? I thought you might do a runner."

The count did not answer, though his eyes widened.

The ballroom's chandeliers were lit and there was a table with a candelabra next to each artist to give them sufficient light for their work. There were four of them and they each had their own corner of the ballroom. Lady Letitia sat on the nearest side and Lord Marchfield was looking uncomfortable having his portrait taken on the far side of the room. Lady Marchfield stood behind the artist, no doubt giving him direction regarding her lord's portrait. That left one free artist on each side of the room.

"There you are, Count," Lord Tramondeley said, "sit with that fellow over there. Lady Valor, I will escort you to the other side of the room. Everyone is to know that I will keep all the sketches to have them properly framed and then delivered to you, as is the Cornwall tradition."

The count was left with little choice on where to place himself. He found himself within shouting distance of Lady Letitia, who did not pass up the opportunity to shout to him.

"Count," she called, "I'm wondering, should I ask this fine fellow to make two likenesses? Tramondeley will demand one of them, that's a given. Were someone else to be devastated…well I could not bear it."

As the count gave some polite answer about being gratified, Lord Tramondeley leaned over her and said softly, "If she makes me keep it, I'm going to put it right over the fireplace. It will be a shame when it falls down into the fire."

"I should say you are unconscionably rude," Valor said, "but on the other hand, you are very hard pressed."

They reached the artist, a middle-aged man who looked kindly upon her.

"Mr. Wiggins," Lord Tramondeley said, "Lady Valor is the daughter of the Duke of Pelham and a guest of honor of this party so do take your time with it."

"Yes, your lordship," Mr. Wiggins said.

"I will circulate and see to the other guests and then return to see how you get on."

"I think I am the lucky artist this evening," Mr. Wiggins said, looking at the situation of his fellow artists. "Pretty as a picture, this will be no trouble at all."

"You are very kind," Valor said. She'd not had a portrait done of her other than when she was very young. Their father had always had an artist come and do a proper portrait when they were somewhere around five years old. He said that age was very suited to a portrait, as well as being able to sit for longer periods. Hers was of her standing by Tulip, who had been a young horse at the time.

She sat very still but let her eyes drift to watch Lord Tramondeley. He stopped at the other artists' stations and then left the room seeming satisfied.

She was rather satisfied too.

WESTON HAD MANEUVERED everybody to where he wanted them. Lady Valor would sit for a portrait and he probably would take Lord Ledderbey's advice to have a copy made. Though especially, the count was sitting for a sketch. That was the real goal and the goal had become more important than ever. The count had tried to resist it, but Weston had made clear it was some sort of Cornwall tradition or expectation.

Of course, Lady Valor knew very well it was not, so she might wonder why he was so eager for the count to sit for a sketch. Hopefully she'd imagine that he all but forced the count to sit for a portrait just to irritate the fellow. He would not like her to think of anything more dangerous than that.

He went back to the drawing room, where Lord Ledderbey

was managing things. Weston found the duke and Mrs. Right with a bottle between them. He had arranged for the waiters to take round the bottles and he assumed the duke had commandeered it from one of them.

Lady Valor's sisters and assorted lords were found in various attitudes around the room while the violinist played softly from a corner. Weston thought that it was a rather odd party and hoped none of them ever went to Cornwall and described it to anybody.

He stopped for a brief conversation with Lord Wembly and Lady Verity. Lord Ledderbey had just now separated himself from the party and examined the books on a small shelf in the corner of the room. Weston presumed this was to give him the opportunity to speak privately.

He walked over and said, "He sits for a sketch."

"Excellent, my boy. Your plan unfolds. I do think, though, that you must be careful. It is one thing to be investigating who was in Cornwall, poking around for the Mosquito. It is another thing to, well what I say is, if that newspaper report is true, he might be a very dangerous fellow. It just struck me, seeing him in this house, that he might be a hornet's nest."

"Which makes it even more important to unravel what he's doing here. If someone in Napoleon's circle is in his father's house, then I will guess he's been sent for some purpose."

"Just be careful. Do not forget you have a lady to secure at the end of this. There is life to live past all this skullduggery and Napoleon will not always be a thorn in everybody's side. Live to see the day, is what I hint at."

Weston nodded. "For now, I will return to the ballroom and see how things get on."

He and Lord Ledderbey parted as if just ending a natural conversation that was to be had at a party and Weston headed back to the ballroom.

He was near assaulted by Lady Letitia waving a paper in his face. "Tramondeley, you must tell me if this is a good likeness. I do not see it myself."

Behind Lady Letitia, the poor artist who'd been forced to sketch her glared at her back. Weston glanced down at it and it was in fact a very good likeness. Not particularly complimentary, but accurate.

"What disturbs you about it?" Weston asked.

"Well look here, my eyes look a bit bulgy when I've been repeatedly told they are my best feature and my face seems rather long."

Weston did not bother to point out that her eyes *were* bulgy and her face *was* long. "I'm sure Mr. Kendall will be happy to make adjustments," Weston said. He was not at all sure about that, as Mr. Kendall looked highly annoyed, but it might send her on her way.

"Good thought, yes, excellent, I'll simply point out the deficiencies," Lady Letitia said, hurrying back to that poor man's side.

Glad to be rid of her, Weston glanced at Lady Valor, who seemed to be having a jolly conversation with Mr. Wiggins. Then he looked to see where the count was in the process.

His artist was still there and still working, but the count was not there. He hurried over. "Where is the count?" he asked, peering over the artist's shoulder.

"Ran out of patience, men often do. It's no matter, my lord, I can finish it off by memory. He's got very angular features, they're easy to replicate."

"Excellent," Weston said distractedly. "When it's finished, on no account let it out of your hands. In fact, take it upstairs and finish it there. Then make me three copies. All the rooms are unoccupied but for the two closest to the stairs. I'll pay you double if you make the copies and stay out of sight for the rest of the evening."

"Very good, your lordship," the artist said hopping from his chair with alacrity.

Where had di Compressio gone? Did he figure out why Weston wanted a likeness? Or had he just become bored?

If he'd just become bored, though, Weston would have

guessed he'd have made a beeline to Lady Valor's side, which he had not.

Had it been anybody else, Weston would assume they'd excused themselves to visit the water closet. Maybe that's where the count had gone, but he would like to be certain.

He turned on his heel and strode out.

CHAPTER FIFTEEN

D AMIANO HAD SLIPPED away from the sketch artist under cover of Lady Letitia's attracting everybody's attention with her loud directives. She must have said four times that Tramondeley would never allow her likeness to leave the premises, that lord must long to keep it for himself.

Better Tramondeley than him was his only thought about it.

He could hear the chatter coming from the drawing room but did not go there. He was far more interested in having a look around the library. If there were any letters or documents connecting Tramondeley to a network of spies, that was the likely location.

He found the right room, slipped in, and closed the door behind him. There was a pile of papers stacked on the desk and Damiano moved silently there and flipped through them.

Most were invitations. It seemed everybody in Town wished to know the gentleman who would someday be a duke. Damiano presumed half of them had unmarried daughters they'd like to pawn off.

Then he came to a bill. It was for docking fees for a sloop. From Bournemouth. He'd have to look on a map to see its location, but that was clearly where Tramondeley had moved the sloop and why he could not find it when he traveled to Cornwall.

Damiano did not suppose it mattered much now. He was already convinced that Tramondeley was the Mosquito and that harrying of the French frigates had ceased. He would send a man to Bournemouth to confirm and perhaps disable the boat if there was an opportunity. That was not the real question, though. The real question was had it been Tramondeley who had discovered that Monsieur Bernard was in his father's villa. Had it been Tramondeley who'd placed that bit in the newspapers. Did Tramondeley have those sorts of connections, which would be dangerous to the marquis.

Out of the corner of his eye, he saw the handle on the door lower. He put the paper back, turned, and pulled out a book.

The door opened and Lord Tramondeley strode through it.

So, the lord had been keeping track of his location. Further evidence that Tramondeley was more than what he seemed.

"Count," Tramondeley said, "are you looking for anything in particular?"

"No, no, just browsing. I like to see what other people keep in their library. The marquis has one of the finest libraries in Europe, but we are always seeking to expand the collection."

"I see, well, you'd best come and talk to Lord Ledderbey, he reads everything under the sun."

"Yes, of course, that would be very helpful," Damiano said. Of course, it would not be particularly helpful, he did not have any involvement with managing his father's library nor acquiring books for it. Nevertheless, he must pretend to be interested.

He followed Tramondeley out of the library and to the drawing room.

"Lord Ledderbey," Lord Tramondeley said, "the count is interested in hearing from you what books the marquis might acquire for his library."

"Oh I see," Lord Ledderbey said, looking very pleased to hear it. "You are in luck, Count, there have been so many worthy books to have been published in the past year. Come and sit by me and I will list them all for you."

Tramondeley smiled and Damiano got the idea he was being pawned off.

"I will go and see how things proceed in the ballroom," Tramondeley said.

Now Damiano knew he was being pawned off. Tramondeley would head straight to Lady Valor. It was exasperating. He'd discovered nothing of note and now he was to be captured by Lord Ledderbey and his various opinions of the books he'd read.

VALOR HAD QUITE the amusing conversation with Mr. Wiggins, the artist who was doing her sketch. It happened that he was forever harassed by family and friends for free portraits, as if he could eat chalk and paint for dinner. Worse, some of the ladies in particular saw something else entirely in their own looking glass than he saw with his two working eyes. Mrs. Ledbetter was entirely unaware that she was very fat. She was. Margaret Paley was convinced her teeth were not bad. They were. Mrs. Weller even went so far as to claim she did not have a long nose. She very much did.

According to Mr. Wiggins, it was a thankless job. Once a lady was apprised that she was not in fact Helen of Troy, the fault of it was all to be laid at his door.

This information, while amusing, did give Valor pause. After all, she could be just as delusional about her looks as the ladies Mr. Wiggins described. Who would ever tell her the truth of it? Mrs. Right would not. Her sisters would not. They would not hurt her feelings for the world.

Lord Tramondeley approached from behind and had a peek at Mr. Wiggins' work. "Ah, a very good likeness," he said.

Valor gulped. Whatever she was to view, good or bad, it was an accurate portrayal.

Mr. Wiggins picked up the sketch and turned it around. Valor breathed a sigh of relief. Her sketch looked very close to what she'd always viewed in the mirror. She might not be Helen of

Troy, but her looks were quite respectable. There was nothing particular that could be pointed to as horrible and she was very satisfied with that state of affairs.

Lord Tramondeley took the sketch and handed it to a waiting footman. "I will have it framed and delivered, Lady Valor."

"That really is considerate. Now, do you suppose we could talk my father into sitting?"

"I have no idea," the lord said with a laugh. "We can try. Prepare yourself, Mr. Wiggins. If the duke sits down for you, he might threaten to set the curtains on fire. And then he might do it."

Unlike most people, Mr. Wiggins did not look at all perturbed to be in receipt of this information. "Dukes," he said, "where would they be without their eccentricities?"

Lord Tramondeley nodded approvingly, then held and arm out. He and Valor strolled across the ballroom.

Lady Letitia was still over the shoulder of her artist, directing him on what to correct. "We've almost got it, Tramondeley," she said, "have a look if you will."

Though Valor would rather not have a look, there was nothing for it.

She peered at the artist's sketch and then worked very hard to put an approving expression on her face. The likeness was nothing like the lady. Lady Letitia was tall and thin with angular features. Her eyes were large and round, sticking out more than most. The sketch was of a lady with soft rounded cheeks and smaller eyes that were not round and bulgy. Even the hair was wrong, there was much more of it than she had in actuality.

The artist had his arms folded, clearly wishing to communicate that he took no responsibility for this alarming transformation.

"Finally," Lady Letitia said, "we have got it right."

Valor stole a look at Lord Tramondeley. There was an incredulous look that appeared and then was quickly covered. "Yes, excellent," he said.

Lady Letitia grabbed the sketch from the artist and shoved it into Lord Tramondeley's hand. "No, my lord, I will not make you beg for it," she said. "Some coquettish ladies might do so, but I have a softer heart than that."

"I see, yes, I will put it with the others for framing." He handed the sketch to the footman. "Everyone will receive their sketches framed."

Lady Letitia whipped her fan threateningly at Lord Tramondeley. "Do you hear him? Pretending he will return it to me when he will do no such thing?"

"Well now," Lord Tramondeley said, looking vastly uncomfortable, "we are determined to see the duke and find out if he will agree to sit for a sketch."

"Very well, I will accompany you," Lady Letitia said. "My work here is quite done. Goodness, never have I had to direct an artist so closely!"

The artist in question looked as if he would shortly have steam coming from his ears. Lord Tramondeley gave him a sympathetic nod.

Valor did not wish to think very dark thoughts about Lady Letitia, but at the moment, her thoughts were rather dark. She really wished the lady would stop flirting with Lord Tramondeley in such a manner. It was really beginning to put her back up.

DAMIANO HAD RARELY been as bored as he was at this moment. Precisely how many books had Lord Ledderbey read that he considered "well worth the time." From the *Theory of the Four Movements*, which was in French and published anonymously though Lord Ledderbey detected Monsieur Fourier's hand in it, to Scott's *Marmion*, and everything in between.

As the old man droned on, Damiano found himself discomfited over this party. He'd not spent any time at all with Lady Valor, but for arriving and claiming his innocence. And then, what kind of party was this? Could anything be more tedious? People milled round the drawing room, being expected to eat small things arriving on trays. Could Tramondeley not even manage a dinner? Perhaps he would convince Lady Tallifer to have a dinner and then Tramondeley could see how it was done. Or at least, how it was done in England. There was no hope of hosting the sort of elegant dinner he was accustomed to at home with these stodgy English cooks on hand. Nevertheless, something far superior to this party could be accomplished.

And then this nonsense in the ballroom, where guests were expected to sit for sketches. It was absurd. How was a guest to be forced into an activity they did not care for? What sort of tradition was that? It confirmed in his mind his already low opinion of Cornwall people.

Was any of this expected to impress Lady Valor? Why would Tramondeley host such a party? Were Cornwall people really so backwards? Of those he'd met when he was in that location, he thought they must be so.

But even if they were, he was an heir presumptive to a duke, just now living in London. Lord Tramondeley was not one of them. He had entry into every good house in London. One might think he'd bring some elegance with him when he relocated to Town. He could not possibly think this shambles passed for a sophisticated London party…

Perhaps he did not. Perhaps he had reason to arrange this nonsense.

Perhaps he wished to see if Damiano would attempt to poke around. Perhaps it was a trap. The idea of a trap swirled around in his mind. He'd been dismissive of the idea, as he did not think Tramondeley would try anything dangerous with Lady Valor present.

And then, what he had not seen, he suddenly saw. What a fool he was. The sketch artists were not there for entertainment. Tramondeley had reason to gather a sketch of him.

Tramondeley had all but forced him to sit for a sketch. How could he have been so stupid?

He leapt up. "Lord Ledderbey, you have given me more recommendations than I could possibly accomplish. I will go to Lackington & Allen on the morrow and see what I can collect for my father. My many thanks, my lord."

"Oh but there are a few others—"

Damiano hurried away, not allowing Lord Ledderbey to launch into what the "few others" might be. He must get that sketch back. He'd use some excuse. He did not favor it perhaps. If it came to it, he'd rip it from the artist's hands and shred it. Damiano did not know what Tramondeley wanted a likeness of him for, but it could not be anything favorable to himself. It would not surprise him if the lord were to distribute it to his network of spies and one fine day the Count di Compressio would find himself dragged into a dark alley, never to be seen again.

He passed Lord Tramondeley, Lady Valor, and Lady Letitia in the corridor, all looking annoyingly jolly.

"Count, you are finished with your conversation with Lord Ledderbey?" Lord Tramondeley asked, feigning innocence.

"Quite," Damiano said, hurrying past them. He raced into the ballroom and stopped short. The chair the sketch artist had been sitting in was empty. He walked over, attempting to seem casual, as Lady Marchfield was still overseeing Lord Marchfield's sketch. From what he could see, Lady Marchfield was determined to capture Lord Marchfield smiling but it was proving difficult.

His own sketch was nowhere to be found. Wherever that fellow had gone, he taken his papers and his graphite and charcoals with him. He approached the nearest artist. "Where has your friend gone? The one who sat right there?"

The artist shrugged. "Lord Tramondeley said something to him and then he was up sticks and gone."

"Up sticks?"

"You know, gone."

Damiano presumed the sticks in question were the graphite and charcoals, and that phrase was particular to artists. He turned on his heel and made his way back to the drawing room, determined to locate that artist and his sticks. He must get that sketch back.

He had expected he would find what he'd left—people milling around aimlessly. Rather, they seemed to be playing some stupid game.

"We're playing Lookabout, Count," Lady Letitia said.

Damiano all but ignored her. The English were famous for running around like idiots and calling it a game. Just now, several people were seated while the others walked around peering at everything.

"It's a letter opener we seek," Lady Felicity said. "The duke hid it for us."

"Hah," the duke said, "they tried to convince me to sit for a sketch, so I had to think fast and suggest a game."

Lady Valor suddenly sat down, so he presumed that was what was done when one located the letter opener. He made his way to Tramondeley, who was still looking.

"Lord Tramondeley, I went to the ballroom to find my sketch artist, as I have decided I do not prefer what he has composed, but he is not there."

"Oh yes, him. He was taken ill and left. I suppose he'll still want to be paid."

"But where is the sketch?"

"The sketch? Well if he did not leave it behind, he must have taken it."

"Taken it where?" Damiano said.

"To wherever he lives, I suppose. We used an agency to hire the artists, so I really have no idea."

"I see," Damiano said. He did not press further, as he did not wish to give away his hand.

"In any case, the sketch will come back to you after it's framed and then you can do what you like with it. Throw it into a fire if you don't care for it."

Damiano would like to throw Tramondeley into a fire. As it was, there was not much he could do about it. He was certain he would get a framed sketch. What he was not certain about was whether Tramondeley would have any copies of the portrait made and, if he did, what he would use them for.

He was really beginning to think that the safest course would be to put an end to Tramondeley. He had wavered when it had just been the question of whether or not he was the Mosquito. The risk had not seemed equal to the benefit.

Now, however, it did.

Tramondeley was making strides with Lady Valor. Tramondeley was likely running a dangerous network of spies. Tramondeley had arranged to capture his likeness.

Tramondeley suddenly gone from the world would solve a whole host of problems. He would just have to plan it carefully. It could not be anywhere near this house, as Damiano had not been fooled by the men attempting to casually mill around out of doors. They were clearly hired guards, which gave further credence to the idea that Tramondeley was a deeper character than he seemed.

Somewhere crowded and chaotic might be ideal. If Tramondeley went to the pleasure gardens it could be done. A sharp knife in a crowd, hitting just the right spot in the back, would take care of everything.

Damiano rubbed his chin. The prince's party would be the most crowded event of the season. Nobody would ever expect something to happen there. It would be dark and crowded in the gardens. As long as he was not disinvited over that item in the newspaper, it could be done. Even if he was, it might be done. There was nothing better than thousands of people to hide what one was doing.

★

Valor was delighted with the Cornwall party. Lord Tramondeley had set up such an interesting way to spend an evening. First the sketches, and then the Lookabout game. As well, his cook was really very good, she had adored the small pastry shells filled with strawberry cream. She had even imagined that Lord Tramondeley might have had them specially for her. She'd mentioned once that she adored strawberries and then when they'd made an appearance he'd motioned the footman holding the tray over to her.

What she had most adored, though, was that Lord Tramondeley had rarely left her side.

He did not leave her side even now, insisting that he would walk her to her door. Her father had snorted over it, but he had not forbidden it.

They had left Lady Letitia waving from her carriage and the count looking very sullen on his horse. Lord Tramondeley gave her his arm while the duke and Mrs. Right followed behind.

As they made their way across the dark square, Lord Tramondeley said, "Will you attend the Carlton House fête on Wednesday?"

"My father says it is to be a terrible crush," Valor said.

"It is," the duke said behind them.

"But we must go," Valor went on, "as we received an invitation for the conservatory where the prince will dine. It would be noticed if we did not attend."

"The burden of being a duke," the duke said.

"Ah, I did not get that special invitation, just a regular one. Lord Ledderbey and I will be under the tents with a thousand other people."

"But I understand there is to be dancing, and then fireworks," Valor said, "before everybody must retreat to their assigned places for dinner."

"Yes, and you have taught me to dance."

"You taught yourself, which you know very well."

"Point is," the duke said, "he can dance."

Lord Tramondeley smiled over her father's comment. "Perhaps we ought to go in one carriage," he said. "It is bound to be a crush."

"Come round for us then," the duke said. "But don't bring your carriage. There will be no point to it as the roads will be littered with carriages trying to get through. It's not too far, we can easily walk."

Lord Tramondeley nodded. "Excellent idea."

They had come to the door and Valor almost invited Lord Tramondeley in, but Mrs. Right had her by the arm. "Goodnight to you, Lord Tramondeley," the housekeeper said, marching her inside.

The duke laughed behind them. "See that, Tramondeley, you've been dismissed by my housekeeper. We will see you on Wednesday. Or sooner if you like, our door is always open to my heir."

"Your Grace."

The door shut behind them and Valor ran to the drawing room and peeked out. She saw Lord Tramondeley smile and turn on his heel. She watched him until he disappeared into the darkness, and then again as he emerged from it and went inside his house.

"Well now, my girl, has a sketch and a game of Lookabout solidified the thing?" the duke asked, coming in behind her.

"I'm sure I do not know what you are talking about, Papa," Valor said, though of course she was sure.

"No matter," the duke said, "I'm sure you'll fill me in eventually."

Valor supposed her father meant that he would be informed if Lord Tramondeley asked. Would he ask? If he would, when?

Gracious, when she looked back on all the things she'd done to avoid being in just this position. She'd even pretended to be consumptive!

And yet, here she was, waiting to be asked.

It did fill her with a sort of terror. But then, an equal terror came over her when she considered the possibility that he would not ask. It was all so scary. Wonderful, but scary.

"I suppose we might have a brandy, Mrs. Right?" the duke said. "I also suppose I'll have to get it myself, as there is no sign of Mr. Huberville."

"I'll take Valor upstairs and then I'll fetch it," Mrs. Right said. "Mr. Huberville will be long abed. A day of nerves and breaking things wears him out, you see."

"Good grief," the duke said.

Valor kissed the top of his head and flitted up the stairs. In her bedchamber, she peeked out the window to Lord Tramondeley's house. She was surprised to see the sketch artist who'd done the count's portrait coming out of the house. Lord Tramondeley had told the count the fellow had come down with an illness and left.

Why would he have said so if it were not true? For that matter, why had the count seemed so aggravated that he could not get the sketch back to destroy it? She could understand one not caring for the likeness, but there was no reason to make such a fuss about it. It had bordered on rude.

And where was that sketch? The artist had nothing in his hands that Valor could see.

It was all very odd.

"Come love," Mrs. Right said, "let us get you into your nightclothes and to bed with you. It's not seemly to be peering out the windows."

Valor laughed and dropped the curtains. No, it was not seemly at all, not that she cared. She was becoming rather daring, she thought. At least, more daring than she ever had been. It might not be another lady's idea of daring, but it felt daring for her.

CHAPTER SIXTEEN

WESTON HAD SENT the copies of the count's likeness to Cornwall for a confirmation that he was the fellow poking around looking for the sloop and the Mosquito. He sent them to Tobias Wright, the local innkeeper. He was a man of good sense, long known to Lord Ledderbey, and knew absolutely everybody in the area. If the count had been there, he would have stayed at the inn. Even if he did not, Wright would show it around. Local people would hear of it and start coming into the inn to have a look. If somebody had seen the count, Weston would find out about it.

As for the original sketches that had been done, he'd had a copy made of Lady Valor's likeness. He'd hesitated in doing it, as he felt there was something underhanded about it. Should not the lady in question approve such a thing?

Lord Ledderbey convinced him otherwise, though Weston was determined to admit to it to Lady Valor when a convenient time presented itself.

The rest he had framed and they would be delivered to each person. He assumed Lady Valor would be very approving of her own as it was a rather glorious sketch. In any case, it certainly beat any Susamelle a foreign count could come up with. He was still annoyed about those stupid *S*-shaped biscuits, though it soothed him that Lady Valor had disdained them.

In the meantime, he'd taken advantage of the duke's open-door policy for his heir. He'd gone the very next day and suggested a ride in the park. This was met with enthusiasm, though it had turned out to be an interesting operation. The duke had brought Lady Valor in his carriage, a groom had taken her horse for a gallop and then returned the mare to the lady. After the saddle was changed, she was helped to mount, and then they walked their horses across a green.

It came out that she did not like to go faster than a walk so it was thought efficacious to tire out the horse, a Dales pony named Tulip, before she got on.

Weston had never heard of a lady who only walked her horse, though he found something endearing about it. He had come to the conclusion that Lady Valor was an easily startled sort of lady. He did not mind it, rather it began to give him ideas of being very protective. He would not mind that at all. He'd spent the past years employing all his bravery and derring-do toward frustrating the French. Perhaps it was time to put it in service of a lady.

Now it was the day of the prince's fête and Weston had begun to wonder if this night might be an ideal time to ask Lady Valor for her hand. He had initially thought he must wait until the count was dealt with, but he'd begun to think differently.

For one, there was no danger to Lady Valor in being engaged—she would still be quite safe in her father's house. For another, it would close the door in the count's face regarding any ideas he might have of winning the lady. For yet another, if the rumors of the prince's party were true, there could hardly be a more ideal place to ask the question. It was said that the gardens were to be illuminated by thousands of lights and flowers would bloom everywhere. It really seemed like the sort of thing a lady would find romantic. At least, that was his best guess. He'd not spent much time in his life thinking about what would be romantic.

He'd put the sapphire necklace in its delicate velvet case in his coat pocket.

The other matter that had to be arranged for was Lord Ledderbey. The duke had claimed they ought not take the carriage as the streets would be crowded for miles. Walking over was no trouble, it would take them only twenty minutes or so, but that was a deal too far for Lord Ledderbey.

The lord had claimed he would stay at home and not mind it, but Weston could not be comfortable with that. He'd finally hit upon a solution. He'd thought to hire a sedan chair but then they all seemed to be hired. Then he realized for the right price he could outright buy one and supply his own manpower. Then he began to consider how muddy the roads were at this moment and concluded that Lady Valor could not be expected to walk through them in delicate ballroom slippers and bought two. Four of his strapping grooms were to get extra wages and days off for carrying both chairs there and being on hand in the early morning hours to take them back again.

Weston supposed that all his years of not spending much money as he'd been too busy on his sloop to gamble or otherwise fritter away his money was paying off, as the price of the whole palaver was exorbitant.

No matter, it was done. The chairs were outside and it was time to go. They'd been kitted out comfortably with very padded seats covered in dark velvet, a footrest, and wool blankets should there be a chill.

"Gracious," Lord Ledderbey said, having a look at his conveyance, "I am to go in high style it seems. I suppose the duke was approving of the idea for Lady Valor?"

"He does not know of it yet, but he will be. The duke is eccentric, but underneath that eccentricity is a deal of commonsense."

"I imagine you're right. Well! Let us get this circus going, as that duke would say."

VALOR HAD PUT on her second-best dress. There was one other that she held back for the moment she might wed, but this was really a close second. It was a delightful seafoam green, very close to the color she'd seen in a book of colored pictures of the islands of the South Pacific. An artist on the *HMS Endeavor* had composed pictures of the various islands visited and there had been one in particular that looked so peaceful and serene—an island dotted with palm trees and surrounded by clear waters. Madame LaFray said her coloring could stand up against it, though Valor might have chosen it even if her looks could not stand up against it. She simply adored the color. The underlay was silk and the overlay a floaty chiffon, with just a simple matching silk ribbon round the waist. It was divine.

At least, she hoped Lord Tramondeley thought it divine. Their time in the park had really been something. She'd come right out and said she was frightened to go on her horse any faster than a walk. Rather than looking with disdain upon that fact, he'd only nodded and said, "If it frightens you, you ought not try it. We are in no hurry, in any case."

She peeked out the drawing room window as it grew close to the time that Lord Tramondeley was to walk over.

"It's dark out, Val," the duke said. "I do not suppose you will see anything of Tramondeley until he is practically at our door."

"True," Valor said, "I can see better out my bedchamber window."

"Been spying on my heir out your window, have you?"

"Once or twice," Valor said, laughing.

"Tramondeley would be flattered to know it," the duke said, "though I certainly hope he doesn't know it. A duke's daughter staring out her bedchamber window to get a look at a gentleman across the way? Your aunt would be apoplectic. Hah! Maybe I'll keep that bit of information in my pocket and throw it at her the next time she irritates me."

Valor suddenly saw the lord coming round the square by the road rather than across the gardens.

"Papa, goodness, he's brought sedan chairs. Oh of course he has, how inconsiderate were we to not take into account how difficult the walk might be for Lord Ledderbey."

"Ah yes, I hadn't thought. You say he's got more than one, though?"

"Yes, there are two. Lord Ledderbey is in one of them and the other is empty."

"Clever lad," the duke said, laughing. "He will have taken into account those flimsy slippers the ladies wear."

"Do you think?" Valor asked, her cheeks burning. She had worried over her slippers, but for Lord Tramondeley to have thought of them too. Well goodness.

"I imagine so," the duke said. "I suppose we ought to go find it out."

Valor did not need any further encouragement. She hopped up and found Thomas waiting in the hall with her pelisse, a pretty, lightweight white velvet trimmed in embroidered lilacs that she'd also worried about. It reached the ground and she had wondered how muddy the hem would be by the end of it.

Charlie helped the duke into his coat. As was becoming usual, Mr. Huberville was nowhere to be found and Valor presumed he'd put himself to bed early on account of his nerves.

The duke led the way out. "What ho, Tramondeley."

"Your Grace, I determined the walk would not be comfortable for Lord Ledderbey, and then when I considered a lady's slippers, well I thought it only right."

"Excellent notion," the duke said.

Lord Ledderbey waved from his perch.

"I'm surprised you found any for hire on this particular night," the duke said.

"I did not, there was not a single one to be had. So I bought two."

Valor was certain her face was as red as a beet. How could it be anything else in the face of such a compliment? She had a great urge to kiss him on the cheek for the kindness of it.

"Lady Valor," Lord Tramondeley said, holding out his hand, "allow me to help you in."

The sedan was lowered and really there was no need for help to get into it, but Valor gripped his hand nonetheless. Her hand felt exceedingly comfortable in his.

Once she was seated, he let go. Reluctantly, she thought. Then the chair was raised and she held on to the sides of it as it rocked back and forth.

They were on their way.

DAMIANO HAD DETERMINED to attend the fête. They had not exactly been disinvited. All that had been received was a note to Lady Tallifer from Lord Moira, a longtime intimate of the prince, hinting that perhaps the count ought not show himself. The fête was to honor French nobles in exile and they might feel uncomfortable in his presence after the scurrilous news report.

Aside from the insult of it, the note did not outright disinvite him. As always with the English, hinting round a thing was meant to accomplish the aim. Had his father wished to disinvite a person to his villa, the note would state the person was not to show themself as the guards had orders to shoot him on sight.

As he was not told he could not attend, he would simply pretend he'd not taken in the hint. Lady Tallifer *had* taken in the hint, she'd taken it rather hard and refused to go. She was too nervous that something untoward would occur. What if the count were stopped at the doors?

The "something untoward" that would occur was a deal more untoward than being stopped at the doors. In any case, Damiano did not think it likely. There were to be thousands attending and all he need do is have an invitation in hand and look the part of an English nobleman.

In any case, it was just as well Lady Tallifer would not be

there to flutter round him. He was determined this night was to be the night Tramondeley met his end. He'd not found out as much about that lord as he would have wished. He did not have any hard evidence that Tramondeley was running some sort of spy network that had access to his father's neighborhood. But Tramondeley wanted his likeness for a reason. This was not a one-sided inquiry—they were pitted against each other. It would be foolish to sit back and do nothing, just waiting around to see what would happen.

He would catch Tramondeley somewhere crowded and dark, the lord would fall and nobody would know what had happened to him until they noticed the gash in his coat and the dark stain of blood. Damiano would be well away from the scene by then.

He'd worn a heavy coat to disguise the blade underneath it. He would bide his time until the night grew late and the guests were all greased with the prince's wine. Nobody would have their wits about them or be on their guard. Sometime during the fireworks would likely be ideal.

He'd thought to take Lady Tallifer's carriage as he would not leave his horse to be tended to by grooms who had a thousand other horses to contend with. Lady Tallifer's coachman could take him to Carlton House and then find a place to park the carriage.

That had been the plan anyway. As he was on Brook Street, he ordered the coachmen to travel through Grosvenor Square in hopes of encountering Lady Valor and the duke's coach. They were nowhere to be found.

They traveled on, but found the roads jammed by the time they reached Curzon Street. It was absolute chaos, with coaches attempting to move forward and others trying to turn themselves around. He let himself out of the carriage and left the coachman to sort it out.

He was carried along by the throngs of people now on foot and making their way to Carlton House. Arriving was no more convenient, as the lines to get in were long. As he toe-tapped and the line inched forward, he spotted Tramondeley well ahead of him. And the duke. Where was Lady Valor?

Then he saw her emerge from a sedan chair. He wondered how the duke managed to secure them, as Lady Tallifer assured him that there were none to be rented on such a night.

She was looking very pretty and Damiano was once more prompted to imagine how the marquis would perceive the lady. It would be very positive. His father had told him that he did not know what the available daughters of duke's looked like, but if he could avoid a blonde, that would be preferable. The marquis claimed that a combination of dark good looks and insipid fair coloring always resulted in a displeasing visage. Brown-haired children were neither here nor there and not to be wished for. The family line was comprised of dark-haired people—the marquis would very much approve of Lady Valor's dark hair.

It was really an annoyance that she was arriving with Tramondeley. That lord had seemed to worm his way into the duke's household, likely with encouragement from the duke himself.

There must be an end to it.

Valor had of course never set foot in Carlton House. Neither had her sisters. She was a bit unhappy that Lord Tramondeley would be excluded from the prince's table, but took comfort in knowing that Winsome and Serenity would be at that table on account of their husband's positions. In any case, there was to be dancing and fireworks before they ever got to dinner.

Lord Tramondeley's grooms had struggled to get the sedan chairs out of the crowd but they'd done it. The lord had given a concerned glance to her slippers but she'd softly said, "They will be fine I think."

Finally, they were at the head of the line being admitted. Lord Tramondeley and the duke handed over their invitations.

Apparently, her father's invitation had some particular marking on it that was recognized. A rather fantastic fellow dressed as a Yeoman of the Guard handed the duke his invitation back to him and said, "Your Grace, once you pass through the hall you will see a room to your right. Show this invitation and you will be guided inside to meet the prince's fêted guests."

He turned to Lord Tramondeley and said, "My lord, go through the hall and continue on through the octagon saloon and that will lead out to the gardens."

Lord Tramondeley gave Valor a rueful look over having been sorted into the gardens rather than introduced to the exiled French noblemen and—women.

Valor dearly wished she could follow him out to the gardens. She felt very sorry for the French who'd had to flee their homes, but goodness she did not need to meet them. Her French was not even very good.

No matter. She and her father would escape to the gardens as soon as was gracefully possible. She was in a terrible hurry to rejoin the lord who had such a concern for her slippers and did not mind that she only walked her horse.

WESTON GAVE HIS arm to Lord Ledderbey and they made their way forward, unfortunately leaving Lady Valor and the duke to greet the exiled French that the prince pretended were the cause of the party. Or the king's birthday was the reason for the party. Nobody could quite decide, as everybody well knew the real reason was to celebrate the regency. His mother, the queen, had made clear she would not even attend, so annoyed over it was she.

The newspapers were probably not helping the case, as they wrote about the costs of such an event. One estimate he'd seen was of one hundred and twenty thousand pounds. Looking about, Weston thought that alarming estimate was probably right. It was typical of the prince, he supposed. There were those men in the world who were like sea lampreys, sucking all the attention toward them inexorably. They were never satisfied; it was never enough. The prince was one of them and when one of them was in a position of power such as he was, it was an endless maw of need. No matter what it cost the nation.

Nevertheless, he was not himself in charge of the royal purse so he might as well enjoy what was on offer. He led Lord Ledderbey to a table so he might sit down.

"Ah, there my boy, I am parked. Here comes a fellow with bottles of wine. I should be quite happy here. Go off and enjoy yourself."

"I will stay here for now," Weston said. "It is in view of the doors and I will wish to know when Lady Valor comes through them."

Lord Ledderbey looked about at the gardens heavy with the scent of flowers and the flickering candles in the girandoles lighting up the night. There were wood planks laid down for a makeshift ballroom floor in the center of it all and it was supposed the prince's ballroom would not hold everybody who wished to take a turn. "Hardly a more conducive place for a proposal."

Weston smiled at the hint and patted his coat pocket by way of an answer.

A footman brought them glasses of champagne. "Well I am very cheered," Lord Ledderbey said. "In the past few years, I've begun to wonder if I'd made a hash of it."

By *it*, Weston knew he referred to acting as guardian to him and his education. "I have been particularly lucky I think."

"And now you know how to dance and understand the meanings of flowers, despite my lack of attention to such things."

Weston laughed, recalling the marigolds. "And the duke is not quite as bad as we imagined."

Lord Ledderbey shook his head. "Gracious, only months ago

I was wishing him dead."

Weston rose. "There she is."

"Go on, my boy."

Weston did just that. He was by Lady Valor's side and said, "How was it in the rarified atmosphere of exiled French noblemen?"

The duke laughed. "They were, as you might imagine, rather down in the mouth. Even more so when they heard our French, I'm afraid."

"The poor Comte de Lille," Lady Valor said. "He is in a wheeled chair as the English weather does not agree with him."

"So he says," the duke said. "I put my money on the gout and he would suffer from it regardless of the weather. These foreigners are forever blaming English weather on their problems."

Weston snorted over that assessment. They proceeded toward Lord Ledderbey's table and were suddenly accosted by Lady Letitia, seeming to come out of nowhere. Blast, she seemed to be everywhere at once.

Chapter Seventeen

V ALOR HAD BEEN very much hoping they would not encounter Lady Letitia in this crowd, but Lord Tramondeley seemed to be her lodestone. Wherever he was, she would find him.

"There you are, Tramondeley," Lady Letitia said. "No, do not say it. You looked for me everywhere, but in such a crowd, well it is quite impossible."

"And yet you found us," the duke said drily. His Grace found himself positively hilarious, though Lady Lititia did not seem to grasp the jab.

Valor was taken aback by the lady's appearance. Lady Letitia always did favor…rather more than Valor would favor. Madame LaFray would downright condemn it. But this was…even more than usual.

The lady was dressed in a bright-yellow brocade with gold thread. If she had stopped there…but she'd not stopped there. There were lace trimmings and ribbons and buttons and it looked very complicated. Then, she wore very elaborate hair ornaments of citrine and even had citrine buckles on her slippers. She carried a reticule of beaded ornamentation, its closure covered in…citrine.

It must have cost her father a fortune, though the whole effect was rather off-putting.

"Oh I see," Lady Letitia said, "we head to Lord Ledderbey's table. Excellent."

Valor was certain she heard Lord Tramondeley quietly sigh.

"Lord Ledderbey, how do?" Lady Letitia said, sitting herself down.

Just then, the orchestra in the garden began to play. Lord Tramondeley took Valor's arm and steered her toward the makeshift ballroom floor with other couples who gathered.

They joined three other couples for a square. "I hope you do not mind that I dragged you away without so much as a by your leave."

Valor laughed. "I do not."

"Then I hope your father does not take offense to it."

"He will not. Though he might take offense to being left to entertain Lady Letitia."

"I would not blame him for that. I do not mean to be ungentlemanly, but I really feel as if she cannot perceive a hint. Where does she think it's all going?"

Valor looked away, as she could not answer such a question and, in any case, did not wish to gossip about where Lady Letitia might think things were going. It might get uncomfortably close to where Valor was thinking things were going. Or at least, hoping about where things were going.

"I'm sure it makes me a bad person, but I really am getting very aggravated with it all."

"Mrs. Right always says there are two kinds of people in the world," Valor said. "One understands the subtlest of hints and the other needs to be clobbered over the head. She says she knows that from our housemaids. Clara will dissolve into tears over a frown and Becky cannot be convinced of something until she's threatened with dismissal. Perhaps Lady Letitia simply needs more of a hint than you have given so far?"

"Perhaps she will get more of a hint with something definite," Lord Tramondeley said.

What did he mean by it? What would be definite? Would she be stupid to imagine an engagement might be the definite thing? What was he thinking?

She did not know. All she could do this moment was enjoy the dance. He really had gotten very good at it. Or maybe she just admired him so much that it seemed so. She did not know and she did not care.

DAMIANO HAD BEEN admitted to the prince's party. He'd covered his disdain when his ears were assaulted with some sort of military orchestra all wearing the most preposterous costumes, or uniforms as he supposed they were.

He'd covered his feelings of insult when it became apparent to him that he was not to be admitted to the special room set aside for the French noblemen. He, a European just as they were. He, in a position to tell them what he'd seen and observed in Sardinia.

He would have told them too. His family were royalists to the end. What else would they be? If there was no nobility, there was no marquis. The prince was an idiot to not have brought him in. If the marquis had a certain Monsieur Bernard in the villa, it was not because he wanted him there. He just put up with it to protect their land. At least, he put up with it when he was not trying to poison Monsieur Bernard.

On the other hand, if he had been brought in and been introduced, it might have brought up some questions regarding that piece in the newspaper. A French nobleman could not be too careful these days. As it was, nobody had taken any notice of him. Insulting, but probably for the best.

He made his way to the gardens. The sun had long set and the place was lit up with candles. There were an endless amount of tables around a second ballroom floor and the scent of flowers hung heavy in the air. Despite his disdain of anything and everything the English did, he was forced to admit it was well done.

What was not well done was noting that Tramondeley had led Lady Valor to the floor for a dance.

He would like to dance with her himself, but for this particular night he must make himself inconspicuous. He did not want Tramondeley or anybody associated with him to know he was there. After Tramondeley was done in, there would be the natural questions about it. After it was done he would slip away as if he'd never been there at all. He took himself off to a dark corner to wait out the time. Let these people drink and drink and drink. When they were all woozily looking up at fireworks, he would strike.

VALOR WAS HAVING the time of her life. Lord Tramondeley had thrown over all of society's rules and danced every dance with her. Her father had not minded, Lord Ledderbey had not minded. Lady Letitia had minded very much, but Lord Tramondeley had claimed it was Valor's birthday and it was a Cornwall tradition to never allow a birthday lady to sit out a dance.

Valor had almost snorted over it. Lord Tramondeley seemed to blame an awful lot on Cornwall traditions. Lady Letitia had sniffed but there was not much she could say. Valor suspected the lady was silently cursing Cornwall, though.

Now the orchestra had stopped and the fireworks would soon go off. Valor supposed they would be lovely but then afterward she would be forced to go inside to the prince's table. She did not wish to be separated from Lord Tramondeley.

She almost took herself by surprise with that thought. Gentlemen had seemed so off-putting until now. She had warned all her sisters about the inconvenience of having a gentleman sleeping in the same room, particularly because they might stare at a person while they slept. Now it did not seem quite so terrible.

Crowds of people had emerged from the house to see the

fireworks. Lord Tramondeley helped her to an open space for viewing while her father remained behind at a table with Lord Ledderbey. Valor had lost track of where Lady Letitia was, but she seemed to have given up on Lord Tramondeley. Valor could not say she was sorry over it.

And then it began. Valor had only seen fireworks once, when her father had hired a man to set them off for Christmas. That particular display had been far smaller and had ended burning down a barn so not a wonderful memory, but for all the horses being saved. She seemed to recall it had cost her father a deal of money to rebuild it and house all the homeless horses that had been the result of it.

This was something different. Fountains of color shot up in the sky, golden suns spun in the air, it was simply stupendous.

"Lady Valor," Lord Tramondeley said, "you cannot mistake my attentions."

Valor took in a breath. Was this it? Was he going to ask?

"I will admit, when I first arrived in London, I was set to be very against the duke. That, however, is over. Upon meeting you, I knew, almost instantly—"

"Count! No!" Lady Letitia shouted behind them.

She and Lord Tramondeley were suddenly shoved from behind.

"You stupid woman," the count said.

Valor turned round and saw the count pushing his way through the crowd toward the house.

"Look," Lady Letitia said, pointing at the ground. A large and very sharp-looking knife lay there, glinting as the fireworks burst overhead. "Tramondeley, he was coming at you from behind, holding it straight out and aiming for your back. He was inches away when I shoved you out of the way and knocked it right out of his hand."

Lord Tramondeley looked down at the knife and said, "This ends now." He began pushing through the crowd after the count.

What ended now? Why would the count wish to harm Lord

Tramondeley? She wished to call him back, he should not chase the count. It was too dangerous.

"Gracious me," Lady Letitia said, "I've never seen the like of that. I realize both gentlemen were competing for your attention, but that was…well I really do not know."

Valor did not answer. She'd wished to call Lord Tramondeley back, but nothing had come out of her. Now it was too late. He was gone.

Her knees felt weak but there was nowhere to sit. The fireworks had ended and the surging crowd carried her forward. Lady Letitia was far ahead of her, both helpless against the hundreds of people who had now turned to get inside. She could not see her father or Lord Ledderbey at all.

She was squeezed in through the doors and began to be afraid that somebody would be trampled in their desperation to get to their table.

Valor grabbed at a door frame and pulled herself inside a room to catch her breath. She closed the door on the surging crowd, she could not think while being jostled like that. She did not know what to do. The count had come behind Lord Tramondeley with a knife and Lord Tramondeley had chased after him. She did not know why, but it seemed Lord Tramondeley had known why. What if the count had another knife? Her father would know what to do, but she did not know where he was.

The room was filled with statues and various pieces made of gold, some large and some small, all on raised marble pedestals. She presumed the prince wished to show off his wealth and royal possessions. Valor walked back and forth to calm herself. The knife, the suffocating crowd, it had all been too much. Her temperament was not made for such things. She must calm herself, let the terrible crowd in the corridor thin out, and then find her father.

Lord Tramondeley had been on the verge of asking and he'd almost been murdered right in front of her! Why did he have to chase after the count? It brought back all her fears about Lord Tramondeley—he took such risks! Was it a part of his temperament that would never change? Could she live with that? Could she live with terror in her heart every other day, never knowing what was to happen next?

What had he involved himself in that would cause the count to approach him with a knife in hand? Lady Letitia had claimed it was because both gentlemen were interested in her. She could not attribute such a violent action to that though.

And what a strange thing for Lady Letitia to say. The lady had seemed oblivious to either one of the gentlemen's inclinations.

Valor stopped her pacing. Out of the corner of her eye she saw the smallest bit of a dark coat disappear behind one of the larger of the statues. She was not alone.

The count stepped out from behind the statue. Valor felt she was almost going blind with terror.

"Lady Valor, do not alarm yourself," the count said smoothly, "Lady Letitia has gone quite mad, as it was *she* that held the knife. When she noted I had seen it, she dropped it and attempted to shift the blame on me."

Could that be true? Lady Letitia might have been irritated that Lord Tramondeley had not danced with her all night. But no, it was preposterous. A lady did not attack a gentleman with a knife. That was a man's work. Anyway, why had he run away and Lady Letitia had not?

"In any case, it is well that all this is to be out in the open now," the count said.

"What is to be out in the open?" Valor whispered. The count was slowly moving forward, as if to calm a skittish horse. Valor was slowly moving backward.

"I have been tracking Tramondeley's movements," the count said. "That story of him harassing French frigates was just that—a story. The truth is he was going out in his sloop at night to deliver messages to the French. It was he who planted that story in the newspaper to discredit me. He understood I had discovered his game."

The count moved ever closer. Valor was backed against the far wall of the room. She did not believe any of it. Lord Tramondeley could be intemperate and too prone to taking risks, but he was not a liar and a traitor. The liar was right in front of her and he was coming closer. She glanced to her right. A heavy gold candelabra sat on a pedestal.

"Now, all this need not trouble you. I cannot know why Lady Letitia made such a move this night, but perhaps she sought to eliminate who she knew to be a spy for the French. There are those ladies the crown employs for such things. But as for you and I, none of this need affect us. These sorts of things do not occur in Hertfordshire, it is very quiet there."

Valor looked at him in horror. He'd moved close enough that she could feel his breath. He was going to try to kiss her.

She grabbed the candelabra and hit him over the head. As he slid to the floor she recoiled, very surprised at her own strength. She picked up the skirt of her dress and leapt over him, running for the door.

As she neared it, four of the prince's guards came through it, followed by Tramondeley. She threw herself in his arms. He caught her just as one of the guards called to Lord Tramondeley. "He's here, my lord. Looks like he fainted."

"No," one of the other guards said, turning him over, "he's got a gash on his head."

"I hit him with a candelabra," Valor whispered.

"Brave girl," he whispered into her hair.

"Well, I had to," Valor said, "you chased after him and he might have had another knife."

"I went for the guards," Lord Tramondeley said.

"Oh, well, that was very sensible."

"I did not think he'd left the premises. I thought he might bide his time and try again. A cornered rat always bites."

The guards had picked up the count, each lifting one appendage. As they passed by them, the lead guard said, "We'll put it about that he's drunk, lock him up, and then see what the Crown intends to do about him."

Lord Tramondeley nodded, and they hauled the count out of the room.

Lord Tramondeley pushed her hair from her eyes as her pins had all come loose. "Now, as I was saying…well let me skip over the whole part of looking askance at your father. Lady Valor Nicolet if you do not agree to wed me, I will get on my sloop and sail into the ocean until I am dead."

Valor shivered at the very idea. "I would on no account allow you to do such a rash and dangerous thing."

"Is that a yes, then?"

"It is a yes, then."

Lord Tramondeley bent over her and touched his lips to her own. He was gentle, as if he understood her.

"Are you frightened of me?" he asked.

"A little," she said. "But not enough to keep you away."

He kissed her again and she most definitely did not keep him away.

"My father will wonder where I am," Valor said. "I should probably go into the prince's table."

Lord Tramondeley held her just a bit away from him and looked her up and down. "First, your hair is in a shambles. Second, there are blood spots on that lovely dress. Third, I would rather get you safely home."

She had been so frightened of Lord Tramondeley's bold nature, but now she was not frightened. He knew just what to do.

"Stay here, do not move," he said. He went to the doors and motioned a footman passing by in the corridor. "Retrieve the Duke of Pelham from the prince's table. Tell him his daughter has been taken ill. Send someone else to the garden for Lord Ledderbey, he will be at the top of the table on the left-hand side."

Lord Tramondeley returned to her and said, "Might I take advantage of our remaining minutes alone?"

Valor nodded and he kissed her again, mussing her hair with

his hands even more than he had done.

"I should go no further," he said, pulling away.

"Just a little bit," she said, pulling him close.

Valor was not entirely certain how much time they'd had alone. It was not forever though, no matter how much she might have wished it.

The duke appeared at the door. He took one look at the couple and said, "My daughter is ill, I believe I was told?"

"Not exactly," Lord Tramondeley said. "You did hint an engagement would be approved."

"I did," the duke said, "though I do not recall any mention of approving a mauling of my daughter."

"Oh, that was not him, Papa. I had to hit the count over the head and well, I got a bit mussed from the exertion."

"Did the count offend you?" the duke asked.

"Not in the way you might think," Valor said.

"Well, I never liked that fellow. Smarmy is what I thought."

Valor did not explain just then that smarmy would be the least of it. She did not know why the count had wished to kill Lord Tramondeley, but she knew that he did.

Lord Ledderbey appeared at the door. "Gracious, what has happened in here?"

Valor glanced around and indeed it did look very alarming. There was blood on the floor and a candelabra laying nearby it. She did not have to look in a glass to know she looked a fright.

"Let us make our way out of the house," Lord Tramondeley said. "Everyone is busy at their respective dining tables and we should have no trouble locating our grooms and sedan chairs."

"Very well," the duke said. "My daughter is in no condition to enter the prince's presence at this particular moment. But I expect a full accounting of whatever has gone on."

THE PARTY HAD hurried past the conservatory to avoid notice by the prince. Weston had got Lord Ledderbey into his sedan chair and then helped Lady Valor into her own.

The duke had demanded a full accounting of what had transpired at the fête, and so he got one. Weston had told his part of it, including that he was known as the Mosquito and that he was certain the count had been looking for that individual in Cornwall. That was why he'd hired sketch artists at his Cornwall party. He then admitted that he'd had a copy made of Lady Valor's sketch and kept it.

She looked pretty pleased about it.

Then he got to a more difficult part of the tale. When he explained Lady Letitia's quick thinking in saving him from a knife attack, Weston thought everyone felt bad about any condemnations of the lady they'd been guilty of. Whatever she wore, whatever she said, she had saved Lord Tramondeley.

Lady Valor told her part of it. She'd been overwhelmed by the crowd and fought her way into the room to catch her breath. She'd not initially seen the count and when he revealed himself she'd been nowhere near the door.

That villain had tried to pin what *he* was guilty of on Weston.

"I did not believe it, though, Papa," she said. "Then he came very close to me and said none of it need affect us and I really thought he was going to try to kiss me."

"The rogue," Weston muttered.

"So I had to hit him over the head," Lady Valor said, charmingly swaying in her sedan chair.

"She was very brave," Weston said.

"Yes, I really was," Lady Valor said, sounding surprised.

"Who would have guessed?" the duke said. "My one daughter who has nightmares about a fox's cries knocks out a would-be murderer."

"Do you have nightmares?" Weston asked. He noted her blush as they passed under a street lamp.

"I'm afraid so," Lady Valor said. "They cannot be helped."

"I'll help," Weston said.

The duke chose to ignore any hint of his daughter being in a position to be helped by a gentleman in the middle of the night.

Weston went on to explain that he had wondered if the count had a foreign spy in his household, thereby leading to the mention in the newspaper. He speculated that the count had become suspicious of him and wished to eliminate him for that reason. Perhaps the count had even imagined he was in contact with the spy in his household.

Lord Ledderbey said, "Well all of this has been very unfortunate, and terribly frightening for Lady Valor, which I cannot like. But I wonder if we might be led by Shakespeare's wise words—all is well that ends well."

"And Papa," Lady Valor said, "your dream of an empty house has finally come true."

"Ah yes, that," the duke said.

Weston did not think he looked quite as enthusiastic as one might when one's dream had come true.

They walked on in silence for a few minutes. Weston walked along Lady Valor's sedan, his hand resting on the side of it. Lady Valor put his hand over his, which he was hoping she would do.

"What do you suppose will become of the count?" Lord Ledderbey said.

"He ought to be hanged," Weston said. "He's in league with the French. It was even in the newspapers, so I am not the only one that knows it, and now the Crown has him."

"As to that," the duke said, "it has recently come to my attention that our housekeeper put that bit in the newspaper. She was afraid our Val would end up miserable in Sardinia, all because the count was promising a quiet life in Hertfordshire."

"I frighten easily," Lady Valor said.

"Yes, I know," Weston said with a laugh. "But you came through it tonight."

She nodded. "Still, very dear of Mrs. Right to try to save me from a terrible decision, even if I never would have done it."

"You'll find, Tramondeley, that there is nothing our Mrs. Right won't do for her girls."

"I'll say," Weston said, a little alarmed that a housekeeper would take such steps. "Though I will soon prove that di Compressio was just as Mrs. Right speculated. I've sent the sketches of him to Cornwall to confirm that it was he snooping around down there, attempting to locate the Mosquito. I am also sure he had discovered it was me. That's why he came with the knife. He'll come to the bad end he deserves."

The duke laughed. "I do not think the count will pay too high a price. The whole thing will be hushed up and he'll be sent home. The Crown will probably take his English estate and explain to him that he is persona non grata."

"Papa! Why would they let him go?"

"Because he attempted a murder at the prince's fête, which was advertised as an honor to the exiled French nobility. Can you imagine the talk that would go round? The prince had invited a murderous agent in the employ of Napoleon to mingle with French nobility?"

Weston took that in and saw the sense in it. The count would probably keep his life, as unfair as that was. However, he would never set foot in England again.

Far more importantly, he was an engaged man. What a night.

A new thought suddenly occurred to him. "I believe in circumstances such as these, the lady receives a token of affection from the gentleman." He reached into his coat pocket and handed Lady Valor the velvet box.

She opened it. "Look, Papa, it is a sapphire necklace. It is simply perfect."

"Well done, Tramondeley," the duke said.

Receiving the necklace necessitated a stop to the sedan chairs to put it on, despite Lady Valor already wearing a necklace. Once that procedure was complete, they set off for home.

LORD TRAMONDELEY HAD seen Valor and her father home and then the duke had invited him and Lord Ledderbey inside for a brandy as it was still on the early side of things.

As it happened, Valor had a brandy too. It was not her usual drink, but she felt some combination of shaken and swashbuckling after the evening she'd had.

Mrs. Right was invited in too, as the duke claimed Lord Tramondeley might as well get used to their way of doing things.

He was very agreeable to it, and even more agreeable to be led to the back of the drawing room by Valor, leaving the duke and Lord Ledderbey to relate the events of the evening to Mrs. Right.

They sat together, sipping their brandies, as Valor made faces over it.

Lord Tramondeley laughed and said, "You do not have to drink it, you know."

"I know," she said. "It tastes terrible, but it will have a good effect, I think. If ever there were a night when I might be woken by a nightmare it would be this night."

"When we are wed, I will wake you up from them and tell you everything is all right."

That was a rather delightful idea. Scary, but delightful.

"I've given up using my sloop to harass the French," he said. "I was reminded that it would not be very responsible for a married man to do."

Valor let out a long breath she did not know she'd been holding. "I can only say I am relieved. I would not be able to sleep wondering if you'd drowned."

"In any case, I think I would find you too difficult to leave at night."

This hinting at what might go on behind closed doors was another scary thing. Interesting, she wished to know all about it, to experience all of it, but scary nonetheless.

"It will be all right," Lord Tramondeley said, squeezing her hand.

She nodded. She believed him.

They spent the rest of their time with Lord Tramondeley admiring her mussed hair and pretty eyes and other such nonsense a man in love is likely to go on about.

The duke finally got the lord and Lord Ledderbey on their way. Lord Ledderbey looked ready to fall over from the exertions of the night and the duke pointed out that the grooms left outside with his sedan chair had likely had their fill of it.

Despite the terror of the evening, Valor did not have any nightmares over it.

CHAPTER EIGHTEEN

THE FOLLOWING DAY, Valor called on Lady Letitia. She had never imagined she would call on that lady and had spent most of her time wishing that lady away.

But then two things must be done. The lady must be thanked for saving Lord Tramondeley. Or Weston, as she now called him in private as Tramondeley was rather a lot to say day to day. As well, the engagement must be broken to her. Valor was very afraid of how hard the lady would take it, but she was determined that Lady Letitia hear it from her and not be blindsided by some report of it out in society or in the newspapers. Considering all the bad thoughts they'd all had of her and how she'd proved her worth when it mattered, it would not be fair.

She was led into the drawing room as Mrs. Right was led to the servants' hall where she would "get a look at how other staff lived," as she termed it.

"Goodness, Lady Valor. I am glad to see you looking well after last evening's shocking events. I did look around for Tramondeley after the dinner but did not see him, nor you or the duke."

Valor had already determined that she could not reveal what had really happened, as her father had pointed out that the Crown would likely wish it hushed up.

"Lord Tramondeley never did find the count, so we do not know where he's gone," she said. She did not mention that she, her father, Lord Tramondeley, and Lord Ledderbey had left the fête early.

"He'll scarper, I imagine. I wondered what had happened to you when I saw Lady Thorpe being helped out by her lord."

Valor also thought better of mentioning the cause of Serenity's early departure, which she'd heard all about the next morning. Apparently, the prince had arranged for a manmade stream with goldfish in the center of the table. It had been an unfortunate idea though, as the goldfish went belly-up one by one. Lord Thorpe had tried to keep his wife's attention away from it, but when Serenity saw the first dead fish floating by, all was lost. Lord Thorpe had taken his weeping bride home, cursing the prince all the way.

That was not why she was here, though.

"Lady Letitia, you were very heroic last evening. If you had not given a warning…"

"Nonsense," Lady Letitia said. "What is one to do when one spots a foreign count slipping through a crowd and then sees the glint of a blade. In any case, I thought all along there was something strange about him. He was trying to keep me on the hook, you see, though it was obvious enough that you were his primary quarry. He thought if he could not succeed with you, he'd settle for me. The jest would have been on him, though!"

"So, you would not have had him," Valor said, "had he asked."

"Not under threat of torture," Lady Letitia said.

A footman came in with a tea tray. They fell to silence until he had departed and closed the doors behind him.

Lady Letitia poured the tea. Valor ginned up her courage. She must just say it and hope she did not have a cup of hot tea thrown in her face.

"Lady Letitia, there is one other matter."

"Yes?" she said, handing over a cup. "What is it?"

Valor put her cup down with a clatter. She just must come out with it. "I am engaged to Lord Tramondeley. He asked last night and I have accepted."

She braced herself for an onslaught of recriminations.

"Ah, congratulations, then." Lady Letitia sipped her tea and smiled at her.

"But I did think, that is I imagined…"

Lady Letitia roared with laughter over her obvious discomfort. "Oh, I know exactly what you thought." The lady leaned toward her and said in a low voice, "It has all been a ruse."

"A ruse? All of it?"

"All of it. The clothes, the loud shrieks, the chasing round of Lord Tramondeley. All of it."

It was true that just now the lady was dressed in a simple white muslin and not talking half so loud as Valor had been accustomed to hearing. But a ruse? Why?

"I see you require more information," Lady Letitia said, seeming to enjoy herself. "Well, my father and Lady Monroe have been in league these past two years to get me married off to somebody, anybody, who would become a duke. My father is a stickler for rank and not particularly practical. He makes pronouncements he expects to come true simply because he uttered them."

"Oh I see," Valor said, though she was not certain she did see.

"Lady Monroe is rather pinched for funds so my father has been paying her to escort me around. Fortunately, she is a rather dim soul. Every time she questioned me about my dress or my mode of flirting, I simply explained that it was how things were done with young people these days. As she did not wish to displease either me or my duke, she's written him glowing letters about my efforts. I feel as if somewhere inside her mind she realizes my mode of going forward could not possibly result in a proposal but she dares not say it. She is frightened of the duke cutting off her funds."

"Goodness, it's all been…very convincing."

"Planning, that's what's required. I was heads together with my oldest friend, Penny Blackington. She gave me all kinds of ideas about how to look as if I wished to wed while guaranteeing I never would. On my last day, Penny said, 'Letty, whatever you do, you must long for things. Whatever it is, long for it. It's highly annoying and bound to do the trick.'"

Valor thought Penny Blackington was on to something. She *had* found the longing for things annoying.

"Mind you," Lady Letitia went on, "neither of us could have foreseen Tramondeley's Cornwall party. When I show Penny how I made that poor portrait artist change my face, she will positively howl with laughter. I had quite the time not laughing myself—everyone seemed to believe that I had no idea what I look like."

Valor blushed as she recalled how incredulous she was over that sketch. "But why? Do you not wish to wed someday?"

"Oh yes, yesterday if I could. However, the gentleman I intend to wed is a baronet from my neighborhood. Not at all up to snuff, my father has said. So, I go through this pointless exercise and then when the duke is convinced I am on the verge of going on the shelf, he will give in to it. My baronet is fully prepared to wait him out. We get on terrifically—we ride all over the county and he does not mind a bit that I own my own fowling piece. We are country people, not Town people."

Valor sat back. Lady Letitia appeared in a whole new light. What a brave lady!

Just then, Lady Monroe came into the room.

"Bad news, Lady Monroe," Lady Letitia said, looking very downcast. "Lord Tramondeley has engaged himself to Lady Valor."

Lady Monroe looked as if a brick had hit her in the head, momentarily stunned. She clutched at her heart. "Oh God, the duke."

"Simply write to him that sadly, another season will be required," Lady Letitia said.

"Yes, goodness, a carefully worded letter. Yes, I must think!"

The lady hurried out of the room.

"I do not blame Lady Monroe for any of it, mind you," Lady Letitia said. "A desperate lady might try anything. In any case, my baronet and I have agreed—my dowry is enormous, we will settle something on the lady so she does not need to get up to these sorts of schemes in future."

Valor was positively stunned. It did strike her that she would never again in her life make assumptions about another person. One really never knew. The last thing she would have gathered from Lady Letitia was that she preferred the country and was in love with a baronet. She found herself ashamed of what she'd thought of the lady. She was determined to take Mrs. Right's advice about shame—it was there to remind you not to do it again.

DAMIANO HAD WOKEN to find himself in a cell. There were chains around his ankles and they were attached to the wall. The place was dank and dim with no window. There was not a stick of furniture in it, just a cold stone floor covered in green slime. He was not certain whether it was day or night.

The remnants of the prince's party came back in bits and pieces. He'd failed to murder Tramondeley, foiled by that blasted Lady Letitia of all people. The only worry he'd ever had over that lady was how the marquis would view her if he were forced to take her home as his bride.

He'd thought he might be able to save the whole situation with Lady Valor by blaming Lady Letitia for the knife and naming Tramondeley as a spy for the French.

Then everything went dark. He believed Lady Valor might have hit him over the head with something. If that had been the case, he would never have been ready for it. How could anybody anticipate that nervous little lady hitting them over the head? How were women to be his undoing?

As he pondered his situation, he could not imagine what would happen. Would he be hanged? Who had locked him up? Had it been the prince? Was he in the tower?

Where was his coat? His shoes? His neckcloth was gone too. He supposed some jailor had made free with them.

He heard the sound of a rusty lock turning and forced himself to sit up despite the ache in his head.

He looked up and found the Lord Chamberlain himself staring down at him.

"Am I in the tower?" he asked.

"Hardly. You are tucked away in a lonely corner of the Marshalsea. You are lucky the prince regent and the queen are in agreement that they do not wish for any talk about this."

Damiano presumed that meant he would not be hanged. At least not publicly.

"You will be escorted by ship to Morocco where you can see what you can do with the sultan to get yourself across the Strait of Gibraltar and then make your way home from there. You nor any of your family are ever to set foot on our shores again and your estate is confiscated by the Crown."

"Morocco?"

The Lord Chamberlain laughed. "You did not expect us to sail you home, did you?"

Damiano did not answer. All he did know was that he had an arduous journey ahead of him and an even more arduous interview with the marquis at the end of it. How was he to explain that their estate was gone, they were barred from England, the Mosquito yet lived, and he would have no duke's daughter on his arm when he arrived?

He would have to think of something. The marquis did not look favorably upon disappointment and Damiano had two younger brothers. He was replaceable.

Weston supposed he was not too surprised that the palace hushed up di Compressio's actions on the night of the fête. He might have been much more aggravated about it than he was, had he not been engaged to Lady Valor. As he spent most of his time in her company, there was not much time to seethe over it.

He did not speak about it much to his fiancée, as he did not wish for her to have any nightmares about it. When it did come up, he just pointed out how brave she'd been. She admitted that it was the first really brave thing she'd ever done. Her rescuing of Sir Galahad had been a little brave, but then Lord Thorpe had been there all along and she'd begun to think the whole thing had been set up by him.

He encouraged her not to care too much about that, as she had not known it was set up when it happened. In any case, it had ended with her having a tremendous dog.

Weston was not certain how tremendous he actually viewed the dog, but he was always rewarded with a lovely smile, so tremendous Sir Galahad would remain.

He sensed that his lady was a bit on edge about the future, which he thought was understandable. A lady gave over her life to a lord who proceeded to decide how things would be.

He decided she would do better with detailed information and he had a long talk with the duke about it. They would split their time between Cornwall and the Dales. Weston pressed the idea that Lord Ledderbey must be brought with them, as he was getting of an age when he ought not be left to bang around his house by himself.

The duke had agreed to it, though he'd laughed that he worked for years to clear his house of daughters and somehow ended inheriting an old man into the bargain.

Just now, Weston hurried down the stairs to find Lord Ledderbey waiting for him and the carriage outside.

Just now, he was getting married.

VALOR PEERED OUT the windows of the drawing room. She'd been dressed in good time, putting on her favorite of the dresses Madame LaFray had composed. It was an elegant lilac silk, cut simply with no embellishments but for tiny little lilacs around the cuffs of the sleeves. Her ideas that it was lovely were confirmed when Serenity arrived and wept over it. Then of course, she wore the sapphire necklace that Tramondeley had gifted her. She very much doubted she'd ever wear anything else.

Tramondeley's carriage was outside his house. He would be here soon. He was such a dear to take Lord Ledderbey in the carriage though it was just around the square.

Lady Marchfield was deeply sighing behind her and muttering, "There is no accounting for it."

"Oh aunt, do cheer up," Valor said. "I know you have always feared for us—"

"And somehow I still do."

"But we are all settled creditably. You must admit that."

Lady Marchfield did not look inclined to admit anything.

"And just think, Papa says we will not get rid of Mr. Huberville because Mrs. Right has explained to him that he's so incompetent that he would starve on the road."

"I probably would, too," Mr. Huberville said cheerfully as he passed by.

"I suppose that's something."

"Look how kind he is," Valor said, leaning forward and watching Lord Tramondeley help Lord Ledderbey to the carriage.

"He is a fine young man and your father's heir. I can have nothing against it."

Valor had nothing against it either. She would wed a glorious man and would never really leave her home in the Dales. She could not wait to show it to him. They would go there for their wedding trip with her father and Lord Ledderbey joining them in a month. After the summer, they would take Lord Ledderbey home to Cornwall, but she had been assured there would be no nighttime forays in the sloop and any danger to Lord Tramondeley was long gone from England.

The carriage had come round the square. "He's here!" she said, leaping up from the sofa. She ran into the great hall and out the doors while her aunt scolded her from behind.

Her lord jumped out of the carriage and she jumped straight into his arms.

They were getting married.

AS ALWAYS HAPPENED to Valor when she was in a new and stressful situation, she was nearly blind with fear during the wedding service. She reminded herself that she was in her own home, as they wed with a special license, and she was surrounded by all her sisters, her father, and Mrs. Right. Nevertheless, she was in a fog of fear. Tramondeley seemed to sense it though and held her up by the arm and whispered to her when she forgot the words.

At one point, the curate from the Grosvenor Church stopped the service and asked Valor if she wed of her own volition, apparently so discombobulated had she seemed. That, of anything, went a long way to calm her.

"Yes," she said. "I am just terrorized, as I always am in new and scary situations. Lord Tramondeley knows all about it." It helped to just say it, for some reason.

The lord had nodded. "It's true, I know all about it."

The curate had not seemed to take a terrible amount of comfort from that assurance, but he continued on.

She was married. They had done it in the late afternoon, nobody in the family liking a morning service. Her father had arranged for a lovely early dinner and Valor drank a large glass of wine to settle herself. Mrs. Right sat on her other side, to the great exasperation of Lady Marchfield, but Valor was comforted by it as the lady had acted as her mother all her life. Perhaps what settled her most of all though was Tramondeley. He was such a calm brick of a man. He'd said everything would be all right and so that must be true.

The far end of the table was taken up by her young nieces and nephews, or Pelham's Pirates, as they had named themselves. Young Miles and his second-in-command, Isabelle, were kept busy keeping the younger ones in order, chasing after them when they escaped, and explaining there was no reason to cry over anything green on their plate as they did not need to eat it.

The arrangements that had been made before Valor and Tramondeley set off for the Dales were that they were to spend the first night in Lord Ledderbey's house, which she had been apprised was really the duke's house, as he had rented it in the first place.

Lord Ledderbey would stay in the duke's house and he'd promised to look after Sir Galahad overnight. Valor thought her new husband had been a little surprised to discover that Sir Galahad would accompany them, but if he was, he covered it very well and said, "Of course he must."

After the dinner, they were cheered by all their family and ran across the square. Valor was both eager to be alone with Lord Tramondeley and nervous about it.

She reminded herself that she had proved she could be brave. She must be brave. She would not allow Lord Tramondeley to ever regret his choice. She must be brave.

Valor knew very well that she was not quite as bold as her sisters when it came time to shut the door to the world and be alone with her husband, but she was determined. As it happened, Tramondeley understood her very well. He had his own particular approach to his skittish bride. Once they were alone, he pulled away after a kiss and said, "I ought not go further."

When he was assured he might go further, he went a bit further. And then he pulled away and said, "I ought not go further."

Valor could hardly say how it happened, but somehow she was up the stairs and she was not frightened. There were stops and starts and it was all up to her. The first time she'd said he might go further and then further again and then even further again was a bit of a shock, even though she understood what was to happen. After that, though, she rather enjoyed herself. A lot, actually.

And so it was that marital relations were more than satisfactorily established between them. Over time, shyness was entirely lost and Weston's strategy became a game in their marriage. He would say, "I ought not go further." She would say, "You really better go further." Or if she wished to hint to him, she might wait until he read the paper or wrote letters or some other mundane activity and say, "Did you plan to go further with that?" His answer was always to throw aside whatever he was doing and chase her up the stairs.

The stairs in the Dales often saw such activity during the wedding trip. Mrs. Right and Thomas had come to run the house, with a cook hired from a nearby village. The staff kept themselves well out of the way of the couple and rather enjoyed themselves below stairs as the duke said the cellars were open for their convenience.

Tramondeley was quite adoring of the house and the landscape of the Dales, as it was so different from Cornwall. They took long walks, hopping over the low stone walls they encountered and one time running from a bull they encountered. They thought about taking some of the horses out, but it turned out that on top of only wishing to go for a horse-walk, rather than a horse-ride, she did not trust any other horse but Tulip and Tulip was still on her way home. They visited the village and Thomas showed them the building that was to hold his and Charlie's little tavern. Once Tramondeley was apprised of the agreement that had been reached with the duke, he vowed to carry on the tradition when the time came.

After a month, the duke and Lord Ledderbey arrived. According to the duke, they'd gone slow as Lord Ledderbey found the journey tiring. According to Lord Ledderbey, going slow had meant more overnight stays at inns and he could not say with any confidence that those innkeepers were happy to see the duke. He'd never seen so many sighs and rolled eyes directed at one gentleman in his life. There had been a very frightening cook at one of them who'd hurled all sorts of threats in the duke's direction.

With the duke and Lord Ledderbey came Mr. Huberville. Much to Lady Marchfield's surprise, the duke finally did have a butler. Mr. Hubert Huberville could not be pawned off on anybody. He remained very terrible at his job but everybody was certain he'd starve on the road if he was dismissed.

He would go on to regularly take what was right and somehow make it wrong. One might imagine Lady Marchfield would feel entirely victorious over it, but the facts of the case proved otherwise. Mr. Huberville was so bad at butlering that it became widely known in Town that the Duke of Pelham employed the most ridiculous butler who ever set foot in London.

The duke, himself, always liking to put people on the back foot, especially his sister, did not mind it one bit. He advertised far and wide that it was Lady Marchfield who had recommended Mr. Huberville. As for the barnacle on a boat himself, once he realized that there was nothing he could do to get fired, he got far more cheerful over his failings.

In any case, the footmen he employed after Thomas and Charlie were gone were always eager to cover up his mistakes because after all, he was an exceedingly kind sort of man. He would go on to supervise a rather lax staff and while he never was very skilled, he intellectually understood the job. He spent much time with his footmen, training them on everything they needed to know. While he might drop anything breakable placed in his hands, he was quite comfortable of an evening sipping his sherry and communicating his knowledge to willing ears. Quite a few of them moved on to become butlers in other houses.

Charlie and Thomas opened a tavern in the duke's little village, paying the duke one pound a year and all the ale he could drink. As the duke kept bottles of his own claret there for his use, he did not drink much of their ale.

The vicar, as was expected, did not look approvingly over the idea of a tavern, as he very much feared the menfolk would be often drunk. He did not get far with his complaints though, as nobody especially cared about the vicar's opinion and most were of the opinion that if God were against ale, he would not have created the ingredients for it. In any case, the women of the village felt free to come in too, as everybody had known Charlie and Thomas since they were young lads. The vicar finally gave up and began joining his congregation at their libations, as he did find that a small glass of the tavern's ale soothed his fraught imaginings of what the duke might say to him next.

When the time came, Valor and her husband and Lord Ledderbey set off for Cornwall. They took their time so that Lord Ledderbey did not tire too very much, making a week's stop in London to break up the journey. To Valor's surprise, Sir Galahad really took to Lord Ledderbey and could be found on his lap more often than not.

The house in Cornwall surpassed Valor's imagination. She had only seen the sea once and this was a different sort of view. High up on a cliff perch she could look out over the horizon and thank her stars that Tramondeley did not sail out to that expanse under cover of darkness anymore. In the warmer weather, they would leave the windows open and Valor found the regular rhythm of the waves coming on shore very comforting.

And so they would go on traveling between Cornwall and the Dales. Over time, Lord Ledderbey stopped making the arduous trip. He met a lady close to his own age who was a voracious reader just like he was and they spent their days quietly reading by the windows and retiring early.

Lady Letitia did finally wed her baronet. Like most fathers, the duke was worn down by time rather than outright defiance.

Lady Letitia began dropping heavy hints about spinsterhood being right around the corner and how she would stay with her father forever. He began to see the sense of the baronet.

Lady Letitia and her baronet would end as close friends to Valor and Tramondeley, as the real lady was not at all like the lady they'd met that first season.

The Count di Compressio, weasel that he was, managed to weasel out of blame for returning home having left the Mosquito untouched, the Hertfordshire estate gone, no bride on his arm, and the family exiled from England forever. He managed all that by writing the marquis that Monsieur Bernard was a double agent working with the English, had exposed him, and nearly had him killed. The count was not at all surprised to discover upon his arrival to the villa that Monsieur Bernard had been poisoned a month prior.

Lady Tallifer was able to rescue her reputation not from what she said but who she was. Nobody at all acquainted with that fluttering butterfly of a lady could for a moment believe she had involved herself in anything dangerous. Further, her side of the family cut off all communication with the marquis.

Though the duke had always claimed his dear-held wish in life was to unload all of his daughters on unsuspecting fools, once he'd done it he did not feel so satisfied. He spent approximately one month alone on his estate and then promptly married Mrs. Right. One might suppose that idea had been brewing between them for quite some time, though nothing had ever been said aloud. Once the girls were successfully launched, the duke could not think what else he'd rather do.

That couple, liking to be on the move, regularly descended upon his sons-in-laws' houses with no notice whatsoever. They also descended upon London during the season and there were those who refused to entertain a former housekeeper even if she *were* a duchess.

The duke understood all too well that there would be no friendly talking into it when it came to accepting his new bride and former housekeeper. Therefore, he'd need to frighten them all into it.

So he did. Hostesses who tried to cut them were shouted at on the street when they were eventually found. Some of the duke's favorite things to shout were: "Lady So and So, what's happened to you? You've aged a hundred years!" or "Lady So and So, do tell me the viscount no longer beats you!" or "Lady So and So, I've heard you were pinched, allow me to lend you some money!"

One might have thought that the husbands of these beleaguered hostesses might step in and demand satisfaction from the duke. They did not bother, though, as they were all perfectly aware that he would swear he would blow them to bits and then sleep through the appointed time.

The *ton* was well-armed to put down all sorts of people, but they found they could do nothing with a man who could not be shamed into behaving. They had also become cognizant over the course of time that crossing the duke could lead to rather bizarre revenge tactics.

It was tacitly agreed in society that when it came to the Duke of Pelham and his housekeeper duchess, one ought to just hurry past, not make eye contact, and invite them to routs and other crowded places. Placing servants in strategic locations during these entertainments also proved savvy, as it prevented a person's curtains from going up in flames.

For whatever discomfort that couple caused the *ton*, the duke and his new lady got on very well together. After all, Mrs. Right was well acquainted with the duke's temperament and did not fan herself over it. As a further bonus, she had always acted as mother to the duke's daughters, and now she was their mother in name too.

Over the years, the duke's house on Grosvenor Square became the center for activity for his grandchildren. They would come at all hours with no notice whatsoever and stay the night if they preferred it. There were times the duke was out and did not even know they were in the house until he saw them at breakfast.

There were other times he arrived from the Dales and found a pile of them already there. There were times he noted a strange dog in the drawing room and then eventually one of his grandchildren would turn up to claim it.

The eldest of them, Grace's son Miles, kept them all going in the same direction and Pelham's Pirates was firmly established.

Valor and Tramondeley added their contribution to the pirates—a strapping young lad and little miss eager to join in. Valor was delighted to have children, though she was shocked to her shoes over the sorts of risks her son would take as if he had no notion that he inhabited a human body and could die. She might have grown more brave than she'd started, but her nightmares continued. She did not dream of foxes' cries anymore, but rather terrible scenarios in which her boy was hurt. That boy would manage to survive just fine, as everybody knows that children are impossibly resilient. Tramondeley acted as an opposing force, as if Valor had her way, her boy would have spent his childhood tied to a chair so he did not get hurt. As it was, Tramondeley taught him how to sail the sloop, but only in the daytime and within sight of the house.

Her girl was less frightening, though Valor would have been happy if she was as fearful of the unknown as she'd always been herself. She was not, however. She might not be as prone to flinging herself off every available surface as her brother was, but that did not stop the worry. There are some parents who fret excessively over the welfare of their progeny, and Valor Nicolet, Future Duchess of Pelham, was a shining example. She soothed herself by peeking into their rooms at night to confirm they were still alive, and nobody had a harder time of it than the nursemaids who had to put up with it.

And so, despite Lady Marchfield's predictions, which even if harsh had always been very sensible, all of the duke's children were settled creditably.

Nobody was more surprised than the duke.

The end.

About the Author

By the time I was eleven, my Irish Nana and I had formed a book club of sorts. On a timetable only known to herself, Nana would grab her blackthorn walking stick and steam down to the local Woolworth's. There, she would buy the latest Barbara Cartland romance, hurry home to read it accompanied by viciously strong wine, (Wild Irish Rose, if you're wondering) and then pass the book on to me. Though I was not particularly interested in real boys yet, I was *very* interested in the gentlemen in those stories— daring, bold, and often enraging and unaccountable. After my Barbara Cartland phase, I went on to Georgette Heyer, Jane Austen and so many other gifted authors blessed with the ability to bring the Georgian and Regency eras to life.

I would like nothing more than to time travel back to the Regency (and time travel back to my twenties as long as we're going somewhere) to take my chances at a ball. Who would take the first? Who would escort me into supper? What sort of meaningful looks would be exchanged? I would hope, having made the trip, to encounter a gentleman who would give me a very hard time. He ought to be vexatious in the extreme, and *worth* every vexation, to make the journey worthwhile.

I most likely won't be able to work out the time travel gambit, so I will content myself with writing stories of adventure and romance in my beloved time period. There are lives to be created, marvelous gowns to wear, jewels to don, instant attractions that inevitably come with a difficulty, and hearts to break before putting them back together again. In traditional Regency fashion, my stories are clean—the action happens in a drawing room, rather than a bedroom.

As I muse over what will happen next to my H and h, and wish I were there with them, I will occasionally remind myself that it's also nice to have a microwave, Netflix, cheese popcorn, and steaming hot showers.

Come see me on Facebook! @KateArcherAuthor